Perchance to Dream

Perchance to Dream

LISA MANTCHEV

Feiwel and Friends
NEW YORK

A Feiwel and Friends Book
An Imprint of Macmillan

PERCHANCE TO DREAM. Copyright © 2010 by Lisa Mantchev.
All rights reserved. Printed in August 2010 in the United States of America by
R. R. Donnelley & Sons Company, Harrisonburg, Virginia. For information,
address Feiwel and Friends, 175 Fifth Avenue, New York, N.Y. 10010.

Library of Congress Cataloging-in-Publication Data Available

ISBN: 978-0-312-38097-7

Book design by April Ward

Feiwel and Friends logo designed by Filomena Tuosto

First Edition: 2010

3 5 7 9 10 8 6 4 2

www.feiwelandfriends.com

For my husband, who not only
learned the tango, but the waltz, the
fox-trot, and the West Coast Swing

Perchance to Dream

CAST LIST

MEMBERS OF BEATRICE SHAKESPEARE SMITH & CO.

Beatrice (Bertie) Shakespeare Smith, a seventeen-year-old girl

Peaseblossom
Cobweb } the fairies from
Moth *A Midsummer*
Mustardseed *Night's Dream*

Ariel, an airy spirit from *The Tempest*

IN THE OUTSIDE WORLD

Nate, a kidnapped pirate from *The Little Mermaid*
Waschbär, a sneak-thief
The Scrimshander
Sedna, the Sea Goddess

AT THE THÉÂTRE ILLUMINATA

Ophelia, daughter of Polonius in *Hamlet,* and Bertie's mother

The Theater Manager
The Stage Manager

Mrs. Edith, the Wardrobe Mistress
Mr. Hastings, the Properties Manager
Mr. Tibbs, the Scenic Manager

CHAPTER ONE

Beginning in the Middle; Starting Thence Away

"It is a truth universally acknowledged," Mustard-seed said, flying in lazy loops like an intoxicated bumblebee, "that a fairy in possession of a good appetite must be in want of pie."

"Yes, indeed," Cobweb said over the rattle of the caravan, "though I awoke one morning from uneasy dreams, I found myself transformed in my bed into a gigantic pie."

"It was the best of pie, it was the worst of pie," was Moth's contribution as he hovered near the gently swaying lanterns.

In the following lull, the mechanical horses snorted tiny silver-scented clouds and the wagon wheels creaked like an old woman's stays. There was no way of knowing how much time had passed since they'd departed the

Théâtre Illuminata. A thin sliver of a moon had risen, recalling the gleam of the Cheshire Cat's smile, while the hours had slipped by them as steadily as the sullen, secretive landscape. Exhausted to her toes, Beatrice Shakespeare Smith leaned against Ariel's tuxedo-clad shoulder, barely marking the continued whinging of the fairies. Drifting along the hemline of sleep, she heard a voice call to her, like the fading remnant of color at the edge of darkness.

Lass.

Bertie jolted as though Mrs. Edith had jabbed her backside with a pin, knowing that it was only a cruel trick her mind played upon her but unable to stop her eyes from scanning the edges of the lanterns' light for Nate.

"We should have had a prologue," Peaseblossom fretted. "Not all this nattering about pie." She paused, but no one offered up any introductory words, so the fairy took a ponderous breath.

PEASEBLOSSOM

A gloaming peace this evening with it brings
In the countryside where we lay our scene.
Toad-ballad accompan'd, crickets sing,
and cupcake crumbs make fairy hands unclean.

An indignant Moth squeaked, "There were cupcakes?!"

Mustardseed, however, was most impressed. "You just pulled iambic pentameter out of your—"

PEASEBLOSSOM
(hastening to add)
Lights up: a caravan incredible.
Nature's moonlit mirror reflects these six:
Four fae, depriv'd of chocolate edibles;
Ariel, winds attending and transfix'd;
And the playwright, named for the Beatrice fair,
Hair purpl'd where it had been Cobalt Flame,
Her many-hued hopes tinged with sad despair
O'er the stolen pirate she would reclaim—

"THAT," Bertie announced loudly, before the fairy could discourse further upon their Sea Goddess–kidnapped comrade, "will be enough of that, thank you kindly."

Under the pretense of driving, Ariel kept his gaze on the horses. Like a maladjusted shopping trolley, they had a tendency to veer slightly to the left toward the open field. On the right, unidentifiable but towering trees kept their own counsel, secrets bark-wrapped and leaf-shuttered.

"This is the first moment we've had alone since I returned from your delivery errand." Ariel's voice coaxed tendrils of enchanted quicksilver from the air.

With one ear trained upon the renewed demands for pie, Bertie tried to brush off his words as easily as she would a wayward firefly. "We are no more alone than Titania was in her bower."

And I refuse to act the part of the ass.

The moon passed behind a cloud, and the swinging lanterns on the Mistress of Revels's caravan flickered; in the ensuing darkness, the world spread out before Bertie in every direction at once. Accustomed as she was to only being able to go as far as the theater's walls, the limitless possibilities should have terrified her.

Instead, she held out her hands in welcome. Their exit page, torn from *The Complete Works of the Stage*, crinkled inside her bodice, just over her thudding heart.

"Perhaps I can appeal, then, to the romantic nature of our situation." Without moving, everything about Ariel reached for her. "The open road, the veil of night drawn over the world, us living as vagabonds."

Usually Peaseblossom played the part of Bertie's tiny little conscience, but this time, she issued the requisite Dire Warning to herself:

Don't think about how close he is, or the fact that all you'd have to do to kiss him is tilt your head. Think of Nate. . . .

"If you're done with whatever fierce internal argument is creasing your forehead—" Ariel's low laugh undid the knot she had tied on her resolve. A bit of his wind pushed her nearly into his lap, and their lips met.

Bertie's brain fogged over until the fairies' collective noises of disgust recalled her to her senses. Pulling away, she muttered, "Vagabonds don't wear crinolines."

"No doubt you would feel more at home in a pair of men's trousers." Every word was a caress. "Something with rips at the knees and a splash of paint across the seat."

"I will have you know that despite the layers in this skirt, I'm freezing and likely to catch my death of cold." She tried to look as though she might perish at any second.

"You're as sturdy as a pony and too stubborn to die of something as minor as a cold." Nevertheless, Ariel let her go long enough to shrug out of his jacket and drape it over her shoulders.

"A pony?" Bertie tried not to revel in either the gesture or the vestiges of warmth and failed miserably. Turning her nose against the ivory lining, she breathed in the scents of wind-ruffled water and moonlight on pearls. Never one to let an opportunity pass him by, Ariel devoted his attention to the cascade of disheveled black-and-purple curls that tumbled alongside her neck. Though Bertie did her best to ignore the gentle tickling, she couldn't help the resultant goose bumps. "Pay attention to the road, please. You're going to drive us into a ditch."

"I won't let that happen."

"Really?" Bertie wasn't thinking of his role as chauffeur when she added, "Not all of our history is good. Why should I trust you?"

"If anyone should hold a grudge, milady, it's me." The muscles in his throat clenched in protest. "When I swallow, I can still feel that damn iron circlet around my neck."

The chill of his winds seeped into Bertie's bones, and she fought the cold with hot temper. "Then I suggest you behave yourself."

"Misbehavior is part of my charm."

"Tearing nearly every page from The Book was hardly what I'd call charming—"

"I paid my debt to the theater, didn't I?" Catching her by the coat sleeve, Ariel pushed the fabric up to kiss her knuckles. "And though you freed me, I am verily still trapped in a prison, for what else is love?"

"Don't be ridiculous." Bertie flapped her hands until they were protected again.

"There is nothing wrong," he said, "with a little romance."

"Sure there is. Look where 'a little romance' got Ophelia." The discovery that waterlogged, oftentimes cryptic Ophelia of *Hamlet* fame was her mother still hovered on the surface of Bertie's skin, beads of moisture yet to sink in.

"You have to respect her nerve, do you not?"

"I do!" Moth said with a tilt of his little head. "The respect inside me is so big there's no room for my guts." He made horrible groaning noises and doubled over. "I respect her so much, I burst. Oh, help! I'm dying!"

The others looked at one another and dropped to their knees with rousing cries of "oh, my innards" and "my spleen!," which led to "my gizzard!" and "no, spleen was funnier."

"What about the man she ran away with?" Cobweb paused to ask.

"The Mysterious Stranger!" Mustardseed frowned and picked his nose, which made it difficult to tell if he was confounded by the matter at hand or the contents of his right nostril.

"As soon as we rescue Nate, we'll find my father and bring him back to Ophelia." But Bertie knew her promise would be difficult if not impossible to fulfill, with no clues to his identity and only the knowledge that he and Ophelia had run away to the seaside.

The sea, Bertie realized, the direction in which they'd already turned their noses to search for Nate.

But stage directions are better than happenstance.

"We need a script," she said without preamble.

"I beg your pardon?" The moment Ariel took his eyes off the road, the caravan hit a pothole.

Wincing at the jolt, Bertie pulled out their exit page.

"Be careful with that," Peaseblossom fretted.

"I am!" Bertie smoothed the softly glowing sheet from *The Complete Works of the Stage*. Back at the Théâtre, before tearing it free, she'd inscribed the page with

Following Her Stars: In Which Beatrice (& Company) Take Their Act on the Road

and paused, long enough for a blot of ink to appear before adding

Enter BERTIE, ARIEL, PEASEBLOSSOM, COBWEB, MOTH, and MUSTARDSEED.

Bertie splayed her fingers over the words and took a deep breath. "If I want to rescue Nate and find my father, I really will have to become the Mistress of Revels, especially the Teller of Tales bit of the job description." She turned to Ariel. "Do you have a pen?"

Catching sight of the page, every line of Ariel's body shifted, resettling into something distinctly uneasy. "Why, yes. I carry a lovely quill and inkpot in my trouser pocket."

"I'll take that as a no then."

With bit of arguing that topped off the lemon pie discussion with meringue, Peaseblossom turned to tug at

Bertie's elaborate coiffure. "The Theater Manager's fountain pen, remember? You purloined it."

Reaching up, Bertie found that she had indeed tucked it into her curls.

"You can use blood for ink!" Cobweb suggested. "By the pricking of your thumbs and all that rubbish."

Bertie tapped the tip of the pen against the page. "Thankfully, there's still ink in it, and I won't have to open a vein."

"Pity," Moth said. "There's magic in blood."

Her hand sought out the scrimshaw medallion hanging about her neck. Thinking of its bone-magic, Bertie scowled. "I'd like to get away from using magic that requires body parts." She spread the paper across her jacket-clad knees.

Ariel leaned over, his breath tickling her ear. "What are you going to do?"

"I . . . I'm not quite sure." She stared at the paper, willing it to whisper some hint as to what she should write.

"Aren't we going to stop for the night?" Cobweb wanted to know. "I fancy a nice campfire—"

"And a meal or three!" added Mustardseed.

Bertie shook her head. "Absolutely not! We have to keep going."

"In the dark?" Moth said, each word more incredulous than the last.

"In the cold?" Cobweb continued to climb the scale.

"Without supper?" Mustardseed tried valiantly to continue the ascent, but his little voice cracked on "supper" and so did the pane of glass in the caravan window.

"Nice going." Peaseblossom applied her knuckle to the back of his head.

"What do you mean, 'without supper?'" Bertie asked. "Isn't there any food in this thing?"

"Afraid not," Peaseblossom said, scuffing her little toe against the air. "I checked every cupboard and drawer when the boys were lighting the lamps."

Bertie suffered a swift pang of regret that she'd not properly appreciated the Green Room's continuous and bountiful offerings back at the theater. "I suppose we'll have to buy some tomorrow."

"Did you bring any money?" came the cheerful query from Ariel.

Mouth falling open, Bertie sputtered a bit. "I ... I ... didn't think about it. I guess I assumed the Theater Manager would ... er ... provide us with ways and means."

Peaseblossom was quick to point out, "But you're the Mistress—"

"I know I'm supposed to be the new Mistress of Revels!" Bertie interrupted her, feeling a myriad of fresh obligations piled about her, like invisible baggage atop the caravan. "But that doesn't mean I have pockets full of muffins!"

"With the title comes great responsibility," Moth said.

"The responsibility of meals at regular intervals!" Mustardseed added.

"We could sing for our suppers, I suppose," Pease-blossom ventured. "Come on, Bertie, let's hear your singing voice."

"Yes, Bertie," Ariel said. "A rousing chorus of 'What Will Become of You?' feels particularly appropriate at this juncture."

"You shut your mouth," Bertie told him. "No singing, no jazz flourishes, and especially no lifts. You keep your hands away from my backside."

He leaned back on one elbow, his laughter low and teasing. "Then cue the pirouetting angel food cakes."

Bertie heard the voice echo again.

Lass.

"Not cake." Though the fairies immediately protested, Bertie barely heard them over the crackling in her ears. "I'm going to save Nate." Possibilities put down roots, each idea a bloom on an unexpected but welcome vine. "I'm such an idiot! All that time wasted having the Players say his line, hoping his page would be acted back into the book . . . I never thought to *write* him back."

"You did have other things on your mind at the time."

If Ariel was striving to sound nonchalant, he almost managed it. "You might try something small and manageable before attempting to drag the man out of the clutches of the Sea Goddess."

"Careful there, you almost sound concerned." Slanting a look at him, Bertie added, "Two seconds ago you didn't lodge a protest over the idea of dancing cake. In fact, you were the one to suggest it."

"I've changed my mind."

"I hate to side with Ariel," Peaseblossom said, her face a study in fretful agitation, "but if you write Nate back, what's to keep Sedna from following? You could put us a thousand leagues underwater in seconds."

Bertie shoved the unwelcome idea away before it could grasp her with tentacle-arms. "That won't happen."

"You don't know that," Ariel said.

"No more than I am certain of anything," she retorted as she penned the stage direction,

Enter NATE.

CHAPTER TWO

A Sudden and More Strange Return

A hushed moment passed, then a thousand leagues' worth of ghostwater rushed around them, tipping over the cart and horses. Currents of air and time cushioned the fall; Ariel and the fairies drifted free of the wreckage, trapped within a wraithlike riptide in which they appeared as though frozen.

Bertie alone was able to move, and so she scrambled to her feet. Twisting in a desperate circle, she spotted Nate standing in the road. The trouble was, she could see *through* him to the vague outline of the trees and waving tufts of grass.

Her fingers clenched the page and the pen as she moved toward him. "Nate?"

"Lass . . ." When he reached for her, the touch of the

pirate's translucent hand was no more than a kiss of salt on her skin.

Bertie peered up at him, simultaneously thrilled and perplexed. "It's like you're the Ghost of Hamlet's Father, come to haunt me."

"Ye can't blame me for that." A rueful laugh caused his form to waver. "Judgin' by how it felt, ye pulled th' soul from my body."

"I wrote 'enter Nate,' not 'rip him in two'!" The horror of what she had done settled into the back of Bertie's throat, choking her.

"How . . . ," He had to swallow before he could finish. "How long has it been? It feels like years have passed, like I was adrift on th' water in a shallow boat, lookin' up at th' stars."

"Only a few days—"

He put a finger to his lips as Time released the others, and everything that had been drifting like foam on the ocean exploded with movement and noise. The fairies circled her, all screams of dismay and tiny, grasping fingers. Nate's shade folded thickly muscled arms over his chest, expression inscrutable, as Ariel's cold hands whirled Bertie around.

"Are you all right?" When she didn't immediately answer, he shook her until her teeth clacked together. "*Are you all right?!*"

"Y-yes!" And it was true; she'd suffered no ill effects,

other than a near heart attack caused by Nate's sudden and incomplete manifestation.

"What were you thinking?" The air elemental looked her over as though cataloguing her limbs. He was as angry as she'd ever heard him, perhaps even more so than when she'd placed the collar around his neck; then he'd been livid and broken, now he was furious and free, floating nearly a foot aboveground with his hair whipping about his face and shoulders.

But he had neither noticed Nate nor acknowledged him, and surely Ariel would have done so . . .

If he could see him.

The fairies flew through the pirate with only wing spasms and random commentary about the sudden chill to mark their spectral passage. Discomfited, Bertie twitched away from Ariel.

"Kindly cease your attentions most solicitous, sir, I'm fine."

The glint of Nate's earring was the reflection of candle-light on a dagger drawn. He and Ariel had never been friendly; their more recent history had been a duel of sharp words and warning looks. "She means keep yer hands to yerself, ye poxy smellsmock."

Bertie choked back a laugh at the insult, and when Nate grinned at her, the brilliant flash of his teeth caused Ariel's breath to catch.

"Did you see that?" The words contained a cool breeze, the sort that held the promise of snow as the air elemental scanned the night-painted landscape.

Moth lifted his nose. "She must have managed something . . . there's salt in the air."

Ariel took a step forward and Nate's expression shifted from amused to feral, swifter than any of the scene changes at the theater. As his lip raised in an unmistakable snarl, Bertie hastened to say, "But it didn't work, did it? No pirate to be seen here."

Turning back to her, Ariel's features relaxed. "I'm sorry."

"You are?" She couldn't help but sound surprised.

"You should try something else." When he trailed his fingers along her cheek, a gesture somehow more intimate than a kiss, Nate growled.

"Maybe something to right the caravan?" Peaseblossom suggested.

"No need for that." Retracing his steps, Ariel moved to the opposite side of the sad conveyance. He squelched a bit, the ghostwater having settled into ruts and pooled in the grass. "All of you, keep clear of the wheels." When he held out his arms, moonlight gathered in his silver hair. The winds collected in his palms, and he used them to lift both wagon and horses from the ground.

Unperturbed, the horses' glowing amber eyes blinked slowly, the light slanting down the length of their silver-metal muzzles.

"Show-off," Nate said as everything settled in its usual upright position.

Indeed, Ariel rounded the caravan, checking the cart and horses for damage but flashing a triumphant smile at Bertie as he did so.

"Now that's taken care of," said Mustardseed, "can't someone conjure a few éclairs?"

"Don't be stupid," Peaseblossom said. "If Bertie writes anything else, it should be something that's actually useful, like kindling a fire."

Something in the distance howled. As one, the boys ceased their snack-clamoring, with Moth making the loudest demand of, "Yes, a fire, and make it a really big one, please."

Bertie tapped the tip of the fountain pen against the paper.

"Careful wi' that thing," Nate whispered in her right ear, the words trickling in like raindrops, "or ye might accidentally scribble somethin' that looks like a dragon attackin' us."

"You shut up," Bertie said with a flash of temper aimed at the pirate that missed and hit the air elemental.

Ariel's confusion manifested as a quirked eyebrow. "I didn't say anything."

"A nice bit of lightning would get a fire going," Cobweb said, oblivious to the pirate's warning.

"Yes," Bertie said, desperately trying to suppress the urge to stick her finger in her ear, "and if I miss, we get fairies flambé. Still sound like a good idea?"

"Not so much, no," he admitted.

"At least we agree on something." She looked about them, trying to conjure the scene in her mind before she put pen to paper to write,

As the night creeps ever closer
to the group of weary travelers—

The moon's brilliant illumination faded, and Nate's voice came from her left side this time. "Lass?"

"Hmm?"

"Somethin' is creepin' this way."

The assertion was confirmed almost simultaneously when Peaseblossom tugged at one of Bertie's curls. "There's something out there!"

"A Big, Dark something," Moth added.

"I think it's the Night," Mustardseed said. "And it has teeth."

Bertie looked in the direction the fairies' fingers were

pointing, and seven sets of gleaming feral eyes gazed back at her, their inquisitive interest directed largely at her jugular. The sizable pack of wolves paced along the edges of the caravan's lamplight, momentarily held at bay by the thin golden curtain of illumination that barely encompassed Bertie and her friends. When the luminous hemline flickered, it revealed patchy fur and canines exposed in snarling mouths.

Nate reached for a cutlass that wasn't there. "Get back!"

The fairies unwittingly obeyed him, darting to the driver's seat where the light was brightest.

"Do something, Bertie!" Moth whimpered above her. "You conjured them!"

"I did not!" Taking tiny steps and trying not to draw their attention, Bertie backed up against the side of the caravan. "I made no mention of anything with teeth!"

"Well, they have them," said Moth. "Big ones."

"You weren't called!" Mustardseed shook his tiny fist at the wolves. "Have the decency to wait for your cue!"

"This isn't the theater," Peaseblossom said. "They don't have to wait for stage directions."

"Makes me almost miss the Stage Manager. He'd have something to say about unauthorized entrances." Bertie was at an absolute loss for what to do. Animals in the Théâtre were portrayed by puppets, actors dressed in fur, or steel-covered clockwork; they certainly didn't exude the promise of a bone-crunching, painful death with every panted exhalation.

"I'm fearin' I'll be no help in a brawl." Moonlight-washed linen bunched as Nate flexed, testing his strength. Crouching, he reached for a fistful of grass and just managed to stir the spectral-dampened stalks. "Even if I had a weapon, I doubt it would do much good."

"It's all right, I can fix this." Biting her lip, Bertie drew a squiggly stripe through the line about the night, but the ink refused to stay put. It wiggled off the page like an inchworm having a seizure and fell onto the ground with a wet *plop*! "I don't get rewrites? Who can write a play in one draft?"

"Shakespeare?" Ariel moved back a few paces, still standing between Bertie and the wolves, but now close enough that she could scent the perfume of his hair.

"This is an inopportune time for a scholarly debate, I think." Casting about them for inspiration, Bertie's gaze came to rest on the lanterns. "The light is the only thing holding them at bay, isn't it?"

Nate nodded. "That's how it works wi' things long o' fang an' sharp o' nail."

"They are most certainly long of fang, and I really don't want to know about the sharpness of their nails."

Bertie could all too easily imagine the damage such claws could do.

Ariel looked at her over his shoulder. Tendrils of his hair brushed her bare arm. "Given the results of your first attempts, you might want to be careful how you phrase the next bit."

"I'm not an idiot." Twitching away from his unintentional caress, Bertie put pen back to paper to scribble,

The fairies kindle a fire.

And the parties in question promptly burst into flames.

"AAAAAH! It burns! It burns!" Mustardseed hollered as he batted at his clothes.

"Stop, drop, and roll!" Cobweb flung himself against the driver's seat.

The wolves scattered, retreating a few feet from the four screaming miniature balls of incandescent light bobbing about like demented fireflies.

"I told you to be careful!" Ariel tried to catch hold of Mustardseed, but missed by several inches.

"That's not what ye meant t' do, is it?" Nate queried.

"No!" Bertie snagged Peaseblossom, bracing herself for searing pain that didn't come. "Are you on fire or not?"

Blue phosphorescent flames curled up the fairy's neck

and shoulders as she considered the question. "I think 'not,' but it does tickle."

The boys, once they stopped screaming, cut gleaming swaths of light against the sky that were noted with interest by the wolves. They crept back, pressing moist-looking noses to the wavering curtain of lantern light.

"You scared me to death!" Snappish in her relief that they were not burning up like pixie-kebabs, Bertie remained tense, watching the predators lick their chops every time the boys swooped past them.

"Sorry," Mustardseed said. "Panic is sort of a reflex response when you're on-fire-but-not."

"Not to be troublesome, but I do believe we're on the dinner menu." Ariel held up his hand. Gathering a wind in his palm, he used it to push the pack leader back to the edge of the lantern light.

Bertie's heartbeat thudded in counterpoint to the *pad-pad-pad* of paws in the grass as the wolves circled, looking for a weak side. "Get ahold of something." The fairies obeyed with uncharacteristic haste, grabbing handfuls of her gown and hair. Nate stood beside her, but he wasn't the one who could help them right now. "More wind, Ariel."

"As milady commands." Every muscle strained under the silk of Ariel's shirt as the wolves snarled and snapped, fighting to breach the veritable tornado that encircled the group. "A bit of help, if you please?"

"I'll turn them into a pile of fur coats." Bertie braced the page against her knee, trying to pin it down long enough to write something, anything.

"Bertie—" Ariel's desperation generated a hurricane blast.

The wind slammed into her like a shock wave, snatching The Book's page from her grasp. Fluttering like a ballerina portraying a dying swan for a half second, the paper then dropped into a puddle of ghostwater. With a dismayed cry, she snatched it up and stared at the running ink in disbelief. "There's barely room left to write my name, much less summon a horde of brigands armed to the teeth, or a legion of soldiers, or a cannon—"

Uncharacteristic droplets of sweat had gathered upon Ariel's forehead, and he spoke through his teeth. "Summon something small, then!"

Inspiration struck, swift as blow. "More paper." Bertie's pen skidded, and the ink blotched as she scrawled,

The winds carry with them a
thick stack of enchanted pages.

A blur landed in front of her with a fur-muffled thump, and the fairies disappeared under the caravan with coordinated yelps. Nate's ghostly arms wrapped around Bertie's waist, pulling her back a full two inches before his strength gave out. She thought the largest of the wolves had made it past Ariel's barrier before realizing the wild creature before her walked on two legs, not four, and the glint in the lamplight was not the creamy yellow of jagged teeth but the obsidian-black of a stone-bladed knife.

"Get away from her!" Ariel shouted, taking no risks with regards to the stranger's allegiance. Concentration broken, his protective winds died, and the wolves were immediately upon them.

"Off with you, curs!" The newcomer turned from Bertie and greeted their attackers, growling and slashing the knife. His movements were a blur of motion, the fight a dance by moonlight. He wore a ragged assortment of leather and fur stitched together in stripes, and his hair stuck out in spiky, black tufts, making him more disreputable looking than most of the pirates she knew. Burlier than even Nate, and that was saying quite a lot. The stranger's weapon—the obsidian knife—was bound with a crimson ribbon that whipped through the air like a streamer of blood.

Recognizing they were in the presence of a greater predator, the wolves fled into the night, thwarted and howling.

From under the caravan, Mustardseed made shooing

motions at their newly arrived champion. "Go on, now! You're supposed to exit, pursuing them!"

The stranger whirled about, piercing black eyes searching for the source of the tiny voice and passing over Nate without marking his presence with so much as a blink. Evidently spotting the fairies, the newcomer addressed his answer to the wheel of the wagon. "Oh, I am, am I? Explanations first, I think!" Turning, he advanced upon Bertie and Ariel. "Let us begin with how you summoned me here. What sort of witchcraft is this?"

"I apologize for interrupting whatever it was you were doing." Bertie folded the still-damp page from The Book into four and shoved it in the pocket of her borrowed coat. "I didn't require a courier. And it wasn't witchcraft." She paused to think over that assertion, then added, "Not really."

The newcomer stalked nearer, vibrating with barely restrained energy. "Only a minute ago, I was about to lay claim to a priceless jewel. Then, without a by-your-leave, I was grasped by Fate's Hand and cast down here like a pebble on the shore. And you claim that was not witchcraft?"

"She said that it wasn't—" Ariel started to say, but a blur of motion knocked him aside.

Before Nate could shout to her, before Bertie could

turn and run, the newcomer had her by the arms, black fingernails like claws curving into her skin through the silk of Ariel's jacket. With his face only a few inches away from her own, she could see the bristles on his cheeks and chin pointing every direction, the depth of the purple-black circles about his eyes. Feral of teeth and foul of breath, he smelled like he'd imbibed the contents of a condemned distillery and looked entirely capable of committing ten sorts of mayhem.

But all he did was sniff at her curiously. "No, you're not a witch."

Nate made a guttural noise of frustration, addressing Ariel's prone form. "Get up an' get in there!"

"Let her go." Unwittingly obeying the command, the air elemental regained an upright position and gathered his winds behind him. His clothes and face were dusty and disheveled, but undiluted fury radiated from every angle of Ariel's body. Bertie shook her head at him, afraid that a sudden, ill-timed blast could startle her captor, who'd brought his nose a bit closer still to sniff at her again.

"No, not a witch," the stranger mused. "Why do I sense something familiar about you?"

"I haven't the foggiest idea." Bertie gave him Mrs. Edith's most Imperious Look, though her voice squeaked a bit when she said, "Unhand me this instant."

Instead, he glanced from the caravan to Bertie, recognition sparking in the depths of his dark eyes. "There was another Mistress of Revels when first we met, and you were smaller, I think. That day, you made it rain jelly beans and peppermint sticks and chocolate humbugs from the sky."

CHAPTER THREE

To Be Acquainted with This Stranger

"You're one of the Brigands!" Moth screeched before Bertie could make the connection.

"I was," he corrected. "No longer am I a member of that particular brotherhood, sadly."

Peaseblossom sniffed her contempt. "If you meet a thief, you may suspect him, by virtue of your office, to be no true man."

"No true man ever got his heart's desire, my diminutive Lady Disdain." Returning his attention to Bertie, he caught sight of the scrimshaw hanging around her neck and squinted at it. "Wherever did you get that?" Before she could answer, he broke into a wide and somewhat alarming grin. "Have you been to the Théâtre?"

"We're *from* the Théâtre." Ariel's winds swirled and

danced behind him, though his shoulders relaxed a fraction of an inch. "But how did you guess that?"

"The lovely medallion the lady is wearing? I took it there myself. Left it as gift for Mr. Hastings." The newcomer's grin broadened, and what had been disconcerting mere seconds ago was now jovial and warm.

Bertie thought of the Properties Manager at the theater. "You left an object for him without filling out paperwork in triplicate? Did you want his head to explode?"

"More like a little joke between associates." The newcomer clapped Bertie on the arms. "Mr. Hastings is a tricky one, he is. Nothing unwanted in that room. Each thing to its proper place."

"It's carved from Sedna's bone," Nate said, hardly able to voice the Sea Goddess's name without choking. "Ask him how a sneak-thief came by such a bit o' magic?"

The title was an apt one, Bertie thought. "Where did you get it from? The scrimshaw, I mean."

The sneak-thief hooked one of his curved, black fingernails under the medallion's leather string, lifting it to the light with an appreciative look. "Perhaps it was a token from a knight I served for a time. Or I chanced upon it in a crowded marketplace." He let it drop, the weight solid and reassuring against her skin. "Or I found it, high in the nest of a bird."

"Which one of those?" Bertie's impatience put an edge on the words.

"It matters not. It was an unwanted thing." He turned, sniffing at the air and following an unseen trail into the field.

"An unwanted thing?" She gave chase past the caravan, fascinated by the cadence of his words.

"Though I left the Brigands years ago, I am still a larcenist of sorts. A bandit, a burglar, a picker of pockets." He paused and held up a finger. "But I have a Code of Honor. I only take things that are unwanted. That's the trick, you see."

"What's the trick in taking unwanted things?" demanded Moth from under the caravan.

With a wiggle and a pounce, the sneak-thief located a leather satchel dropped in the grass upon his untimely arrival. "The trick is knowing the difference between when they are not wanted and when they are."

Nate snorted at the exact same time Ariel did, and it was all Bertie could do not to laugh at the disconcerted look the pirate gave the oblivious air elemental.

Peaseblossom peered at the newcomer from between the rear wheel's painted spokes. "Have you a name, sir?"

"Waschbär." Nose aquiver with amusement, the sneak-thief bounced on the balls of his feet, as though prepared to bound away at the least provocation. "And whom do I have the pleasure of addressing?"

"I am the Mistress of Revels, also known as Beatrice Shakespeare Smith." When one of the fairies cleared his throat, Bertie added, "And Company."

Waschbär's chest rumbled, a precursor to laughter. "But of course. Emissaries from the Théâtre, on a grand and merry adventure through the countryside. Am I right?"

"Precisely." Bertie didn't think they needed to get into the particulars just yet. She tried to maintain eye contact with him, but her gaze kept sliding to his pack.

He caught her staring and flashed another mouthful of teeth at her. "I have many nice things. Mayhap you find yourself in need of something?"

"That's why you were . . . er . . . summoned here." She pointed at the still-flaming fae. "You gather what dry wood you can find." None of them moved. Bertie sighed and added, "Once there's a fire, we can see about food."

"Aye, Captain!" Four sparks of light immediately scattered and disappeared into the bushes. Their enthusiasm for snacks overcame Bertie's previously kindled blue-fire, much as a tidal wave would douse a candle: flames smothered all at once without even a wisp of smoke to mark their passing.

"And I, milady?" Ariel asked. "What would you have me do?"

Bertie slanted a look at Waschbär. Despite the new-comer's change of mood, she had to repress the urge to use Ariel as a shield. "I suppose you should check on the horses. Make sure their upending didn't knock all their bolts loose."

The fairies returned with armloads of twigs that might, with conviction and hard work, become sticks someday. Aided by Waschbär, who could obviously see better in the dark than any of them, and a box of matches the sneak-thief pulled from the unseen depths of his pockets, a fire soon crackled merrily. Illumination expanded like a spot-light until the area around the caravan was included in the ragged-edged circle.

Nate skirted the fire, loathe to walk through the con-flagration though it could hardly do him damage, seeing as Bertie could see every spark through him as he walked. "Watch yer back, lass, ye don't know what he'll do next."

Waschbär gestured to the merry blaze. "Let us sit, enjoy your fine fire, and share both food and safety in numbers."

"We have the numbers if you have the food," Mustard-seed said.

In response, the newcomer nudged his pack over. Apples, sugar buns, and little brown nuts rolled in every direction. A very dead rodent landed on the ground as well, eyes gummy and mouth hanging agape.

Bertie wrinkled her nose at the sight of it. "That's nasty!"

"No, that's a squirrel." Waschbär considered it a moment, sniffed it twice, and set it to one side.

The fairies ventured closer to the provider of sustenance, more afraid of skipping a meal than of possible death and dismemberment. Ariel managed to step between Bertie and the stranger without making a noise, but Waschbär acknowledged the defensive gesture with a chortle. The rumble moved down his chest to dislodge a pair of furry slippers from his pockets, which proceeded to scamper about his ankles.

Startled, Peaseblossom flicked her fingertips at the unwelcome arrivals. "Shoo! Go on, you nasty things."

The animals hissed and retreated in a series of humpity steps, backs arched and teeth bared, but they did not flee.

"What are they?" Bertie held out her hand and got bitten for her trouble.

"Dinner," Nate said.

"Ferrets," Waschbär supplied. "They've been my only company these many years."

"I say we poke them with sticks," Mustardseed said.

"Be my guest," Cobweb said. "You'll be lucky to not get eaten."

"They've never eaten anyone. Well, not to my

knowledge, at least." Waschbär said with a nod. "This one is Pip Pip and the other Cheerio."

"So they're British ferrets," Peaseblossom said.

Moth perked up a bit. "Perhaps they're royal ferrets."

"'Her Majesty's Ferrets' certainly has a ring to it."

"What do you think, Ariel?"

"I have no opinion on ferrets, royal or otherwise." The air elemental reached out his hands and pulled, as though upon an invisible rope.

"Oh, oh, are you pantomiming a tug-of-war?" Mustard-seed hopped up and down.

Ariel's glance would have withered an Opening Night bouquet. "No." Another pull, this time accompanied by a dragging noise.

Startled, Bertie jumped. "What are you doing?"

"I have no intention of sitting on the ground." One last pull, and he hauled a fallen log into their midst. The ferrets immediately clambered upon it, chattering their approval.

"Perfection. Now we shall break bread." Waschbär located two sugar buns and picked up one in each hand. Casting about, he took three sure steps through the tallest of the grass and crouched down. When she squinted hard, Bertie could see a tiny, slow-moving stream lazily traversing the field. Humming to himself, the sneak-thief plunged the buns into the water. After much sloshing and splashing, he turned and offered the damp bits of bread to Moth and Cobweb.

They couldn't conceal their disgust. "What did you do that for?"

Waschbär marveled at their dejected countenances. "But I washed them just for you! Do you not clean your food?"

"No," said Moth. "Most people don't. At least not like that."

"To heck with most people, I sure don't," said Cobweb. "You want to dunk them in jam, fine. Frosting, you don't even have to ask. But water?"

"I don't even like to drink water, much less soak my food in it," Mustardseed said.

"All right, then." Waschbär selected two more buns. The boys accepted them and retreated to the other side of the fire to share out the spoils while the sneak-thief sat back on his haunches, his musk more pronounced as the fire warmed his variety of furs. "What would you like to eat, Beatrice? Rough bread? Sharp cheese? Joint of roast mutton?"

"This is fine." Not wanting to appear rude or ungrateful, Bertie picked up a rosy red apple and took a tiny bite as she crossed to the improvised bench. Nate leaned against the log, looking wholly disapproving when Ariel moved closer. Now that the situation wasn't dire, Bertie could appreciate the unfamiliar scent of the countryside: hay and campfire smoke and what she assumed was a distant cow. Stars winked into existence overhead, as though eager to keep an eye on her. "And you can call me Bertie. Unexpected use of Beatrice makes me think I'm in trouble."

"As you like, Bertie." Waschbär studied her across the fire while his nimble fingers cracked nuts with a rapidity that defied logic. "So what thing is wanted here?"

"Paper." The bit of fruit stuck halfway down her throat, and Bertie had sudden sympathy for Snow White. "But not your average sort—"

With a gleeful noise, he turned his pack completely over. Bits of twine threaded with shiny beads spilled out alongside a gold ring that gleamed with opal-fire. A glass vial scattered colored sand into the grass.

Peaseblossom peered over his shoulder. "The ring is lovely."

Waschbär nodded as he polished it on the front of his shirt. "From the jewel cask of a castle on the Lightning Ridge."

"What's with the sand?" Moth wanted to know.

The sneak-thief let a bit dribble through his nimble fingers. "The sands of time."

Bertie would have reached for that, drawn by the glittering flecks of stone, but Ariel's words caught her wandering attention.

"The lady asked you for paper."

"There's paper, and then there's paper." With a wink and a nod of acknowledgment, Waschbär tossed aside a piece of ragged silk to reveal a journal. The leather cover was tooled in designs that shifted with the firelight, and the thong closure held an ebony fountain pen against the edge of the pages. . . .

Pages that glowed.

Nate cursed under his breath, then added, "Just like Th' Book."

"Oh, my." Bertie leaned forward to get a better look. "How could that be 'unwanted'?"

"Ah, that's a story. That's a story for certain!" Waschbär chortled. "Mayhap a wizard left it lying on a stone bench near his tower. Mayhap it fell from the pack of a scribe journeying to his holy land. Mayhap it was locked away in the darkest recesses of a dimly lit sanctuary." He stroked the cover, softly, so as not to scratch it. "The trick is knowing when something is wanted and when it is not."

Even across the fire, Bertie could sense its power. "It's wanted."

"Oh, yes?" The two words held the suggestion of countless deals brokered in sun-warmed marketplaces.

"I would trade for it."

"Of course you would," the sneak-thief said.

"I have nothing," she said, "to equal the value of such a thing."

"There are the usual promises," Waschbär said. "A kiss."

Caught between Nate and Ariel, Bertie's cheeks flamed. "Kisses are nothing but trouble."

The fairies jeered. "I thought you said boys were nothing but trouble."

"Yes, and who do you think she's kissing, stupid? Certainly not the fence posts!"

"Your hand in marriage," Waschbär suggested with a teasing grin. "Your firstborn child."

"I'm too young to get married and have kids," Bertie protested, desperately trying to avoid making eye contact with either of her male bookends.

"Come, come, there must be something!" Waschbär leaned back on one elbow, looking deceptively nonchalant. "If you cannot make the standard offerings, then you must make an unusual one. A dream, mayhap. A secret yearning of your heart."

Unable to do more than whisper, Bertie asked, "What happens when I give something like that to you?"

Nate made a rude noise through his nose. "Naught good, I can tell ye that."

"Nothing good will come of this." Ariel tried to keep the warning between the two of them but didn't quite manage it.

"Now then, air spirit, do you fear that you are the unwanted thing at this fire?" The sneak-thief's eyes were bright, black buttons, if buttons could be amused. The firelight didn't quite illumine their depths, so looking into them was like waving a flashlight around the under-stage area at the Théâtre.

"Why don't you give it to her out of the goodness of your heart?" Ariel let slip a blast of hot air, and the fire blazed before dwindling to embers.

In the shadows, Waschbär chuckled. "If you've nothing to trade me, Beatrice Shakespeare Smith, you will have to steal the journal from me."

"I beg your pardon?" Bertie stared at him, not quite sure she wasn't hallucinating due to lack of food and a surplus of campfire smoke up her nose. "You want me to what?"

A hidden owl hooted as Waschbär lifted the journal to his twitching nose and sniffed it. "Yes, yes, this is the thing that's wanted here. A place to write your hopes and dreams, eh?"

"And pudding," Moth said. The others elbowed him but he wouldn't recant. "If it were mine, I'd write about treacle tarts and jam roly-poly."

"Might I see it?" Bertie held out a hopeful hand, fingers nearly grazing the leather cover before the journal disappeared into the folds of Waschbär's furs.

"I think not." He gave her a wink and a nod.

"Of course it wouldn't be that easy." Mustardseed hammered two walnuts together with an aggrieved air. When they cracked open, he picked out the meats and wore one of the shell halves as a hat.

"The very definition of stealing would suggest I take it against your will," Bertie said with a frown.

"There are many ways to use a word." Ariel offered guidance as though it were no more than a bit of bread and cheese. "Reflect a moment upon *Much Ado About Nothing*. Act Two, Scene Three."

"Beatrice's line," Nate supplied. "'Against my will, I am sent t' bid ye come in t' dinner.'"

"'There's a double meaning in that,'" Bertie said, completing the quote. "A double meaning."

The sneak-thief took a coin from his pocket and flipped it over and about his fingers. The flash of silver changed to copper in an instant, then to gold. "Why, 'tis a cockle!" The coin morphed into a shell, heart shaped and striped. "Or a walnut shell. A knack, a toy, a trick; they are all words."

"Not just playthings," Nate said, ghostly fingers seeking out the nape of Bertie's neck. "We know better than that. They can be used as weapons, t' cut and t' wound."

There were so many things she wanted to say to him, none of which could be uttered before this audience.

Vowing that the next thing to be stolen, after the journal, would be a moment alone with him, Bertie selected her words with care. "There are many ways to steal something. I might steal it the way I steal a glance." She looked at Waschbär from under her eyelashes.

"Yes, you might," he said.

"Or there is the way I might steal a kiss." Plucking Mustardseed from the air mid-flight, Bertie planted her lips on his cheek, much to his chagrin.

Waschbär smiled. "Yes, it might be stolen in that fashion. Perhaps with a bit more enjoyment, in some cases." His gaze flickered over Mustardseed, who had rubbed his face nearly raw and was still making disgusted noises and rude comments about girl germs.

"A heart might be stolen." Ariel's soft suggestion was nearly lost to the crackle and hiss of the fire.

"I might steal someone's thunder," Bertie said, then held her breath when lightning ripped through the canvas of the night and the promised noise rattled her very bones. This was no sound effect, wrung from a sheet of metal in the flies; the real thing settled in the back of her skull and tasted of ozone.

"Almost there," Waschbär said.

"Mind what you say next, Bertie," Ariel said, sounding far more cavalier at full volume. "I don't care to be burned to a crisp by an errant lightning bolt."

"Hush," Peaseblossom told him. "This is the important bit."

Bertie clasped her hands about her knees until her knuckles turned white. "But I think I need to steal . . . the show. My show."

The journal appeared in her lap, a sudden weight upon her legs and mind.

"That's it, that's it!" Waschbär clapped his massive paws as he reclined against his pack, at ease with the universe now that the game was done.

Bertie ran her hands over the leather cover, nerve-clumsy fingers untying the knot that bound the journal closed. "It *is* like The Book's paper, albeit less wrinkled and smeary." Pulling their exit page out for comparison, she was gratified to see how its glow matched that of the journal. "See? 'Following Her Stars'—"

With a sizzle and a hiss, the page from The Book fused into the binding of the journal. Sparks of light flew every direction. All four of the fairies froze midair, Bertie's hair frizzled with static electricity, and a hollow noise echoed around them, like an enormous door slamming shut.

Ariel reached toward her, then thought better of it and let his hand drop. "Did you not stop to think that reading that line out loud might have acted us back to the theater? Why would you do something so foolish?"

"I . . ." Bertie swallowed. "The Book is part of the Théâtre, the outside world is the journal, and my story belongs to both places." It was one of those lies that, once spoken, became truth.

"You're truly the Teller of Tales now." A shudder rippled through Ariel. "I hope you understand what that means."

Mustardseed flailed his arms about. "Won't SOME-ONE think of the PUDDING?!"

"I don't think that's a good idea at all." Bertie closed the journal. "Caution whispers in my ear."

"Would that ye'd thought o' that a bit sooner, eh?" Nate's soft words eased over her shoulder.

With a glare at the ready, she turned. The last remaining sparks of The Book's golden light clung to him in places, flaring, burning bits of him away. The desire to speak privately instantaneously transformed into Necessity. Leaping to her feet, Bertie trumpeted, "I'm exhausted. I vote we make camp and get a fresh start in the morning."

"At the cock's crow?" Mustardseed said behind her.

Moth opened his mouth, but Peaseblossom pointed a stern finger at him. "Don't you dare!" she admonished. "Not before company!"

Waschbär stretched until several vertebrae popped like champagne corks. "It would be good to start your merry romp on the morrow," he said with a yawn that revealed his back molars. "It's full dark, and the hour is late."

Ariel slanted a wicked look at Bertie. "And let's not forget that there are dangerous creatures afoot."

The sneak-thief mistook his meaning but still concurred. "Lurking beyond the firelight are things larger and more fearsome than our friends the wolves."

As though summoned, the shadowy silhouette of an enormous bird dipped low over the campsite. Its cry sent dark, curved talons down Bertie's spine as she followed Nate's vague shape toward the caravan.

Already settled upon the ground, Waschbär nestled deep into the folds of his furry overcoat and gestured to the ferrets, who came at a run and dove into his pockets. "No more proper bed than a soft cushion of earth and the night sky for a coverlet."

Running, Bertie called out, "Good night, everyone!" She feared the fairies would give chase, but a glance revealed they were already constructing impromptu nests of twigs and brambles, as though setting a scene from *A Midsummer Night's Dream*. There was no time to stop and appreciate the pretty picture they made as she climbed the diminutive back stairs. Inside, Nate wavered in the center of overturned boxes and cabinet doors hanging ajar. Far worse than the mess, he'd gone as fuzzy as a spotlight diffusing across a stage.

How can he look paler than a ghost?!

"Bertie?" came the soft query behind her.

Though she didn't want to, she turned around in the doorway to see Ariel standing just below her, a Romeo of reduced circumstances now that they were without the necessary balcony.

"Would you like to me come inside?"

"Whatever for?" Before Ariel could explain, the answer slammed into her chest. "Oh. No. No, thank you."

"Are you certain?" When the air elemental placed one foot on the staircase, the caravan began to vibrate.

Standing just behind her, Nate strained to close the door. The journal's sparks had burned tiny holes in his shirt, his hands, his cheeks, and bits of light gobbled yet more greedily as he expended what energy he had left.

Bertie hastened inside, not wanting him to wink out like a candle. "I am. But . . . er . . . thank you for the offer."

"Good night, then—" Ariel managed to say before Nate succeeded in slamming the door shut in his face.

CHAPTER FOUR

Darkness Like a Dream

While **I** don' like th' idea o' him sniffin' about ye," Nate said, his voice crawling out of a dark so blue that it could only be found at the bottom of the sea, "I hope fer both yer sakes all he's done is sniff."

"Never mind that." Entangled in unseen debris, Bertie lost her shoes as she tripped over what felt like a table leg, a jumbled pile of bedding, and an open drawer. She fumbled her way along one wall, locating the wooden bracket that contained a tiny glass oil lamp and a box of matches. Once she'd banished the shadows, the interior of the caravan reminded her of a doll's house that had been upended and rattled about. The sleeping berth tucked along one wall had belched half its bedding upon the floor, the pocket-size breakfast nook was a jumble of embroidered place mats and crockery, but she gave the amenities only a perfunctory glance. Setting the journal and pen in the center of the table, she turned to address a more important issue. "You're fading."

Nate leaned against the cabinetry, though he wasn't solid enough to rest any weight against it. His poltergeist act had apparently drained him of yet more strength, causing his features to waver then resettle upon his spectral bones. "I'm not long fer this place, I fear."

Bertie would have traded any number of things to be able to reach out and take his hand. "Your soul isn't meant to be separated from your body. I'll have to write you back."

"T' Sedna's cave?" Nate surged forward and attempted to grab the journal, though his hands merely stirred the cover. "Like hell ye will!"

"I have to! Do you want to die here?"

He hesitated before admitting, "I'm already dead, lass."

Everything went hazy around the edges, and the floor tilted up to meet her. When Bertie sat down hard upon the crooked mattress, she cracked the back of her head against the wood that framed the sleeping berth. "What do you mean?"

"Sedna drown'd me, don't ye remember?"

Instantly Bertie was transported back to the theater.

Hanging from the chandelier, she saw him sucked under by the saltwater currents. She remembered holding her own breath until her lungs burned, reaching desperately for him as the Sea Goddess claimed Nate along with the glowing paper-fish that was his page from The Book. "Why?"

"She couldn't take me t' th' underworld, unless my physical body was dead." The words had more substance and power than he did. "That's all she has now: that empty shell." The sounds of spectral expectoration. "May she curse it till she's blue instead o' green."

"But you're *fading*."

He fell to his knees alongside her, half drifting through the floorboards. "I'd rather fade t' nothin' here wi' ye than be trapped there wi' her."

Bertie's stomach clenched painfully and, along with it, her fists. "I'll *kill* her."

Nate rested the suggestion of his shaggy head on her knee. "Leave it be, lass. I'll not have ye risk yer life fer th' sake o' revenge."

"If you think you can order me about, you've forgotten much in your time away." She tried to touch him then, but all she could feel was the cold.

"I've forgotten nothin'." Then, before Bertie could say anything, he mumbled into her skirts, "Ye need t' change. Ye've got dirt on yer face, an' this gown's fer th' rag bag."

"Tsk." It took every bit of Bertie's restraint to stay the threat of tears. "Mrs. Edith would have a fit, should she learn I changed clothes in your company again."

"Yes, if by 'fit' ye mean she'd have my head on a pike." Nate's shade was now as thin as a bit of tissue paper held up to the light. He reached for her again, and this time his hand drifted through hers. "Lass—"

The whisper trailed off, a bit of rope slithering across a wooden deck and falling overboard without a splash to mark it. Surging up from the mattress, Bertie scrambled to open the journal.

"*Not again.*" Two fierce words, strong enough to cause the lamplight to flicker as she wrote,

> They were transported to the place where her powers would be strongest, the place where she could hold on to him with both hands.

A gust—*of wind? of water?*—snuffed out the lamp. Underfoot, the caravan's floor was suddenly slick, a midwinter pond etched with ice-skating patterns, furrows raised and sharp like scars against the bare soles of her feet. Setting the pen down atop the journal, Bertie didn't expect the table to immediately glide away from her like a sleigh. She reached for it, stretching her arms out in front of her, fingertips expecting to meet something, anything, but the bed was gone now as well, as though the Stage Manager had called a scene change, summoning a Great and Icy Nothingness to replace her bedroom. Trapped in the memory of black velvet curtains, Bertie took a tentative step, shoving against fabric that wasn't there.

"Nate?"

Her piercing whisper prompted no response, and Bertie's teeth started to chatter. The cold crept up her bare legs in icy ribbons, and the hem of her ruined evening gown crackled with frost. About the time she would have started screaming for help, a pinpoint of light appeared in the distance. Squinting, hoping it wouldn't disappear, Bertie sidled forward. The fleck of gold dilated until she realized it was a single brilliant spotlight focused on a kneeling figure.

Then she began to half run, half skate across the treacherous black ice. "Nate!"

His head came up, and she was thankful to see that, though scruffy and wild-eyed, he was no longer transparent. "Don't—"

Too late; she'd passed through a thin sheet of amber gel, the sort used to color the theater lights. Nate was on his feet just in time to catch her, and never before had Bertie been so thankful to painfully collide with someone in her life. Grasping his face in her hands, she wished for better words than the ones that tumbled out of her. "Are you all right?"

Nate nodded until hair came loose from his plait. "I think so."

Bertie counted fingers and toes and eyes in a frantic bodily inventory that thankfully ended with everything where it should be. He had no wounds, either. Not ones she could see, anyway.

"It worked!" she crowed, as loud as Peter Pan. "Something I wrote finally turned out the way I wanted it to!"

"Ye kept me from fadin' t' nothin'," he said. "And fer that, I owe ye my thanks."

The kiss wasn't unexpected, but the moment his lips touched hers, Bertie realized something was still not quite as it should be. Nate's mouth, the rough linen of his shirt, the solid weight of his chest under her hands . . . everything was slightly askew, reminding her of an ill-fitted costume. Pulling away from him, she put a hand over the scrimshaw. "You're still not properly you."

"I'm wearin' yer memories o' me like a second skin." He tilted his head to the side, as though testing muscles newly strung. "Ye did well, though I feel a bit taller than before."

Now she could see the small differences she'd wrought, the details she'd neglected. Beyond angry with herself for conjuring only the illusion of him, Bertie spat curses upon the ground.

Nate stepped back, giving her temper a wide berth. "Mrs. Edith would wash yer mouth out wi' soap, if she could hear ye."

"I don't give a fig for Mrs. Edith right now." Bertie went to kick something and realized they stood in a tightly focused spotlight. Slowly it expanded to include a tiny circle of stones, streamers of red and orange ribbon snapping to life within. Immense roots crept over the ground, the tangled tresses of a captured dryad. Bark-clad legs and gnarled torsos formed the trunks of ancient trees, their branches reaching through the darkness to form a massive canopy.

Nate's breath caught at the sight of the trees. "Do ye know this place?"

"Yes."

The last time I stood in a grove such as this, Ariel had torn all the pages from The Book, the Théâtre was falling down about our ears, and I used the trees to keep the ceiling from crumbling in upon us.

She'd conjured an exact duplicate of that set, and once again she drew strength from the ancient grove. A few minutes more, the branches might be her own arms, able to protect her and Nate both from time and tide.

"I want ye t' promise me somethin', Bertie." The softly

voiced words drew her attention away from the forest's foliage.

She turned to face him, thankful she didn't have to lie about this. "Nothing happened with Ariel."

Nothing too bad, at any rate.

The stern look he gave her was exactly as she'd remembered.

Of course I got that bit right.

"I can't deal wi' him as I'd like." Nate's right hand reached for a sword she'd forgotten to give him. "Until that changes, I want ye t' promise me ye won't go lookin' for Sedna."

"Can't exactly go looking for her here, can I?" Bertie thought she'd neatly skirted the issue, but that only led to another bit of difficulty.

"An' how will ye get back t' th' caravan?"

"You can't think I'm going back without you." Not phrased as a question, Bertie's words came out flat, the edges sharp, a dare to contradict her.

"Stow yer weapons, lass, ye won't cut me wi' that tone." Nate's arms encircled her, pulling her against a reassuringly solid chest. "Th' longer ye tarry, th' harder it will be t' get back."

"And how do you know that?"

"Th' same way I know how t' find th' North Star."

Putting a hand over hers, he raised it to gesture at a sky devoid of light. "Ye don't belong here."

"Neither do you!" He was a page torn from her own book, held maddeningly just out of reach in the hand of a goddess.

"Go." As though it pained him, Nate released her. The gentle shove that followed put her within inches of the spotlight's edge. "I'll keep."

"I won't leave you here—"

"Ye will!" He pushed her out of the light then, and everything beyond was the same brittle crackle of black ice.

Feet shooting from underneath her, Bertie fell upon her rear with a solid *thunk!* Pain shot up her spine. She was sliding, the already-terrifying downward slope growing steeper with each passing second. Her hands scrabbled at an impossibly slick surface until the ice ended, and a Void began.

Flung into it, Bertie screamed, loud and long, but now there was not so much as an echo for her trouble. She was Alice falling down the rabbit hole, without the niceties of a harness, counterweighted cables, and a dozen stagehands to guide her descent.

"Little One, what have you done to yourself?" The voice came from every direction at once, then there was the brush of feathers against her cheek.

Bertie windmilled at the darkness with both arms, her

fears tangled about her like a winding sheet until she ceased her flailing to grab the medallion with both hands. "Help me!"

"You're having a nightmare." This time, the voice came from just above her. Fingers like talons closed over her shoulders. "Calm yourself and open your eyes."

Without knowing why, Bertie obeyed, then wished she hadn't. The creature standing before her was more bird than man, taller even than Ariel. Moonlight streamed through the window and over his broad shoulders.

"Who are you?" Bertie's skirts were twisted about her, waist to ankles, thwarting her efforts to scramble away from him. The caravan—for they were indeed inside the caravan now—was pitiably small, the sleeping berth a tiny prison in which she was trapped by a demented stranger. "What are you doing in here?"

There was a horrible clearing of his throat, as though bird and man fought for use of the same muscles. Man won. "I was flying overhead. Your nightmare pulled me in, even as the medallion called to me."

"Why would it do that?"

"Because I carved it." There was the flare of a match as he relit the lantern. "I'm the Scrimshander." With those words, the stranger began to tremble. The feathers obscuring his face drifted free from his skin to reveal tattooed swirls and flourishes. When he adjusted the lamp's wick, Bertie saw that which she'd mistaken for a beak was only his nose, shadow-exaggerated. Cold sweat trickled down the small of her back when he reached out a tentative hand to caress her cheek, as one would comfort a small child. "I mean you no harm, Beatrice."

Bertie backed into the sleeping berth, as far away from this man, her curious rescuer, as she could possibly get. "How do you know my name?"

"I was trying to reach . . ." He swallowed hard against something, then managed to say, "To reach the Théâtre." Another shudder, another drift of feathers upon the floor. "But it's difficult to be anything but a bird when I'm flying." Standing in the narrow aisle, the Scrimshander shifted from one foot to the other, his head grazing the ceiling. Agitated, he shook himself, settling his remaining feathers—*his wings!*—back into place. "Why did you leave the nest? You were safe there, warm and cared for."

"The nest?" It took her a moment to understand what he meant by that. "You mean the Théâtre?" The shock of it all settled into her bones, and Bertie pulled the bed's narrow coverlet around her shoulders. Tracing the quilted squares so she wouldn't have to look at the Scrimshander, she noticed in a detached, mind-wandering-the-lily-fields way that they'd been cut down from worn-out costumes: here a bit of pink silk that reminded her of Titania's robes; another of moss-soft green velvet, the sort that edged Puck's tunic. The stitches, though perfectly straight and even, were hand-wrought. For a moment, Bertie could feel Mrs. Edith's arms around her, could smell her lavender eau de cologne. . . .

I mustn't cry.

Tears would never do, not with the scrimshaw still hanging about her neck. The last time salt water had fallen upon the medallion, the Sea Goddess had manifested.

And kidnapped Nate.

Bertie sucked in a deep breath; only then did she smell the star-shine and salt upon the birdman, the wild promise of freedom that threw open every door in her mind. For an instant, she was Ophelia, fleeing the theater, her arms clasped about his neck. A second later, Bertie was four years old again, throwing herself off the highest cliff she could find, trying to fly.

Like a bird.

"You're the Mysterious Stranger." She could hardly vocalize the second half of the realization. "You're my *father.*"

He raised his voice to an insistent squawk. "You must go back!"

"Keep it down, unless you want the others to come running!" Bertie wasn't about to be lectured by some stranger, father or not, even if he was large and intimidating. She peered up into glassy black eyes that were like something sewn on a child's toy. "I can't go back until I rescue my friend. He was kidnapped by Sedna."

The birdman went very still, as though he'd been struck by a hunter's arrow. When next he spoke, he struggled with words caught in his throat. "The Sea Goddess?"

"Yes."

"Whatever business your friend has with the Sea Goddess, it is his own."

"That's not true." Her mind was like a puzzle box, suddenly opening. "It's *my* fault. For crying on this medallion . . . that *you* said you carved."

For a moment, a glimpse of the Scrimshander was visible in the birdman's face: the pride of an artist; the terror of a father. "You won't be able to get to him. One must be dead to travel through the gateway to Sedna's Kingdom."

Bertie sat up on her knees. The blanket slipped down her shoulder, and she wished she was wearing something more than a much-maligned evening gown as armor against his piercing gaze. "That means there *is* a gateway, and you know where it is."

He squawked and retreated half a step. "I don't."

"You're lying." Bertie wrapped her hand around the scrimshaw, hearing Nate's words just as he'd whispered them to her in the Properties Department.

Sedna learned, in th' hardest o' ways, t' look beyond th' surface o' a man, t' see what hopes an' dreams an' fears lay nestled in his heart o' hearts.

Except the medallion showed her a heart that beat simultaneously in both man and bird. He was bound with two water-ribbons, one the color of the moon reflected on a drowning pool, the other brilliant sunlight on the ocean's waves. Following the silver one immediately to his right, Bertie found a woman, eyes sparkling with sequins, hair twined about with flowers, floating in the eddies of her own salt tears.

My mother.

When the Scrimshander-within looked at Ophelia, his face in profile was that of a man in love, as unmistakably human as it was vulnerable.

Bertie swallowed, not wanting to tear her gaze away from the pair of them, standing together just as she'd always imagined, but the golden ribbon led in the other direction. Turning, she saw that the sunlit streamer danced through sparkling sand and disappeared into the waves. Just beyond the surface, the Sea Goddess beckoned to the birdman with her starfish fingers, calling to him with whale song.

Bertie's father turned to look at Sedna, the other side of his face that of a bird.

"Sedna ran away from her family to be with you." Bertie's accusation caused the scrimshaw's vision to dissipate. Easier to see him now that the pink light of dawn teased its way over the window sash. "You were married to her."

He didn't deny it. "You must return."

"I can't." Bertie scrambled out of the berth and backed him against the door, armed with only her anger and an accusatory finger she pointed at his face. "You saw to that the day you coaxed my mother away from her home. You stole Ophelia, Sedna stole Nate; twice pages have been torn from The Book and taken into the outside world."

"Your story belongs at the Théâtre."

"Not anymore, it's doesn't." Reaching over to the table, she snatched up the journal to show him their exit page bound within.

He recoiled from the unearthly glow, filling the caravan with his panicked cry. Through ringing ears, Bertie heard Ariel's matching shout, muffled though it was by wooden walls. The Scrimshander beat his wings at her, sending the journal flying. When the air elemental jerked the door open, her father flung himself skyward.

"What's going on!?" Ariel peered, wild-eyed, into the caravan.

"Never mind about me, catch hold of him!" Shoving past Ariel and nearly falling down the stairs, Bertie caught sight of the enormous winged creature overhead. Bird instincts warred with those of a father, and indecision caused him to circle, dipping and wheeling but unable to break free. She stamped her bare foot in the grass. "Come down here at once!"

"Are you all right?" Ariel immediately followed his first question with an encore. "What the hell was that thing?"

"He's—" The idea filled her throat with cinders and ash, choking her before she could finish.

When the Scrimshander keened again, Ariel turned, lifted his hands, and sent all his winds to knock the bird-creature from the sky. Thrown back by one current and then slammed forward by another, it panicked.

Bertie lunged at Ariel, grasping his arms and forcing his hands down. "Don't, he's my father!"

The air elemental stared at her as though she spoke in tongues. "Your . . . father?"

"He knows where to find Sedna," Bertie said. Overhead, the Scrimshander circled again, free of the caravan's confines but seemingly undecided about fleeing. Spiraling up then dipping down, his flight pattern matched the heaving of her midsection as she waited for him to break away.

By now, the fairies had rounded the corner of the caravan, flying full tilt into Bertie's hair. "What's going on?"

"We were making breakfast!"

"The porridge is going to burn."

"Never mind the porridge." Bertie turned around, scanning a floor littered with feathers, the bedding half-dragged from the sleeping berth. The journal was nestled on the limp goose of a pillow, a most unusual egg. She fell upon it with a cry, then reached up for the fountain pen, still atop the table. Ariel caught her around the waist as she came through the door, and the two of them nearly fell down the stairs.

"You're going to kill us both—"

"Get out of my way!" She shoved him aside and, gaze still locked upon her father, opened the journal. "I don't want any misunderstandings this time."

Ariel assessed their reluctant guest circling overhead, one hand twitching to stir a faint breeze. "I don't think you have time for fancy turns of phrase, milady."

He's right, damn him.

Uncapping the fountain pen, she scribbled:

Father and daughter are still linked, as
though by a finely wrought chain of gold.

Pink flooded the valley, and with another raucous cry, the Scrimshander's indecision evaporated. He fled the grasping fingers of first light. Bertie watched him go, tasting bitter disappointment over her most recent written failure.

"We have to follow him—" But she didn't get to finish the command. With a jerk like a tightrope walker's wire gone taut, Bertie dropped the journal and the pen into the dew-damp grass when the Scrimshander began to tow her in his wake.

CHAPTER FIVE

Our Valour Is to Chase What Flies

Bertie caught a glimpse of the encampment, everything angled Down Center Stage to face an imaginary audience, but only as she kicked over a cooking pot, leapt over the campfire, and tripped over a mound of furs that might have been the still-sleeping sneak-thief.

"AAAAAH!" the fairies screamed directly into her ears, clinging to her hair and rattling about her shoulders like Cleopatra's beaded headdress.

At the edge of the clearing, Ariel caught Bertie under the arms. The Scrimshander towed both of them forward a half-dozen steps, though the air elemental dug his similarly bare heels into the ground.

"Cut him loose!" Ariel strained to hold her.

"I can't!" Bertie managed to say before pain swallowed

the protest. As the Scrimshander struggled to flee, the connection she'd wrought threatened to tear her heart from her chest. "For God's sake, let go!" Another tug that pulled them farther afield. "Get me the journal!"

Ariel's arms tightened, then released. He shouted to the fairies, "Stay with her!"

"Aye, Captain!" Moth said as Bertie was pulled into waist-high grass. It slapped at her skin, leaving welts along her arms. The heavy skirts of her evening gown protected her legs somewhat, but rocks dug into the soles of her already-abused feet, and each unwilling step felt like—

The little mermaid, walking on her human legs.

"Tell me when it's over!" Peaseblossom screamed, her tiny eyes squinched shut. To underscore the plea, Cobweb hummed a dire tune, the sort a string quartet would play aboard a sinking ship.

Abruptly the Scrimshander circled overhead, his avian instincts perhaps warring between the need to protect his hatchling and the desire to flee. Bertie couldn't help but notice the beauty of his flight, couldn't help but wonder what it must be like to soar, but she dared not stop running, even when unexpected company joined her.

"And what are we fleeing this fine morning?" Waschbär's jovial greeting belied the ridiculousness of the circumstances under which it was uttered. Naught but twitching noses protruding from the sneak-thief's right-hand pocket,

Pip Pip and Cheerio added their own good-mornings between Waschbär's nimble leaps.

"Not fleeing," Bertie said between gasps for air. "Following." She tapped the scrimshaw. "Found this high in the nest of a bird, did you say?"

"I might have," he admitted.

"No mere coincidence, I think." Pressing one hand against the cramp in her side, she pointed with the other. "That bird-thing is going to lead us to the Sea Goddess."

"Appropriate enough, since that 'thing' is a seabird. A fulmar." The sneak-thief moved through the grass as though accustomed to unscheduled jaunts across the countryside. "And now one is bound to the other, bonds both familial and spiritual."

"Only one of those bonds is my fault." Landing on a particularly pointy rock, Bertie used a word that would have caused the stagehands to blush.

The ferrets looked at her, tiny expressions appalled, but Waschbär only grinned. "How long do you think you can keep up this brisk pace, pray tell?"

"Not much longer," she was forced to admit. "But it will be easier to keep up with the caravan."

"Naturally. Until he flies where such a conveyance cannot follow, and then what happens to you?"

An escalating rumble swallowed the end of the query, and Bertie nearly tripped when she caught sight of the foot-high letters on the side of the caravan: "BEATRICE SHAKESPEARE SMITH & COMPANY" painted in red with "TOURING PLAYERS OF THE THÉÂTRE ILLUMINATA" under it in blue.

"I did the bit in Crimson Lake!" Moth said into Bertie's right ear. "Free advertising."

Mustardseed sounded aggrieved. "We only managed to do one side last night before we ran out of Prussian Blue—"

"Ascension first, discussion afterward." The sneak-thief neither blinked nor asked permission before he grasped Bertie by the waist and tossed her at the still-moving vehicle. "Allez-oop!"

It was the cry of trapeze performers and trampoline jumpers, but there was nothing graceful about the way Bertie smashed into the railing alongside the driver's seat rather than triumphantly atop it. Pain bloomed in both knees, shins, and elbows on impact. Ariel clasped her by the wrist and heaved her the rest of the way aboard.

"That's going to leave a mark," was Moth's wry observance.

Not waiting for her to settle, Ariel shoved the reins at her.

Bertie had no choice but to grasp them. "What are you doing?"

"Taking precautionary measures." He looped a sturdy leather belt through the wrought-iron railing and buckled the strap around her waist. "Otherwise an untimely change in that thing's flight pattern might pull you right off." With a glance at the sky, he guided the caravan onto a road of packed dirt, a welcome change from the field. The only sign-post marking their new route was tilted and time-scabbed, thickly grown over with moss.

Behind the seat came the scrabble of fingernails against wood and a thud as Waschbär boarded. The fairies, finally convinced Bertie wasn't going to be dragged off to oblivion, emerged from her hair.

Peaseblossom zipped about Bertie's face and hands. "Are you hurt?"

"She's not gushing blood." Mustardseed looked disappointed. "Not that I can see, anyway."

Moth jabbed her nose with his finger. "Who are you, and what have you done to the Bertie who doesn't get out of bed before noon?"

"That bird-thing worked better than an alarm clock—"

"That bird-thing is my father," Bertie said without preamble. The fairies fell several inches as they all forgot to fly, but she paid them no mind, turning to Ariel. "Did you find the journal?"

With his gaze still fastened upon their airborne compass needle, he handed it to her. "What are you going to do now?"

Bertie stared hard at the bird-creature, and when her

eyes watered a bit, she wiped them carefully, blaming it on the sun.

The connection between them lengthens, every unspoken hope forging a link that she adds to the invisible chain.

I hope you can lead me to Nate. I hope you don't break free.

When the Scrimshander wheeled away again, the tugging upon her heartstrings was delayed by a few seconds. "Better, but not perfect."

Peaseblossom patted Bertie on the cheek. "Are you all right? About meeting your father?"

She couldn't bring herself to share the tone of his voice, the regret in the words "Little One," the feeling of having his hand touch her gently upon the cheek even if it was only for a moment. The bone-disk was warm against her skin, and the etching of the Théâtre on the surface shimmered. "Not just my father. He's the Scrimshander who carved the medallion, too."

"Golly," Mustardseed finally managed. "D'you think Nate knew?"

Bertie's arms came out in goose bumps. "I don't know."

That's certainly something to ask him, when next we meet.

The troupe bounced along for a minute, everyone catching their collective breath and wincing with each jolt of the wagon, each rock caught under the wheels. While Ariel sat easy in the seat, one booted foot up and shoulders relaxed, Bertie clung to the wooden armrest and braced her feet against the running boards. She could have hooked her arm through his and been far more comfortable, but the few inches of space between them was a chasm filled with unasked questions and urgency.

Her chest constricted, the invisible tether pulling her forward. Held in the seat by the leather belt around her waist and her white-knuckled grip on the armrest, Bertie snapped at Ariel, "Can't this thing go any faster?"

"Perhaps you'd like to write something to that effect in your journal, milady?"

"There's no need for sarcasm."

"Of course not! I was merely minding my own business, getting dressed—"

Bertie interrupted. "I note you managed to tuck in your shirt and do up your trousers since last I saw you."

"—when both the poetically quiet predawn and my ears were assaulted with screaming and chaos."

Bertie jabbed a finger at the sky. "'If I chance to talk a little wild, forgive me; I had it from my father.'"

"Don't you start quoting *Henry the Eighth* at me!"

Waschbär popped up behind them. "None of this is strictly her fault, if you consider the circumstances."

"No one invited you." Strands of silver hair moved

over Ariel's shoulders alongside his irritation. "We've no valuables to steal, so you might as well be off."

Twisting around, Bertie grasped a handful of Waschbär's fur coat to make certain he didn't scamper away. "I need you to stay with us. In case the connection breaks."

"You want me to join your merry band?" The sneak-thief peered at Bertie with black-button eyes that reminded her uncomfortably of her father's.

"Yes. Please." Trying to recall any part of the previous night's conversation that might sway him, Bertie was inspired when Pip Pip and Cheerio poked quivering noses out of Waschbär's coat pockets. "Sharing food and safety in numbers."

The sneak-thief studied each of them in turn, taking in something more than the troupe and the caravan with his steady gaze. Bertie did her best to project fellow-feeling and camaraderie, letting warmth pour from her smile like a spotlight. Waschbär's grin was her answer, though all he said was, "Will there be dessert?"

Bertie tried not to contemplate how much a six-foot-tall raccoonlike man could consume in the way of sugar-coated edibles. "As much as you can eat," she promised rashly. "With meat and cheese and bread, besides. I have to feed the fairies . . . one more mouth won't make much of a difference." When the ferrets chattered, Bertie amended, "Three mouths, that is."

"In that case, it would be my greatest pleasure to join your group!" Waschbär whistled a merry tune as the ferrets clambered onto his shoulders.

"This is a theater troupe, not a menagerie." Ariel gave the sneak-thief a withering look that he then shifted to Bertie. "You don't know anything about your newest recruit, except that he's a criminal."

"And a tracker. So, against the dire moment the Scrimshander breaks the connection between us, he stays." Looking up, Bertie could almost see it: a thin gold chain running into the sky like a kite string. Attached to a most unusual kite, though.

If you wanted to protect me, why did you abandon us at the theater?

And why are you running from me now, right when I need you the most?

"Perhaps we ought to contemplate breakfast." Waschbär's casual statement recalled her to their foodless plight.

Peaseblossom squeaked in outrage. "The porridge! What happened to the porridge I was cooking?"

Bertie thought of the cooking pot she'd kicked over during her hasty exit. "I'm afraid I might have trod upon it."

"Do not suffer these oats to be eaten," Mustardseed said with grim satisfaction.

"'Ceres, most bounteous lady, thy rich leas,'" Moth quoted. "'Of wheat, rye, barley, vetches, oats, and pease.'"

"Tee-hee, *Pease*." The boys rolled about, holding their stomachs and laughing at their own terrible pun until Cobweb sat up and said, "Bertie, would you please conjure some pancakes?"

"Now?" She thought of what she'd done to Nate, of the pain in her chest with every tug of the chain, and fear—of the words, of the journal—filled her from her maligned toes to her considerably rumpled hair.

"Chicken!" Moth put his thumbs in his armpits and strutted down the length of the armrest.

"I didn't say I was afraid."

"You didn't have to." Waschbär leaned over the back of the seat and placed a finger alongside his nose. "Your scent did."

What does fear smell like? Perspiration and iron-tang and—

"Lemons," Waschbär said.

"I beg your pardon?" Bertie said.

"You smell of lemons."

"Of course I do." She frumped around in her seat, fairly certain her posterior was also riddled with splinters. "Then my discomfort should smell of grapefruit, no?"

Waschbär reached out a single curved claw and traced it down the journal's spine. "No sense having something with that sort of power without knowing how best to use it. Otherwise it's of no more use to you than a sword too heavy to lift." His voice held no hint of reprimand or coaxing, but nudged her all the same. "You'll feel the strain of its weight, its power upon you."

Bertie placed a hand on the leather cover. "Could you feel it? The power, I mean."

The sneak-thief lolled back, managing to look at ease despite the rough condition of the road. "I'd have to be ten sorts of fool to miss it."

"And only one sort of fool to steal it." Ariel's breeze caught the cover of the journal, ruffling the pages.

"Could you not use the journal to transport us, bag and baggage, to your desired destination?" Waschbär suggested.

"Because the link to my father fared ever so well." Bertie gestured to the leather belt looped about her waist even as she checked the sky. A mere speck far above them, the Scrimshander had gained altitude if not distance. "Do we fancy a nice plummet that ends with us landing on the Sea Witch?"

"I wouldn't mind," Moth said, "as long as we can sing 'We're Off to See the Scrimshander' first."

"I say you need rehearsing, and lots of it," said Cobweb. "I suggest you rehearse up some fruit pies and chocolate buttons!"

"What do fruit pies have to do with anything?" Bertie couldn't help but laugh at the idea.

Mustardseed held up an admonishing finger. "Remember your *Titus Andronicus*, Bertie! 'I of these will wrest an alphabet, and by still practice learn to know thy meaning.' That's wholly applicable here."

"Yeah!" Cobweb crowed. "Applicable in layer cake."

"Unless whatever cake I conjure has poisonous frosting." Something that couldn't kill them might be a safer option, never mind that Mrs. Edith's upbringing had cultivated a deep-seated need for clean underwear. "Perhaps I should pen some clothing first?"

Ariel shook his head, dislodging bits of grass from his hair. "A change of attire will be mandatory at some juncture."

"Clothes are a waste of a perfectly good word-wish." It was difficult to understand Mustardseed, given that he was mumbling through a sulk of colossal proportions. "Such a girl thing to do."

"Just for that, I should conjure you a cancan skirt." After carefully considering the wording—and deciding to omit anything that might cause a chorus line to enter Stage Left—Bertie wrote,

Atop the caravan appeared luggage filled with tools, spare parts, and clothes of the sensible sort: nothing made of silk, and nary a corset to be seen.

"Incoming," Waschbär noted as he deftly leapt off the caravan.

A low whistling noise increased in pitch and volume. Following the sneak-thief's lead, Ariel looped an arm around Bertie's waist and pulled her as far forward as the leather belt would permit, then shielded her when something heavy landed behind them with a *thud!*

"Would you kindly remove yourself, sir?" Shoving Ariel aside, Bertie sat up and spotted a steamer trunk, stickered on all sides and scuffed around the edges.

Clickity-clack! Its latches popped open, while valises, carpetbags, and linen-wrapped bundles of all shapes and sizes rained down upon them. The moment the baggage deluge tapered off with a reticule dripping bead fringe and a gilt cage large enough for a hummingbird, Waschbär's quivering nose reappeared over the edge of the caravan.

"Should you decide to write about foodstuffs," he observed, "give me enough warning to ready some buckets."

"Of course," Bertie said, loosening her belt strap enough to twist around in the seat.

"What's in all that junk?" Cobweb asked just before a late incoming messenger bag nearly felled him.

"Let us rummage." Bertie's aching toes tapped in anticipation of mary janes, but the uppermost folded garment in the open trunk was a nightdress, less substantial than the sunlight shining through it. "What sort of frivolous nonsense is this?"

Ariel considered the soft lace and pale ribbons. "The sort that a lady wears to bed."

Cheeks flaring, Bertie flung the nightgown back, noting with relief the presence of a pair of jeans, a knit pullover, and assorted underthings that she hoped were her size. She dearly wished she could stop here and change, but it would just be a waste of time and she certainly had no desire to be dragged half naked down a backcountry road. The clean clothes would have to wait, at least for now.

"That went rather well," Moth said. "No one was killed by a high-heeled shoe to the noggin."

"Still," Mustardseed said worriedly, "if you're going to make with the eats, you might want to start with muffins."

"Pancakes!" said Cobweb.

"Croissants are soft," Peaseblossom ventured, "like little buttery pillows."

Four fairies tipped their heads back and opened their mouths wide, waiting for a rain of breakfast foods. Watching them, Bertie realized that, since leaving the theater, she'd only partaken of three reluctant bites of apple. Her head was suddenly a balloon on a string, drifting up away from her shoulders, and she felt faint. The hair-dye fumes sometimes did the same. . . .

But when's the last time I keeled over from hunger?

She couldn't remember, because such a thing didn't happen at the Théâtre. Though they were only a day's journey from that place, they might as well have been a million miles away. Reminding herself that she'd managed the clothes, albeit with an unexpected manner of delivery, Bertie started to write.

With bellies grumbling...

She paused, uncertain what to say next. In the lull, Something Happened.

"I could certainly do with a bit more scenery." The voice was unfamiliar: a low sort of rumbling filtered through a few yards of intestine and with a touch of acidic sarcasm.

Mustardseed clapped his hands over his belly. "What did you do?"

Similar complaints rumbled through everyone's middles, and Bertie's own stomach spoke sotto voce. "Her diet is deplorable, if I may say so. None of you have any idea what this girl has put me through over the years."

Peaseblossom had her hands pressed to her front as her stomach bellowed in a startling, deep voice, "Don't play the martyr. This one can eat an entire chocolate cream pie all by herself."

The fairy's mouth dropped open. "I've never!"

The stomachs commiserated in a series of burps and belches that had Bertie blushing crimson to the tips of her ears. Waschbär's stomach didn't speak in any recognizable language but carped and nitpicked in a tongue all its own. Pip Pip and Cheerio, thoroughly embarrassed by the goings-on in their midsections, retreated to the sneak-thief's fur-lined pockets.

"An addendum might be in order, milady." Even Ariel looked discomfited, though his own innards had yet to tattle on him, and Bertie wondered just what, if anything, he did eat.

"No kidding." She tapped the end of the fountain pen against the journal until she thought better of it. "I need to be specific. And put everything on tables."

With bellies grumbling *silently,* a veritable wedding feast appears upon roadside trestle tables: a banquet of roasted chicken and cold ham, pigeon pie and leg of lamb.

Their suddenly silenced bellies gave her hope, and Bertie lifted her eyes to the landscape, fully expecting the manifestation of such abundance. But she was disappointed by the same rolling green grass, the same outlying purple mountains, the same avian-shaped figure now fleeing as fast as his wings would take him away from her.

79

"No matter," she said, telling herself it was the truth. "We don't have time for a blissful repast on the roadside, anyway."

"Maybe you need to write more," Moth said, shading his eyes from the sun. "Say something about jam puffs and pound cake."

"I'll give you a pound cake!" Cobweb punched him in the back of the head. "How was it?"

Bertie ignored the fistfight that broke out with cries of "knuckle sandwich!" as she tried to determine a way to word "hardtack" without maiming someone.

Sandwiches, knuckle or not, are a good idea. We can cobble them together without hardly stopping.

Orange wheels of sharp cheddar
rest alongside bowls of fresh butter.
And the bread! Rolls and biscuits
and braided loaves.

"Still nothing," Mustardseed fretted. "Be more specific!"

"Don't forget the napkins," Peaseblossom said. "And niceties like plates."

"Who needs plates?" Moth scoffed. "There isn't any food to put on plates, anyway. The Teller of Tales messed something up."

Bertie didn't know what was worse, the prospect of getting pelted with pickled eggs, or the fact that it hadn't happened yet. Scowling up at the sky, she allowed her rumbling stomach to get the best of her.

Plain glass bowls brim over with
fresh fruit and stewed, served with
trifles and whipped cream, ladyfingers and
sponge cake. Alongside that is horseradish and
mint sauce and salad dressing, mustards and oils
and salts and peppers. And when hunger
is slaked, thirst must be addressed, with tea
service for a hundred or more, alongside
lemonade, ginger beer, soda water...

Stomach protesting the as-yet-imaginary feast, Bertie capped the fountain pen with a scowl. "I'm just torturing all of us, writing like this."

The fairies drummed their heels and howled. Waschbär turned up his collar to deflect the terrible noise, and Ariel put on his introspective face. Now that he was ignoring her, Bertie had the sudden, perverse desire to ask him what he was thinking.

Such an ingénue thing to do!

When they crested the next hill, Bertie lost interest in

speaking with Ariel as a tiny town came into view. Thatched cottages dotted the green slope, while plumes of wood smoke flavored the air with a spicy reek.

"Are those sheep?" Moth squinted at the wooly things far afield.

"How quaint," Cobweb said.

"If quaint means smelly, sure."

"Maybe this is where the food is!" Bertie leaned as far forward as her belt permitted, trying to get a better look. Red-painted Dutch doors stood half open to the sunshine. Flowers bloomed in window boxes, and the aforementioned sheep chewed mouthfuls of long, sweetly scented grass with all due consideration.

"It's a hamlet," Ariel supplied, then pointed his finger at the fairies. "Don't even think about it."

Geared up to deliver jokes at the expense of the Danish prince, they deflated.

Peaseblossom tossed her hair over her little shoulders. "Not all of us go for the easy quip."

"But three out of four fairies agree that *Hamlet* puns are funny," Moth said.

"Plus there are corollary ham jokes to be made—" Before Mustardseed could finish the thought, all four fairies lifted their noses and screeched, "I SMELL BACON!"

And they jetted away, leaving trails of glitter in their wake.

CHAPTER SIX

To Preserve Mine Honour, I'll Perform

The Scrimshander didn't pause simply because the fairies had disappeared in search of sustenance. Only the leather strap around her waist prevented Bertie from being dragged from her seat as he surged forward, and her surprised cry was matched by one of frustration from her father as he was forced yet again to circle overhead.

Leaning over Ariel, Bertie snapped the reins on the backs of the mechanical horses. "We can't stop to let the fairies gorge, bacon or not."

"You're going to get between them and food? Try not to lose a finger."

About to say something cutting, Bertie caught the intoxicating scent of freshly baked bread atop the starch-crisp bouquet of Morning in the Countryside and relented half an inch. "Maybe we can trade for a picnic hamper? Then we could eat without stopping."

"Trade what, exactly?" Ariel squinted as they rattled down the main road. "And with whom?"

Bertie tried to peer through the window of the next cottage they passed. "It is odd we haven't met anyone yet."

"Perhaps they're waiting in the wings with pitchforks and flaming torches." The air elemental turned his head and gave the sneak-thief a pointed look. "Have you anything in your pockets they might be missing?"

"This is not a place riddled with unwanted things," Waschbär answered. "Each item has a purpose, each tool used daily and put away clean, every scrap of food hard-won from earth and animal."

"That's good to hear." Especially since Bertie had spotted several farmwives swarming around the open village square. The crowd cleared a bit to reveal laden banquet tables, and Bertie pointed a finger in triumph. "You see? The journal *did* conjure food! Just not quite the way we expected it."

"I suppose you never imagined it was appearing elsewhere," Ariel said. "Nor that the fairies will probably be knee-deep in it by now."

The villagers approached the caravan, their expressions a varied study in Grim, Ominous, and Disapproving.

"Something's run through the raspberry blancmange," the closest of them shouted.

Another chimed in. "Two cold cabinet puddings in moulds completely ruined!"

"What in the blue blazes is cabinet pudding?" Bertie asked.

But "do those small, obnoxious creatures belong to you?" was not the answer she was looking for.

For a moment, Bertie was tempted to say, "Why, no!" and set the whip to the mechanical horses, but her sense of duty—and a horrible curiosity—won out. "Yes, I'm afraid they do."

Fanned out across the road, the villagers gave Ariel the choice between stopping or trampling someone. He brought the caravan to a halt, and Bertie braced herself, expecting a pull upon her that didn't come. Peering up at the ballerina clouds in gray-edged tutus, the blue of the backdrop faded somewhat, it was easier to spot the Scrimshander weaving through the overcast like a needle through cloth.

Surrounding the caravan, the village women continued listing the damages. "Every drop of the whipped syllabub . . ."

"Bites taken out of the candied ginger."

"There's a debt to be settled!"

"We haven't any money," Bertie said, prompting a low

rumble from the irate crowd. "Perhaps we can offer something in exchange?" With a glance at the sky, she added, "I'm afraid we're in a terrible rush—"

A man in a drab-colored uniform, apparently the constable, pushed his way to the front. "Come this way, please."

His expression was the same worn by Mrs. Edith and the Theater Manager when they would not be budged. Wondering if the connection to her father was still intact, Bertie unbuckled the leather strap binding her to the caravan. Seconds later, she was heaved from the wagon. The villagers stared as Bertie swung to and fro like a trapeze performer, carefully clutching the journal to her chest as she slowly drifted to the ground like a bit of thistledown.

"One of our many illusions." Ariel mimicked her elaborate dismount with the aid of his winds.

"Never mind your illusions!" A woman wearing daisy-sprigged green silk and the darkest of the frowns immediately seized Bertie by the elbow and dragged her toward a collection of trestle tables. "How will you compensate for such damage? Have you any idea how long it takes to prepare a wedding feast?"

Ariel caught up with them. "Longer, I would guess, than it takes my young friend here to write 'a veritable wedding feast.'"

"Surely there wasn't that much damage done . . ." Bertie's

voice trailed off when they reached the trestle tables. Horror deprived her of her own words, so she borrowed some of Mr. Tibbs's. "How in the name of the sweet god's suspenders did you wreak so much havoc so quickly?!"

Three fairies sat in the wrack and ruin, heads hanging in shame. "We're sorry, Bertie, honest."

"But there was the pigeon pie—"

"The cheesecakes—"

"The fruit turnovers . . ."

"You treated these tables like the ones in the Green Room! This isn't the Théâtre, if you've forgotten already." They tried to apologize again, but she was having none of it. "Shut up. Where's Peaseblossom?"

Three fingers pointed, and Bertie turned. The last member of the ravaging horde sat atop a thankfully undamaged confectionary masterpiece. Dark fruitcake peeped between ornate scrolls of royal icing and meringue, which in turn was interspersed with orange blossoms, but it was the sight of Peaseblossom clutching a marzipan groom that caught Bertie unprepared. "Pease!"

The fairy didn't bat a lash, so busy was she making doe eyes at the manikin. "Yes?"

"Get down from there!"

Peaseblossom turned slowly and gave Bertie the most Evil of Eyes before hissing like a tiny spiteful cat.

Bertie was shocked down to her toes. "Peaseblossom!"

"You don't understand! You've never been in love!" The fairy clutched the marzipan figurine, subsiding into mumbles of "I won't let them separate us" and "never fear, my beloved" while the boys made gagging noises.

"He's not real, Pease," Bertie tried to reason with her normally rational friend.

"I don't care! I like the strong and silent type!" Pease-blossom clutched the tiny groom until his almond-paste head fell off. Over her disconcerted *eep!* Bertie grabbed both fairy and her beheaded paramour.

"You've *ruined* someone's wedding feast—" Bertie started to remonstrate before the Scrimshander towed her face-first into the cake. For several seconds, Bertie's entire world was candied fruit, nuts, and meringue. Though she'd managed to close her eyes, her mouth had been ajar to scream and the frosting had not only filled that but gone up her nose as well. Flailing, she inadvertently dropped everything: fairy, marzipan groom, journal.

A set of strong arms extracted her, and it was to Ariel's credit that he did not laugh has he did his best to wipe off Bertie's face. "No one at the theater would ever believe that was an accident."

"It *was* an accident!" She choked on what turned out to be a stray orange blossom as she located the journal in the grass. Peaseblossom had disappeared with her newfound love, but the boys hovered near Bertie's frosting-bedecked face, trying to get their licks in while the village women clucked over this horrifying new development.

"We'll need time to prepare another cake."

"I could manage a new meal in a few hours."

A young woman dressed in an ivory gown appeared on the fringe of the crowd. "Performers for the celebration?" She clapped her hands and turned to the woman in daisy-sprigged silk. "Thank you, Mother!"

"We didn't hire them," the woman protested. "They arrived without warning, and I'm afraid there was some damage to the luncheon."

"Pah!" The girl—for she couldn't have been older than eighteen—waved at Bertie with great enthusiasm. "I would sooner have dancing and music and a play than food."

Ariel knew a cue when he heard one. "'If music be the food of love, play on.'" He made her a lovely bow. "I take it you are the bride to be?"

She colored prettily under her flowered wreath. "I am."

Ariel started to hum a song of spellbound honeybees. The air around him shimmered and turned faintly gold, and his familiars emerged to settle around his brow like a crown. When he lifted his hand to his hair, a perfectly white butterfly walked with delicate legs onto his finger.

"Oh, how lovely!" the bride exclaimed.

"Not so lovely as you." Deftly transferring the compliment along with the unusual adornment to her carefully arranged curls, Ariel spoke with a purr. "Permit us, fair maiden, to work off our debt with songs and storytellings."

Bertie broke between them. "Would you excuse us for a moment, please?" Without waiting for an answer, she grabbed Ariel by the arm and dragged him away. "Have you lost your mind? We can't stop to sing for the fairies' suppers—"

"Breakfasts."

"Whatever!" Spinning like a compass needle, Bertie sought out the Scrimshander, though the growing cloud bank made it difficult to spot him. "I could be dragged off at any second!"

Behind them, the mechanical horses whickered, matching metallic whinnies that were a prologue to the rattle and shake of the caravan lurching forward. Bertie twisted around in time to see their clockwork livestock led away by a man with a blacksmith's musculature.

"That's ours!" she shouted as Waschbär's nose peeped over the side. Bertie flapped a hand at him in a silent if agitated order to get down and stay put. "Just where are you taking that?"

"In lieu of payment for the damages." But he halted, looking to the constable for orders.

"I didn't say we'd trade the caravan!" Bertie tried to

calculate how many people they might trample if she put the buggy whip to the mechanical horses.

"They are going to perform for us instead," the bride said, intercepting the constable. "As part of the wedding celebration!"

"A limited engagement. One hour only!" Ariel nudged Bertie aside and ran back to the caravan, leaping atop it.

"Ah!" The constable and the blacksmith shared a whispered conversation that ended with the latter unhitching the horses and leading them away.

"Until the debt is paid," the constable said in passing. "We'll permit you to retain use of the caravan, since it no doubt stores your costumes and properties."

"A thousand thanks, kind sir!" From one of the bags, Ariel had produced a black silk top hat. Buoyed by the shifting tides of excitement below his perch atop the driver's seat, he rolled it deftly up one arm, across the back of his neck with a bounce, and down the other arm. "Ladies and Gentlemen, we are but a group of humble thespians, traveling the fair countryside in search of an audience to astound and amaze!"

Hat firmly in place, Ariel began juggling scarves of brown-patterned silk which, midair, transformed into flaming billets of wood.

"Oh!" said the crowd.

As the sticks turned into green-glass wine bottles, Bertie hoped the villagers' subtext was "Oh! How amazing!" and not "Oh! They're witches! Someone fetch the ducking stool!"

Ariel hasn't been the King of All Games around me for a long time.

It was years ago that they'd crawled through the catwalks, played leapfrog over the auditorium chairs, whistled in scene changes that transported them to any fairyland they liked. Her nostalgia was short-lived, though, as the Scrimshander towed her several feet away from the crowd surrounding the performing air elemental. Contemplating a return to the lap belt, Bertie circled around to the side of the caravan.

Out of the corner of his smiling lips, Ariel hissed at her and the fairies, "Get a puppet show set up," before raising his voice back to a ringmaster's bellow. "We are performers of all sorts: mimes, mimics, and mummers, with a little magic thrown in for good measure!"

"I absolutely and unequivocally refuse to mime," Cobweb announced, landing on Bertie's shoulder.

She turned her head to glower at him. "You got us into this mess, you can help us get out of it."

He deflated, but still managed a sassy "mimes are creepy. All that time spent not talking is unnatural."

"Mimicking is fine," Moth said, "but we don't have enough bandages for mummers."

"We could rip up some of the clothes," Peaseblossom said. "I would like to be the Queen Mummer."

They flew atop the caravan, where they put their little heads together and set to rummaging in the boxes and bags. Snippets of satin, sequins, and string drifted about them like gaily colored dust motes as they argued in undertones, pausing only to shout, "We need a stage!"

Casting about her for something that could serve as a performance area, Bertie asked "Will a hatbox do?"

"Cut a proscenium arch into the side for an opening!" Mustardseed ordered as the fairies pushed, shoved, pinched, and, in Moth's case, bit Cobweb in the backside to be the first into the Dressing Room.

"You weevil-ridden bastard!" exclaimed Cobweb from the depths of the carpetbag decorated with vivid, pink roses.

"What's a theater without a proscenium arch?" Bertie said with a dribble of sarcasm as she ducked into the caravan and rummaged in the drawers. A sudden tug from the Scrimshander landed her on her bum, hindering her search momentarily. In the mess on the floor, though, she located an ancient but wicked-sharp knife, the sort meant to cut meat tough as shoe leather and stale loaves of bread. Carrying it gingerly outside, she sat upon the stairs and braced the hatbox against her knees, sawing away at the cardboard until a scalloped proscenium arch emerged, somewhat crooked for her haste to finish and set the knife down before a wayward tug caused her to pull an inadvertent Juliet.

"Is the stage ready yet?" demanded the carpetbag.

"Only just." Bertie placed the hatbox on an upturned barrel and dumped the contents of the talking luggage inside the miniature theater without further ceremony. As they took their places, she caught glimpses of trailing yarn and rouged cheeks. "Where'd you get the makeup?"

It was Peaseblossom who answered. "Moth found a lovely bit of red satin. When he spat on it enough, the color came off."

"That was certainly creative, if not quite hygienic."

"We are improvising, after all," Peaseblossom said before rushing to whisper something in Ariel's ear.

His patter drowned out even the fairies as he beguiled the crowd. "Marvel at the World Premiere of *The Montagues and Capulets Are Dead!* The first four rows are forewarned . . . there will be spatter!"

The children in the crowd detached from their parents and surged forward, drawn by the promise of bloodshed. The adults followed, and Bertie sidled over to Ariel to watch the performance.

After a bit of scuffling and a protest of "you're standing on my costume," the curtain went up. The fairies had tied bits of twine to their wrists and elbows for an ingenious sort of puppet show. Cavorting about the stage and posturing in wicked imitations of the other Players, they launched into their version of *Romeo and Juliet* with gusto.

"Two households, both alike in dignity..."

There were difficulties, of course. Their strings got tangled up in the fight scenes, and there was an unfortunate costume malfunction that exposed Moth's nether regions to the audience.

"Your bum is showing!" Cobweb hissed at him.

"My what?"

"Your bottom!"

"Bottom is in *A Midsummer Night's Dream*. I thought we were doing *Romeo and Juliet*!"

"Your arse! Your arse is naked!"

Moth looked over his shoulder at it. "Fancy that! Why didn't you say something?"

Peaseblossom, left to handle all the women's roles, handily managed to perform the scene with Juliet, her mother, and her nursemaid.

"The schizophrenia works for me, somehow," Bertie whispered to Ariel.

He nodded his agreement. "I am horrified to admit that it has a certain perverse charm."

The fairies then butchered themselves and the lines with enormous quantities of fake blood and groaning, killing every last Capulet and Montague, an acceptable revision as far as Bertie was concerned. The miniature actors took their curtain call to a hearty round of applause.

Less pleasant was the expectant hush that followed.

"My guess," Ariel said in a low voice, "is that a puppet show and a bit of juggling isn't going to settle our debt."

"I'm at a loss as to what to suggest for an encore," Bertie said, "because my guess is the fairies are out of fake blood."

"Right then. There's no helping it."

"Helping what?"

"This." He grinned and turned to the crowd. "The lovely Beatrice, Mistress of Revels, will now tell you a tale."

All the villagers turned as one to scrutinize her, and Bertie froze, pinned against the side of the caravan by the unexpected nature of the attack. With a glance that inferred she would repay him thrice over for this fresh humiliation, Bertie managed to stammer, "I'll be just a moment" before fleeing inside.

Bolting the door shut was her first priority, and lighting the tiny lantern her second. Cherry-tinted glass filtered the light. For half a heartbeat, Bertie was backstage at the Théâtre Illuminata again, where the red-gelled glow of the running lights was the color of secrets and compulsory quiet. She could almost hear the hushed whispers of the Players waiting in the wings.

The illusion was broken when she had to shove detritus out of the way with her foot in order to open the latch on the closet; while the backstage area smelled strongly of ironwork and rope, it lacked the musty, nostril-tickling tang of mothballs, and Mr. Tibbs would have never permitted it to remain in disarray.

The tiny alcove housed only one change of clothes, and though she half expected it, Bertie was still taken aback to see the Mistress of Revels's costume hanging inside: the dress of emerald and black silk with embroidery extending from belt to hem, all moons and stars and mystic symbols. The metallic threads winked in the half-light, and Bertie reached out a hesitant hand to stroke it. A gentle jingling of metal proved to be the belt a-dangle with golden disks. The perfect costume for a rhymer, a singer, a Teller of Tales.

The same costume Mrs. Edith had worn all those years ago when, at the Theater Manager's behest, she'd taken Infant Bertie away from the Théâtre. Away from Ophelia.

Closing the closet door, Bertie exchanged one persona for another, shucking her sadly tattered and muddied Opening Night dress and underthings. If wishes were washcloths, she would have bathed first, but she still managed to hurriedly splash off the worst of the frosting facial with the contents of a battered ewer. Only then did she reach for the Mistress of Revels's vestments.

While she'd had the occasion to wear all sorts of costumes over the years, none of the spangled capes or thigh-high pirate boots changed Bertie so instantaneously. The moment the silk slithered over her skin, she was someone else: a person as much at home in royal halls as in the village. Campfire smoke kohl-rimmed her eyelids, while the kisses of a thousand courtiers reddened her cheeks and lips. Bertie found a pair of delicate golden sandals, perhaps more appropriate for the Pantheon than a village performance, yet the moment the long ribbons were tied, they were as much part of the ensemble as the countless bronze bangles she threaded on one arm.

When Bertie was done, someone else's face stared back at her from the tiny, green-tinged mirror: the water-wavering image of another woman ready for her entrance.

I look like Ophelia, the ever-drowned, she of the broken memory.

No flowers twisted in her hair, no gown of floating chiffon, but the shape of Bertie's face was the same, as was the tilt to her eyes, the bow of her rouged mouth. It seemed impossible she'd never noticed the similarities before, but makeup and lighting—the sort that illuminated thoughts as well as features—made all the difference indeed.

Turning away, Bertie went to slip the journal into her pocket and realized she was still without one. The alternatives—the waistband of her skirt or tucked into the golden belt—were woefully insecure. A second glance at the belt, and clarity jangled like the disks decorating its hem.

I can pay for the fairies' damage with some of the gold disks!

Hastily adjusting her laces, Bertie managed to squeeze the journal down the front of her bodice. Then, with a deep breath that was almost a gasp, she quickly opened the door of the caravan.

During her hasty costume change, Waschbär had drawn the crowd off some distance with tales and tricks. Bertie spotted Ariel, his back to her as he supervised the sneak-thief's turn, but before she could tell him about the money, a swift, dark shape dipped out of the sky. It caught hold of Bertie by the back of her fancy dress, talons scratching down her back as it gripped the fabric. The ground fell away from under her feet, her panicked scream lost to a sudden happy roar of the crowd, delighted by some new sleight of hand. There was only time for a single, fleeting glimpse of the troupe, the caravan, the village, before the Scrimshander tilted his massive wings and the trees stepped between Bertie and the possibility of a rescue.

With the wind rushing around them, the Scrimshander lifted her into the sky and spat with ill-concealed fury, "I never took you for a fool, Ophelia."

CHAPTER SEVEN

You Should Be as Your Mother Was

A moment of twisting panic as Bertie kicked her gold-sandaled feet and tried desperately not to look down. "Take me back at once!"

"I will not," was the grim response. "Then I will—" Here, a squawk threatened to swallow the words, but he forced them out. "I will return and carry Beatrice to the theater as well."

About to shout that she'd pull every one of his feathers out if he did that, his words penetrated Bertie's swirling haze of panic. "I'm not—"

"Oh, you *are,* make no mistake!" The Scrimshander's furious shriek accompanied another surge in height, and the terrible noise was the ragged edge of Waschbär's obsidian dagger jammed into Bertie's ears. "Had I realized you were with her, I would have—"

"You would have what?" Seizing an unparalleled opportunity, Bertie took care to pitch her voice a scant measure higher, to soften the edges of her consonants. *If it's Ophelia he wants, Ophelia he gets.* "You would have kidnapped me earlier?"

"It's a rescue, whether you understand that or not."

"A girl will wonder about her father." Not entirely true, but it didn't take a trained musician to pluck heart-strings, if only to slow him down a bit. "She simply wants to get to know you."

"One so young knows not what she wants." A noise of disgust, ill-muffled by another massive downbeat.

"You underestimate her."

A moment of breathless gliding passed before he said, "I haven't the luxury of entertaining any notion about her at all."

Bertie's stomach clenched. "Of course not. Easy enough to shove her back into the theater, to shove all your responsibilities aside."

"Seeing the both of you to safety *is* my responsibility."

"Careful now, you almost sound concerned." Equal parts Ophelia and Bertie that time.

"Seventeen years since we parted, but some things are

impossible to forget. Like the fact that there's no reasoning with you when you're in this stubborn mood." The jewel-toned edges of his anger bled color so that, under the vehemence, there was a pale wistfulness.

She didn't want to feel sympathy for him, but the same would-that-things-had-been-different pricked at the skin around her eyes. Quickly clasping one hand over the medallion, Bertie wiped angrily at her traitorous tears and running nose. The scrimshaw thrummed in response to her touch, a reverberation that moved through her and opened a space inside her chest.

The rhythm of flight settled into that empty place. Heartbeat and wing beats synchronized.

Pieces of her—including the useless, human fear of falling—tumbled to the sullen earth. Aspects of Ariel she'd never understood came into sharp focus as the air grew thin and infinitely more sweet. The wind kissed her skin until it glowed, and her thoughts grew more disjointed as she took in the quilt of the fields, the last sunshimmer smothered on the horizon, the sky's loom weaving gray yarn over fading blue.

She stretched out her arms, and time slipped from her grasp. Instead of minutes, hours, she noted the changing position of the sun, the distant presence of other birds, the subtle shifts in the air currents. Only when the Scrimshander adjusted his grip on her dress, scratching Bertie through the rents in the silk, did she recall her human form. A warm trickle wormed its way down her back where he'd drawn blood.

Then she remembered what it was like to fall. "Maybe we should land somewhere."

He struggled to maintain their altitude. "It's been some time since I carried you, but I promise I haven't forgotten the knack of it."

Below them, the terrain had changed. If her father was a stranger to her, the landscape was just as foreign and unfriendly: Water-filled marshes like holes poked in a pie crust, with ragged cattails and miserable, stunted trees growing at sporadic intervals.

I know it was full dark, but I would remember if we'd passed such pitiful excuses for trees last night.

"This isn't the right way."

"'As the crow flies' is faster than the twisted abomination of the road." But his voice was strained, as though he carried more than her weight as a burden, and there was a sudden, stomach-knotting dip.

"You're going to drop me!"

"Never."

But the word was a lie; she could feel it in her bones. Bertie reached up, trying to catch hold of something besides thin reassurances, and the journal wiggled its way free of her bodice, spiraling away like a pirouetting ballerina.

As she twisted about, trying to see where it had fallen, they encountered another air pocket and plummeted toward the ground. When Bertie screamed, abject terror stripped away the thin veneer of her mother.

The Scrimshander stiffened, scrabbled to maintain his hold upon her. "You're—"

"Not Ophelia!" Her fingers closed around a handful of feathers; fractal and stiff-soft, they tore free as he struggled against the revelation and the winds.

He immediately headed for the ground, angling over the brackish green dimple of a pond before an icy down-draft hurtled them at the water, tearing Bertie from his desperate grasp even as it tossed him back into the sky like a child's toy. She fell, the rush the same as it had been when she jumped from the cliffs: hair whipping about her face, her skirts like the unfurling sails of a ship. The Scrimshander cried out, an anxious bird calling to a hatchling precipitously shoved from the nest before Bertie hit the water with a smack and sank like a stone.

The shock of the impact deprived her of all reason as she drifted down, down, Gertrude's voice from *Hamlet* ringing like a clarion bell in her head:

"'Her garments, heavy with their drink, pull'd the poor wretch from her melodious lay to muddy death.'"

Eyes squeezed shut, Bertie understood why Ophelia never fought the written pull of the water that had dragged her under: Everything inside was sharp bits of broken glass from a shattered spotlight, the dull throb in Bertie's head the same as the time a trapdoor had slammed shut atop her. She held very still for a moment, entangled in pain that was like the rough, coiled ropes backstage, then realized her options were to swim or to drown like her mother.

Opening her eyes, it was impossible to tell which direction was up, but the slime of waterweeds tangled about her ankles gave Bertie one clue, then a glimmer of the fleeing sun overhead gave her the second. Kicking hard, she surfaced seconds later, gasping for air. A few feeble thrusts put sand underfoot, and she staggered from the pond, thinking only one thing:

Ariel wouldn't have dropped me.

She stood a moment, dripping water from the Mistress of Revels's skirts, once a lovely emerald green, now sodden and three shades darker than midnight. Twisting around, Bertie tried to get her bearings, tried to pinpoint where the journal might have fallen and prayed it hadn't been in the pond. When a shadow flickered over her, she tilted her head back, Raven's Wing Black dye dripping from her bangs into her eyes.

"You aren't taking me back!" Her hand swept the ground nearest her and closed around a rock.

But the Scrimshander dipped low, no doubt meaning to catch hold of her again, so she threw it with all her strength.

The years spent flinging glitter bombs, water balloons, and stale pastry made her aim true; the jagged edge of the rock struck him between the eyes, and he reeled back with a squawk.

"Leave me alone!" For an encore, Bertie threw another rock, larger than the first, and hit him in the breastbone. The Scrimshander only just managed to evade a third projectile. "If you touch me again, I'll kill you!"

He must have taken her at her word, for he wheeled about and flew, hard and fast. Bertie could hear a thin, golden noise, like a chain hissing along the ground, dragged in the dirt: a reminder of the link between them.

"Not again." Wrapping her arms about the nearest excuse for a tree, Bertie braced herself for the painful tug that came only seconds later. She ducked her head and pressed her cheek to the rough bark, trying to imagine she had roots that went deep, roots that would tether her to this place. Another tug, harder than the first, that jangled her bones within her skin.

That's when she spotted the journal, leather cover half buried in the loam. Only a few feet away, it was still too far to reach unless she let go of her anchor. She'd have to time it just right and have luck on her side. Thankful to find the fountain pen still firmly stashed in her bodice, she pulled it out and took a deep breath.

Deadline indeed.

The third time the Scrimshander pulled at the chain connecting them, Bertie waited for the exact moment the line went slack and dove upon the journal. On her knees in the dirt, she fumbled with the cover, traitorous hands trembling as she scrawled,

A single link in the chain breaks.

Bertie felt the *snap!* when their connection gave way. With his tether to humanity severed, the Scrimshander raced from her, taking with him her hopes of finding Sedna, of reaching Nate. Had she been onstage, a tragic, broken heroine, she might have performed a moving soliloquy, a heart-rending aria or, at the very least, crumpled to the floorboards and wept. But she couldn't cry on the scrimshaw.

And you're not a soprano, so get moving. You have to find the others before you can even think about rescuing Nate.

She paused only a moment to check her arms and legs, fingers and toes. Though the shock of the water had been frightening, it had also saved her ending up a brilliantly dressed pancake upon the ground and left only a residual ache. Then, cradling the journal and wincing with every step, Bertie picked a delicate path through the worst of the marsh, stumbling twice, refusing to cry out both times.

The terrain was treacherous: uneven and damp in the best of places. Without warning, the ground would drop away into sinkholes filled with noisome and brackish water. The Mistress of Revels's golden sandals were a mucky green-brown, the hem of her damp skirts similarly filthy by the time Bertie climbed a short, steep bank and found herself on a deserted country lane. Although not the road they'd been traveling on, it was nevertheless a welcome change from the mind-numbing slog.

Which way?

She missed the fairies, who surely would have provided ridiculous commentary on her situation. However annoying they might be, however much she'd once longed for quiet and solitude, she'd trade the gold belt around her waist to hear that cascade of infectious giggling, the perfectly pitched straight line of "Shall we go west?" so one of the others could immediately demand, "Your west or mine?"

"True west, I think." Bertie peered down the road, trying to ascertain which route might lead back to the village. Surely the others would have noted her absence by now, but they'd have no idea which direction she'd been taken. Bertie didn't like to think what the irate air elemental might do when, or if, they managed to find each other.

"And this wasn't even my fault."

Wasn't it? he might as well have whispered in her ear.

Shoving away the unwelcome thought, Bertie trudged down the lane. Though she had a lovely view of the mist-enveloped fields, the road rolling out like a rust-colored ribbon before her, she soon learned it wasn't at all like an idyllic traveling scene at the Théâtre, where a continuously moving backdrop would indicate the passage of both fields and time, and set pieces would fly on and off the stage on wires and wheels. Even after a hundred steps, the distant rock she had chosen for a marker appeared just as distant. And her feet! Heels blistered within the Mistress of Revels's ridiculous sandals. The sun disappeared, a spotlight switched off, and a chill wind taunted Bertie with icy fingers along her hemline.

"I shouldn't like the journal to be ruined." She gazed up at the ominous gathering clouds. "Though it's not like I can get wetter than I already am."

No one shared the road with her, neither coach, nor cart, nor rider on horseback.

"That's a little odd. The bit about not having met anyone else yet, I mean."

The solitude grew progressively more disconcerting. A thick layer of fog crept over the fields, and Bertie didn't need the Theater Manager's pocket watch to know hours had passed since the Scrimshander had so unceremoniously dumped her in the marsh.

A few more steps. Reach that cursed rock, then you can have a moment's rest.

Her teeth were chattering by the time she collapsed atop the pert granite square marked MILE 478. Opening the journal, Bertie thought of summoning the troupe to this spot, but feared the caravan might land on her, finishing her off for good.

"Not the sort of finale I'm looking for, not after the day I've had." Surrounded now by shifting layers of fog, she uncapped her pen and wrote,

All roads lead to Bertie.

and crossed her fingers, wondering how long it would take Ariel and the others to reach her.

"I should have eaten something in the village." She'd had nothing at all today, and a strange buzzing set up between her ears.

The mist swirling about her shifted, revealing a tiny stone cottage that had not been there three seconds before. A large tree crouched over the house, and a woman bustled out to gather the clothes flapping upon a laundry line.

It was a scene straight out of *How Bertie Came to the Theater*, the place she'd always imagined her Mother lived, before the startling revelation that Ophelia was her mother.

Bertie rubbed a hand over her eyes, but the vision remained. "I like to imagine she was a simple person," she whispered, rising to her feet and drifting across the road, "with an uncomplicated life. She married her lover and raised a family. She looked beautiful, even when doing her chores." Leaning against the low rock wall that surrounded the garden, she couldn't find the words to call out.

The woman turned nonetheless, the dark braids twisted about her head the same Raven's Wing Black as Bertie's shaggy mane. "Can I help you?"

Though Bertie knew the line, she could not speak it aloud.

I picture her with my father, along with five or six of my brothers and sisters. And—

The Family Dog came running. A huge, hairy beast, it dashed past the woman and lunged at the wall, barking madly. With a scream, Bertie dodged back only to whack her funny bone against the trellis. The woman grabbed the slobbering thing and dragged him back.

"Good gracious!" she said with a gasp. "Down! Get down!" Bertie was tempted to throw herself to the ground, so stern a command did the woman issue. The dog backed up with a reluctant whine and another bark. "Sit!" It planted its hindquarters on the ground, tail sweeping through the dirt like a janitor's broom.

"My apologies," Bertie finally managed. "And greetings to you, goodwife."

The woman righted her apron, twisted askew by her canine intervention. "Who are you?"

Bertie took a deep breath and stepped into her proper role. "I am the Mistress of Revels, Rhymer, Singer, and Teller of Tales, on my way to a distant castle to perform for the Royal Family."

As though on cue, the Incoming Storm arrived. Bertie's free hand covered the scrimshaw medallion just before a droplet splashed down her nose, immediately followed by a dozen of its brethren. Squinting up, she marveled that the real experience felt exactly the same as the rain machines.

"You're wet enough already, and it wouldn't be right for me to leave you out here to drown." Rushing back to the laundry line, the woman pulled the remaining clothes from their pegs and tossed them atop a wicker basket. "Follow me."

"Er," Bertie said, forgetting to be the Mistress of Revels, the Teller of Tales. "That is most kind of you."

"Come along, I haven't all day to stand about the yard."

Keeping a wary eye upon the dog, Bertie followed the woman to the thatched-roof cottage and hesitated in the doorway. A merry fire burned in the hearth, string-tied bundles of dried herbs hung upside down from the rafters, and small pots of wildflowers dotted the table, the windowsills, and the mantelpiece with the sort of haphazard charm that indicated they'd been gathered by chubby fingers. "You've a lovely home."

"My thanks." The woman's voice dropped to a whisper as she jabbed at the cradle set in the corner. "It takes a lot of work to make it so, especially with the other children, thanks be they're yet at school."

Bertie lowered her voice to match, sitting on a bench at the nearby table and setting the journal before her. "How many do you have? Children, I mean?"

"Six, plus the wee one." Passing the hearth, the farmwife dropped the basket on the swept-clean stone floor, removed lids from pots, and set the contents a-swish with a long-handled wooden spoon. Though she moved with the silent efficiency of one of the stagehands, a strange noise nevertheless turned into the hiccup-cry of a startled newborn. The woman sighed, and her voice returned to a normal volume. "This one's hardly let me get a moment's rest since she arrived."

Lifting the tiny thing from its cradle, she afforded Bertie her first glimpse of a real baby. There were no infants at the Théâtre; for performances, swaddled dolls took their place, and Bertie had never been a child who played with dolls. Mr. Hastings had offered a parade of teddy bears and dainty porcelain-faced beauties, but why would Bertie want an inanimate sawdust-stuffed thing when she could frolic with the fairies?

Thus she was completely unprepared for the farmwife to ask, "Hold her a moment for me?" Without waiting for an answer, she deposited the baby in Bertie's arms.

Startled by the soft, heavy weight of it, Bertie stared down into the child's tiny face. Surely not every baby had hair like golden peach fuzz, milky blue eyes, or brilliant flakes of pink on such fat cheeks. "She's beautiful."

"Thank you." The woman opened a cupboard door to sort through a selection of medicinal liniments and powders. "Where did I put that ginger? You ought to have something hot to drink." The ingredients the farmwife culled reeked of heat and spice, and she muttered to herself as she pulled a gently steaming kettle off the hearth.

Cautiously shifting the child, Bertie realized everything about the creature was as damp as her own skirts, from the spit bubbles the baby blew on berry-colored lips to her suspiciously soggy posterior. "I think she needs a change."

*Tsk*ing under her breath, the woman moved to take her progeny. "Oh, Beatrix, again?"

All roads lead to Bertie.

Bertie-the-elder got chills down her arms from something other than the cold outside. "Such a pretty name."

"After my mother." The farmwife whisked the child

away, removing the soiled cloth diaper and replacing it with lightning efficiency. Wiping her hands on a towel, she shouldered the tiny thing before handing Bertie a humble ceramic mug filled to the rim. "That will help with the chill."

My line. I know I have a line here.

"A debt paid today is one that cannot be called in tomorrow, so I will give you something in return. I can weave your daughter's story on this . . . er . . . evening's loom."

The woman hesitated. In Bertie's imagination, a violin held a long, high note; as it descended the scale, the farmwife took a deep breath and joined the Mistress of Revels at the table.

Long fingers flicked the gold belt dangling around Bertie's waist. "One of these coins would pay for the drink, and a meal as well. There's bread and stew, a bit of new cheese. Ale, if you're thirsty."

Not the line Bertie was expecting, and so the farm-wife's words took a moment to sink in. "Oh. Yes, please." Bertie pried one of the glimmering discs from her belt and held it out.

The woman bit it, seemed pleased, then spirited it away into her kirtled apron. "Wash up. There's a pump in the corner."

There began a dance of plates and pitchers, knives and

forks. The farmwife set out a bowl of thick stew, half a loaf of bread still warm from the brick oven, a small wheel of soft cheese. There was butter molded into the shape of a clover, and a stein of dark, home-brewed beer. Trying to remember she had any manners at all, Bertie fell upon the food, dipped up rich broth with the bread, consumed vegetables the fairies wouldn't have touched even had they been dying of starvation. Between bites, she grinned at the baby, now nestled firmly in the laundry basket atop a pile of clean-but-rumpled shirts, and tried to keep up with the farmwife's small talk.

"So you're a performer?" The woman held a heavy iron up to her cheek to test the heat, then ran it over a pillowcase thick with embroidery. "Where's the rest of your troupe?"

"The next village over," Bertie hazarded, not knowing for certain if that was indeed the case. "I need to get back on the road soon."

"Not with the weather as it is."

"Oh, the rain." Bertie glanced at the window and saw it was slashed with silver streaks. "Have you a bit of oilcloth I could purchase? I shouldn't like my book to get wet."

The farmwife nodded and went to fetch it, then, with a noise that was equal parts laughter and "silly child," she took up a napkin. "Hold still, you've butter from ear to ear."

Eyes squinched obediently shut, Bertie could almost imagine she was Beatrix, that she'd grown up in this house, that this woman—

"For another coin, you can stay in our barn. There's plenty of hay in the loft." The farmwife returned Bertie's napkin to her. "More stew?"

Bertie wanted to say yes, but her ribs were already creaking. "No, thank you. I've had all I can hold." Spreading the oilcloth between salt cellar and pickle jars, she managed to wrap it about the journal and secure all the edges without needing to pay for a length of twine, too.

The woman nodded, gathering the plates. "Just as well. The rest of the family will be back soon, and I'll have another supper to serve. It's a burden, I tell you, having this many mouths to feed."

Not quite the right line, but Bertie understood it as her cue. Journal in hand, she rose and looked at the tiny Beatrix, sleeping in the basket, thumb firmly lodged in her mouth. "Does she have stars in her eyes?"

"I beg your pardon?" The farmwife looked up from the dishes.

"Stars?" Bertie's head swam with the combined effects of her fall, the long walk, the beer, but there was no gainsaying Destiny. "You know, like those in the heavens above?"

Pulling another loaf of bread from the brick oven, the

farmwife paused to think over the question. "I suppose so, though I thought it was but a teething fever. . . ."

"She will want a life greater than this, you realize."

"You mean the farm?"

"I mean upon the stage."

The woman frowned. "You speak like the village idiot." She abandoned the food to herd Bertie toward the door. "It's none of my never mind if you don't want to pass the night, but you'll have to go now."

The scene wasn't playing out as she'd imagined it, though Bertie gave it a valiant effort, holding out her arms and summoning inflections not quite her own. "It's not all roses and curtain calls and champagne on Opening Night, I fear. The bright lights mask the sorrow, but the sorrow is still there."

"Sorrow?" The farmwife looked alarmed now, then shifted so her stance was that of a warrior ready to do battle. "I don't know what nonsense you're speaking, but you're no longer welcome here."

Bertie hastened to reassure her. "It's all right if you have nothing to send with her, besides a mother's love and best intentions."

"Send with her? Just where do you think she is going?"

Too late, Bertie realized something had gone terribly awry. "With me?"

"Are you *insane*? Get out of my house! Go on! Shoo!"

The woman shoved Bertie through the door, letting loose an ear-splitting whistle. The dog came charging, as yet a distant blur in the rain-soaked fields but rapidly approaching.

Bertie stumbled down the front path, the baby's cry pursuing her. Twin slams: the cottage door, under the hand of the irate farmwife, and the gate, under Bertie's own power. Seconds later, the hellhound leapt against the wooden boards, adding a barrage of doggy threats, punctuated by snapping teeth and flecks of spittle.

Running through the intermittent raindrops falling on the storm-darkened lane, Bertie threw fearful looks over her shoulder, worried the awful thing might figure out some way of leaping the stone wall that bordered the garden. With every footfall upon the road, a truth shook loose in her head to rattle about.

A child is not a thing given up easily . . . a knack, a toy, a trick.

Bertie had believed it was Ophelia's broken memory that had separated them—

But could she have really forgotten me, as though I were no more than a flower on the current?

Body aching and head swimming, she stumbled over a stone she couldn't see and sat down hard in the dirt.

A hand clamped down on her arm. "There you are."

With a scream, Bertie kicked out at her would-be attacker only to get hauled to her feet by a familiar man-shaped heap of fur. "Waschbär, you just scared five years off my life!"

"My apologies, fair Mistress." The shadows under his eyes seemed to spread across the surrounding fields. "We've been searching for you for hours. Thankfully the road led us right to you."

Out of the darkness behind him came the rumble of wooden wheels, accompanied by a roll of thunder and a fresh downpour. Squinting into the gold puddles of lantern light, Bertie could make out the dim outline of the caravan, the fairies' enthusiastic waving, and the incensed expression on the air elemental's face.

"Heave me into the ditch and be done with it," she told the sneak-thief, "because Ariel's going to wring my neck."

CHAPTER EIGHT

Till of This Flat a Mountain You Have Made

Far from looking worried, Waschbär hailed the caravan with a piercing whistle. As it drew closer, Bertie could see that Ariel had summoned the necessary winds to create a wavering bubble, tinted gold by the lantern light. Neatly encapsulating the caravan, air currents formed a constantly swirling roof against which persistent needles pattered. Four sparking incandescent orbs careened through the night and smacked into various parts of Bertie's travel-frayed anatomy.

"Where have you been?!"

"We've been so worried—"

"There's dessert in the hamper!"

"I'm not hungry," Bertie told them.

Utter silence, composed of equal parts incredulity and

shock. Then Moth found an explanation. "Something must have fried her brains."

Bertie couldn't even argue with that. "All I want is a few minutes rest."

"Good luck with that," Mustardseed said, clinging to her hair.

"Consider, if you will, giving her two seconds to breathe." Waschbär helped her onto the caravan with far more care than the last time.

Sliding into the driver's bench alongside Ariel, Bertie saw his expression was even worse close up.

"Such a romantic way to travel, don't you think?" she ventured, though the next second she didn't quite manage to suppress a sneeze. "You look awfully debonair, considering." Her skirts stuck to her legs, clammy and discomfiting.

"Damp and debonair are two different things." A slight movement of Ariel's shoulders sent a ripple through his black silk shirt. His butterflies ventured out of his hair, took one look at the limp and bedraggled scene, and retreated whence they came. "Surely a wordsmith should know that."

"This wasn't my fault."

"I didn't say it was." Not waiting for her to settle, Ariel snapped the reins smartly. The caravan started up again with a lurch.

"Then why do you look as though you've been drinking vinegar? It's not like I wandered off into the fields to sing and shove flowers in my hair, shades of Ophelia."

"I knew well enough you'd not wandered off," he said with a scowl that should have shredded the clouds from the skies. Indeed, they parted for a fleeting moment, then coalesced, unconvinced he was their master in such matters. "I've been cursing myself all afternoon for not keeping a closer eye on you, not realizing until too late that he'd pulled you away from the group—"

"Bertie," said Moth, sounding faint, "is that *blood* on your shirt?"

"Oh, just look at your bodice!" Peaseblossom cried.

Bertie understood, when next he spoke, that Ariel's fury wasn't directed at her. "Did the bird-creature do that to you?"

"Yes." A hesitant twitch of the shoulder blades resulted only in mild discomfort and certainly nothing in comparison to the ache in her feet. "But it was an accident."

"Where is he now?"

"Long gone." *And a good thing, too!* Ariel looked as though he could murder someone midair. "I broke the connection."

"How are we supposed to follow him, then?" Mustardseed wanted to know.

"I haven't the foggiest notion." The warm weight of a

wool blanket settled on Bertie's shoulders, placed there by Waschbär, and she smiled her thanks at the sneak-thief.

"Don't linger on the notion of fog," Peaseblossom said. "The weather is inclement enough as it is."

Cobweb heaved a sigh. "It would be ever so much easier if a stagehand ran in with a map."

The hoped-for moment of silence came and with it, inspiration.

"That just might work." Bertie took a moment to squeeze her eyes shut and say a silent prayer before unwrapping the journal and uncapping the pen. "We don't need the Scrimshander . . . just something that will chart his path. Something that will show us where he's going."

"I'm less concerned about his whereabouts than I am about your well-being," Ariel argued. "Let me see the damage done to your back again." Taking advantage of his distraction, a few raindrops wormed their way through his wind-shield. Ink immediately ran in rivulets down the length of the page, and the world around them melted to match, streamers of blue-black twisted about the bubble of light.

"Ariel! Mind the rain!"

With a frown, he exhaled upon the paper to dry it, but now the night's ink painted the world into shifting curtains of dark velvet.

"We have to find him," Bertie said softly.

Ariel scowled sidelong at her. "And when we catch up with him? What's the sense in chasing him if he doesn't want to help you?"

"Badinage and persiflage, Ariel. I just need the chance to speak with him." She had to believe that now. "At the very least, he owes me that."

A map most marvelous charts their course...

An otherworldly vine of brass and gold clambered over the lip of wood at their feet.

"A man-eating plant!" Moth retreated behind Bertie's left ear.

"No, nor a fairy-eating one," Bertie promised. She watched, fascinated, as unfurling metallic tendrils twisted up and over and down until a golden casing spanned the width of the driver's bench. Within the frame, thousands of countless counterweighted brass rods rolled an enormous piece of parchment up, and to the left, constantly adjusting for their position.

"That would be the perfect little picnic table," Moth observed, "if it didn't have so much junk on it."

"That junk," Bertie said, "is the important bit." Decorative steel engravings appeared on the map: vignette views, armorial shields, a scale, and a pair of crossed flags, one bearing Thalia's mask of comedy, the other Melpomene's mask of tragedy. Fixed in the center of the map was a miniature caravan, finely wrought in silver.

"It's charted our course all the way back home." Cobweb walked along a line, as thin as spidersilk, to a tiny façade of the Théâtre.

"That's all very well, but we know where we've been," Moth said.

Recognizing her mistake, Bertie hastened to add,

...even as it charts the Scrimshander's position.

A tiny silver bird appeared on the map, skimming over the surface of the paper. A thick series of peaks indicated an approaching mountain range and the circuitous route they would have to take to cross it.

Peaseblossom heaved a tiny sigh of relief. "In any case, I'm glad we found you, because I've had just about all the excitement I can stand."

"Oh, please!" Mustardseed nudged her. "You stole two extra bows tonight at curtain call."

Before a fight could break out, the sneak-thief put a finger alongside his nose. "You did well, and performers require nourishment, do they not?"

"The villagers packed up the remains of the morning feast and sent it with us. Waschbär put on quite the show once we'd realized you were gone," Peaseblossom explained. "Colored smokes and showers of sparks and sleight of hand, the likes of which I've never seen, not even back at the theater!"

"I couldn't have competed with that," Bertie said, a bit rueful as the sneak-thief chortled and dragged the basket into his lap.

"There are tricks, and then there are things of importance," Waschbär said, wicker rummaging, "like currant buns and cheese," here the boys dove headfirst into the hamper, "and quite a lot of wedding cake—"

"Oh, I forgot about Henry!" Peaseblossom fled into the carpetbag. Thereafter were muffled mumbles of "My dearest, I'm so sorry" and "I do hope this frosting will do to keep your head on." The boys, after gathering a late-night snack, followed her in, prompting dire warnings of "don't you dare lick him again."

The mechanical horses began towing them up a slight incline, and within minutes, the rain falling beyond their golden bubble had turned to slush. The sway of the lanterns cast waltzing shadows, the particles of half-frozen water like the sequins on a ballroom dancer's skirts, swirling around them only to disappear into the night's black tuxedo jacket.

Bertie consulted the map, tracing their route from the cottage with one tired finger. "Now that we've entered the mountains, the road will fork into three paths. One along the top of the range, heading north. A second curving like a lady's hairpin, and leading back the way we came."

The sneak-thief's arm appeared between them to trace the circuitous third route with a single curved claw. "And the third goes west, to the White Cliffs."

"The cliffs?" Bertie's skin prickled at the mention.

The sneak-thief nodded. "Yes." Some sort of understanding passed between them like a flash of summer lightning. "Fowlsheugh."

"Fowlsheugh." She mouthed the word like a magic spell, and it tasted like salt and chalk. "I would bet all the coins on my belt that's where Ophelia went with the Scrimshander. Where I went with Mrs. Edith."

"The place where you nearly died," Ariel said, in case she'd forgotten.

The Wardrobe Mistress of the Théâtre Illuminata had saved her that time. Remembering her more recent freefall, Bertie considered tying herself once more to the seat of the caravan.

Ariel studied the map, looking for options that weren't there. "Perhaps he'll veer in another direction."

"He's going home." The way Waschbär settled in amongst the luggage, hamper between his knees and ferrets on his shoulders like a duchess's stole, closed the door on conjecture and supposition. He reached past the fairies to extract a rose red apple, which he then peeled with the wicked-sharp obsidian knife. A coiled crimson streamer dangled from the fruit alongside the matching silk ribbon, the apple's flesh laid bare to both the chill of his gaze and the night air. He offered fruit and knife to Bertie. "They nest in the cliffs, looking out upon the water."

"Where the air meets the sea. A between-place." Cutting a wedge of apple, shoving it into her mouth and tucking the knife into her skirts, she pulled out the journal and uncapped the pen. "The sort of place we might find a portal to Sedna's world."

Ariel tensed. "What are you going to do?"

"Hurry us along, just a bit."

Following the mountain road, the horses pick up speed until the landscape is a white blur around them.

There was a hushed moment, then, with an icy exhalation of breath, the mountains urged them forward. The terrain twisted and turned, but instead of jolting them from their seats, the wagon eased around the corners and up the slight incline as though it floated rather than rolled. The horses ran at a gallop now, necks stretched and limbs dull silver in the occasional flashes of light from the lanterns. Their hooves should have made a terrible noise, but

Bertie could only make out scraps of muffled thunder between lengthening intervals of crackling silence.

"Don't you worry we'll fall into a ravine?"

She could tell Ariel was shouting at her, that his winds whipped his hair about his shoulders, but the space between them filtered his voice and his motions through thick bubbled glass. It was as though she peered through the Theater Manager's Office door, trying to catch a glimpse of the shadowy figures within, had her ear pressed against the sturdy wood, trying to eavesdrop on a conversation not meant for her.

"I said we'd follow the mountain road. We'll be—" She was going to say fine, but couldn't bring herself to voice the lie. As everyone else moved at the speed of starlight, she slowed, able to sense the presence of every stick, every stone, every bit of the passing countryside, not just what skimmed underfoot, but to the pinnacle of the mountains surrounding them. Placing the obsidian knife alongside the fountain pen in the journal, she swallowed hard. "I feel terribly odd."

"You're exhausted." Ariel's words were drawn out like warm molasses taffy. "Of course you feel odd." Another moment passed before he added, "Why didn't you use the journal?"

Trees she couldn't see called to her, and everything

tangled together: branches, journal, knife-ribbon. "I just did."

"I meant before. When the Scrimshander took you."

"I used it then, too." Her synapses fired at half speed now, worn out with the lethal combination of confusion and exhaustion, and Bertie shoved the journal back into her bodice, fearing she might drop it.

A soft sigh stirred her hair. "Wait, don't tell me. You summoned food of some sort."

"You could say that." No need to tell him about the cottage, the Beatrix-not-Beatrice, the misunderstanding with the farmwife and her rabid dog. Bertie turned her nose into the warmth of the wool blanket, head swimming. "Life is certainly not like a play."

"No, that's become quite apparent over the course of this day." A long pause, during which Bertie nearly fell asleep. "You should have . . ."

She tired of waiting for him to sort through all the things she ought to have done. "Should have what?"

He made a frustrated noise. "Found a way to call me to you faster."

"I tried to find the right way to word it, but I didn't want to risk hurting anyone."

More than I've already hurt Nate.

"There is that. I suppose I should be thankful."

Wrapping an arm about her waist with his free hand, Ariel pulled her closer. "Scratch that. I *am* thankful."

"I'm only permitting such familiarity," Bertie said in tones borrowed from Mrs. Edith, "to prevent a swift and sudden tumble over the side." It wasn't an idle fear, as the lanterns' light threw long shadows over the edges of the mountain's road. "Perhaps I *should* write something about us not falling over a cliff."

"You've written enough already, and the horses are managing nicely." A low chuckle. "Rest your head."

"All right, then." She leaned against Ariel and closed her eyes. Dual heartbeats like drums; Ariel's pulse was the faster of the two, and Bertie struggled to keep up. The medallion pressed hard into her chest, or maybe that was the ache in her lungs—

"Little One, what have you done to yourself?" The scrimshaw reverberated with her father's voice.

"Leave me alone. I haven't done anything." Bertie clenched her jaw, and the dark shifted around her.

"Little One—"

"Shut up, shut up." The medallion hummed against her skin as she imagined the landscape as piles of words, glittering like beetles' wings. Faster and faster the horses galloped, their whinnies the protest of steam locomotives charging ahead.

"We have to slow down." The brake on the caravan

was an enormous fountain pen. Bertie tugged at it, and the barrel broke off in her hand. Blue-and-black magic stained her fingers; when she rubbed them over her eyes, the darkness was there as well, the same as it had been the last time she'd seen Nate.

The pirate's words were softer than the flip of a mermaid's fin in the water. "Yer bleedin' from a thousand soul cuts. What have ye been doin'?"

"Chasing a waking dream."

"What happened after ye left me? I thought I heard ye cry out."

Bertie opened her eyes to the damp black of an ink puddle, a place without edges or echoes. "I fell into a great, big Nothing."

"An' then?"

For a moment, she couldn't remember anything beyond the utter terror of falling through the void.

Little One.

"My father rescued me." She reached for the scrimshaw. "Did you know?"

"Know what?" Nate's voice was closer now, growing in strength.

"That it's all connected: the scrimshaw, Sedna, my father." She walked forward, arms outstretched, until she bumped into the solid weight of him. The story fell out of her in dribbles of gold and silver light until the ground shimmered. "Did you know he'd carved it, when you gave it to me?"

"Nay, I didn't know." The touch of his fingertip traced the edge of the medallion, curving around the bone disk to burn a circular path on her skin.

Something inside Bertie cracked. Or maybe it had cracked when the Scrimshander had told her in feather tones that he was her father. She needed so many things: to feel safe again, to rescue Nate, but most important, she needed to see him, to look into his eyes. "We need more light."

The moment she said the words, there was once again a bonfire. Only then was it evident how much Nate's soul had weakened in her absence. Forced to abide within her memories of him, he would have been helpless to stop the fraying along the edges that reduced his linen shirt to tatters at hem and cuffs. The bit of leather holding back his queue had broken, allowing strands of hair to become tangled and wild. His boots were gone, his earring missing, the laugh lines around his eyes and mouth had smoothed.

But, worst of all, the light in his eyes had faded, replaced with the dancing flames of a real fire rather than a stage artifice. Its smoke wended a path through trees that rustled with living leaves. The ancient grove was coming to life, roots running deep into soil that was dark and rich.

It filled Bertie's nostrils with the promise of seedlings and spring, but she had no use for it, not when she'd rather press her nose to Nate's chest and smell salt and soap and leather. Resting her cheek against his shoulder, Bertie could detect nothing of him at all.

Thankfully the feel of his arms around her had not yet changed, for all that Nate was but a walking shadow. Their fingers met at the tips, then slid one alongside the other until interwoven. The steady thrum of his pulse against the base of her wrist was some reassurance, at least, as he pressed his forehead against hers.

"It's been so long since I saw ye last."

"Only a day." Bertie thought of everything that had transpired. "The longest day of my life, I'll grant you, but just a day."

His hand tightened upon hers. "Yer days might be spent in Ariel's company, but yer nights belong t' me."

The thought came, unbidden, unwelcome, as prickly as a nettle against Bertie's skin:

Then what is mine, and mine alone?

"This night, at least." Nate looked down at her, eyes filled with equal parts jealousy and despair. "I don't think I can last much longer."

Whatever prickling disconcertion she'd been feeling disappeared, replaced by a more immediate threat. "I need to pull you through."

His voice was hoarse, this time with hope. "Do ye think ye can manage it?"

"I have to try, before you're no more than a dress-maker's mannequin." Bertie didn't want to summon Sedna, and so she did not use her name. "Where is she keeping you?"

Nate tilted his head back, the bobbing of his Adam's apple visible when he swallowed hard. "A cavern. There's water all around, an' a throne o' dark stone."

"What did it feel like, when I pulled you from that place?"

"It hurt," he said with a wince. "Like I tore open, slow an' soft, an' stepped out o' myself. And then I . . . passed through."

"Like through the curtains at the theater?" It had felt the same, stepping into the soft glow of the spotlight, falling through the Void and back into the caravan. "There are thin places, I think. Between what's real—"

"An' what ye've conjured."

"Yes." Now that she'd given the idea words, Bertie could feel the different layers of the world come together, one atop the other, like the old bits of tissue paper Mrs. Edith kept in the Wardrobe Department for wrapping delicate costumes. She held her arms out, convinced she could touch them, if only she reached hard enough. "Distance is only a matter of perception."

"Ye make it sound easy," Nate said. "But yer words weren't enough th' last time."

Bertie's exhalation of breath slowed everything, including her heartbeat. Underneath them, the earth shuddered. "No, the words weren't enough. It takes something more. Some kind of sacrifice."

"Blood-magic is powerful." His thumb found the hollow of her throat, pressing hard enough to count off her pulse, if he wanted. "Yer father helped bring ye through, and ye share the blood."

"Then we'll do the same. We'll make a blood vow." When she pulled the journal from her bodice, the ribbon-tied obsidian knife fell from its pages and into the grass.

"That's quite th' bookmark." Though Nate crouched down, he didn't move to touch the blade. "Unless ye just summoned a knife from thin air."

"Oh, happy dagger." Kneeling, Bertie scooped it up.

"Ye don't fancy yerself as Juliet, do ye?" Nate caught her by the wrist.

"I'd prefer less death and more results, if that's all right with you." She rotated her hand over and unfurled her fingers, the knife's streamer of silk like a blood trail. "Hold this." After a long moment, he took it, and she was able to open the journal. "What should we say?"

"Yer th' one wi' th' words." The muted dance of the

fire's light played over his face, softening his surprised expression. "Why would ye think I'd know?"

Heartened by her success with the map, Bertie still wondered how best to word it. "There should be no misunderstanding that I want you with me."

Cradling her left hand in his, Nate tracked her life line across her palm with his fingertip. "Forever?"

The question gave her pause, but only for a second. "Of course."

"Then I have the words." His voice dropped, as though he feared someone might overhear him. "Blood o' my blood."

The rightness of the phrase echoed in her head, and she wrote it without hesitation.

Blood of my blood.

Though she expected the pain, it still startled her when Nate carved a thin line into her palm. She held out her hand for the knife and made a mirror cut on his broad hand. Her palm against his, the knife's crimson ribbon twisted about to bind them at the wrist, the blade dangling like a man from the gallows. Their gazes met, then their lips; the firelight flickered and died. As the kiss ended, the grove of trees behind Nate disappeared into the blackout, and dark scrim curtains rushed to encircle them.

A pale blue light came up beyond the thin gauze, and

Bertie caught her first glimpse of Sedna's lair. The Sea Goddess's spell upon Nate's inert physical form was a ribbon bow that bound his hands behind his back and wound about his legs. "I can see you." The Nate standing before her jerked with surprise, and she hastened to add, "Don't move."

His hand, already tight in her grasp, clamped down upon hers in panic. "I can smell th' water."

"Don't. Move." Without taking her gaze off either Nate, Bertie wrote,

Knots unpicked by unseen hands,
he was free to leave.

"It isn't good manners to trespass, nor to steal." The Sea Goddess stood behind Nate's body, all ink trails of deepest purple, the flash of scales, and flickering glimpses of creamy yellow bone that matched the medallion hanging around Bertie's neck. "If you want him, you will have to take his place. You will have to drown to save him."

"Not all the rules are yours," Bertie said.

(The words pull him to her.)

BERTIE
Blood of my blood.

The echo shook the walls of the cavern, shook her, shook both Nates.

"It's working—" he gasped.

She didn't need him to tell her; she could feel the difference as the blood they'd shared pulled his physical self through the thinning curtains.

The Sea Goddess screamed her displeasure, wrapped her arms about her prize, and retreated into the gloom with a snarl. "Though it's but a shell, it's mine nonetheless."

Next to Bertie, Nate choked, as though Sedna were drowning him again.

"Blood of my blood!" But Bertie needed something more than blood-magic. "Bone of my bone." Left hand still clasping his, she shoved the journal into her bodice and caught up the scrimshaw in her right. With the rustle of leaves, of pages, of sheets of tissue paper, the curtains skimmed around them. "Don't let go!"

"I won't!"

Tiny, crystalline bits of white drifted over their skin like a lighting special. Bertie clasped Nate with all the strength she possessed, her grasp on the scrimshaw tightening until the only thing separating the bone medallion from her own bones was the thin layer of flesh on her fingers.

"Say ye love me," Nate choked. "Even if it's not true, let me keep th' words."

"I'm not giving up!"

"Three words, lass. 'Tisn't much."

He's wrong. The words are everything. I should have written these down as well.

"I . . . I love you." Bertie fell forward, resting her head against his shoulder as his face faded into the blackout. In the place between light and dark, she shifted, taking the words with her. "I love you." Still she leaned on his shoulder. Still she held his hand, fingers interlaced. "I love you."

A gentle breeze settled around Bertie's shoulders like a warm cloak as he pressed his mouth to the top of her head. "I think I've waited all my life to hear you say that."

Bertie opened her eyes, wincing at the brilliant white light that slanted over his shoulders.

Ariel's shoulders.

CHAPTER NINE

Snow upon a
Raven's Back

Ariel's arm encircled her under the blanket, pulling her against his chest and settling them both more comfortably on the narrow driver's seat. Around them, a winter's tempest stirred the air, as though a giant hand shook a snow globe and set it down in their path, white flakes aswirl.

At least, if I cry, the tears will freeze before they fall.

Heart aching over her failure, she wished she could put her head back down on Ariel's shoulder, fall asleep again, return to that place armed with something more than a mere knife and a mouthful of words—

"Did you have pleasant dreams?" was his softly spoken query.

There was no way in Hades to properly answer that

question, so she pressed her own lips together, swallowing the secret. The inside of her mouth tasted as though something small and furry had clambered in there while she slept. *And died.* She would have suspected the ferrets, but a backward glance revealed that Pip Pip and Cheerio snored under Waschbär's chin. "When did it start to snow?"

"A soon as you wrote about the landscape passing in a blur, but it's ten times worse now that we're clear of the mountains." Peaseblossom looked guiltily from Bertie to her almond-paste boyfriend, propped against the hatbox proscenium arch. "We did try to wake you."

The boys jumped up and down on Bertie's knees. "All the usual things—"

"Pinching—"

"Punching—"

"Hair pulling!"

"We were just about to wave the smelly cheese under your nose." Mustardseed looked thwarted.

"Thank you for refraining." Bertie pulled away from Ariel, but her palm came free from his with the crackle of dried blood.

"Oh, we didn't refrain," Mustardseed said cheerfully as Ariel recaptured Bertie's hand and made a series of *tsk*ing noises. "Moth ate the last of it!"

"You've hurt yourself," the air elemental said.

The crimson ribbon bloomed in the folds of Bertie's skirt, still wrapped around the knife. "Just a scratch. Probably from this." She lifted the blade gingerly.

A furry paw appeared between them and then the knife disappeared, better than a conjurer's trick. For his part, Ariel pulled out a clean handkerchief and bandaged her wound deftly, finishing off the procedure with a gentle kiss, causing some part of Bertie's soul to wither.

"Please don't."

"That's not hygienic!" The fairies made gagging noises. "Tell me the point of wrapping it up if you're going to get your GERMS in it."

"Yeah, keep your lips to yourself!"

Ariel only laughed at them, his smile brighter than the dawn. Peaseblossom, however, alighted on Bertie's shoulder like a tiny rain cloud of despair.

"I didn't think it possible, but the weather's getting worse!"

Frost flowers bloomed on the arched necks of the mechanical horses, their inner workings struggling under the harsh conditions. Blue diamond crystals skimmed along the harnesses and enveloped the caravan. Beyond that, Bertie could see only a few feet of white-powdered road.

She pulled the woolen blanket atop her head in a

makeshift hood, her exhaled breath tinkling like sleigh bells. "Where are we?"

"No way of telling." Waschbär leaned over the seat, his breath furring the edges of his hood with ice. "I'm afraid the map's delicate machinery froze up some time ago."

No longer able to fly for the cold, the fairies burrowed deep under Bertie's blanket to warm their icicle extremities in her elbow crooks and under her hair. Peaseblossom's nose had turned the bright pink of her namesake. She clutched the marzipan groom to her, tiny teeth chattering. "This is t-t-t-terrible. We can't stay out much longer in this, or we'll freeze—"

A heart-stopping screech interrupted the fairy: The legs of the mechanical horses had locked up stiff, but the wheels missed the memo to stop. The caravan slid to one side and slammed into a snowdrift.

Moth spoke from under Bertie's hair. "What are we supposed to do now?"

"This never would have happened in the theater." Peeking out from the protective wool of the blanket hood, Peaseblossom's lips were blue, and Bertie wondered just how long they could survive.

Except I'm not about to sit here and wait to find that out.

Tucking Peaseblossom farther into the blankets with her Henry, Bertie thought of the baby Beatrix and gave silent thanks they weren't also contending with an infant in this sort of weather. "I'll have to write something." Nearly numb, she pulled the journal out.

"Sooner rather than later," Waschbär advised, "if you value your fingers and toes."

Though the cottage scene from *How Bertie Came to the Theater* was not as she'd expected, there was another bit to that tale Bertie could use now. "We'll take the train."

"Can't you just write us out of the storm?" Cobweb had worked his way under her left ear, which tickled when he spoke.

"Would you like to end up a hundred miles away? A thousand?" Bertie put the fountain pen to paper. "With my luck, the journal would pick us up, shake us around a bit, then plop us down in the Bermuda Triangle."

"Never mind," was his muffled rejoinder.

Intending to write "An Ordinary Station" before her fingers cracked with cold, Bertie panicked when she couldn't get the ink flowing. "Ariel . . ."

He leaned over in the seat, understanding the unspoken plea. Lips brushing her hands, he exhaled a soft summer wind into the tiny shelter between her palms, thawing the ink long enough for Bertie to write,

The train station is a carriage
clock of a building.

When she looked up from the journal, she thought she could make out a distant structure between the shifting flurries of blinding white.

"Well done." Cobweb peeped out of the blanket. "Except that there's a goodly amount of space between 'here' and 'there,' Bertie."

"I'll take care of it." With a gallant leap, Ariel descended, not sinking into the white powder so much as hovering atop it. He moved between the horses, agile and surefooted as though there wasn't an inch of ice covering the road now. Hands outstretched, he summoned equatorial winds and tried to surround the caravan the same as he had during the rain. Snow and ice turned to slush, metal gears warmed and began to turn again. Slip-sliding, Ariel coaxed the mechanical horses to move forward. The caravan followed, wheels dragging through the half-melted snow instead of rolling as they should.

Bertie clutched the journal and her seat both as they approached the station. Built of wood that had the same dark gloss as freshly baked gingerbread, it was well suited to the elaborate whorls and carvings around the eaves and archways. A fine layer of ice decorated the roof with sugar powder. Beyond the main building, train cars like icing confections beckoned.

"Glorious," Waschbär said.

Plucking the fairies from her hood, Bertie shoved the

four of them and the marzipan groom into their carpet-bag. "Find something warm to wear, all right?"

There were immediate cries of dismay from Pease-blossom. "Bertie, the boys are trying to eat my boyfriend!"

Automatically Bertie said, "Leave Peaseblossom's boyfriend alone."

"He doesn't need *all* his toes."

"Stingy!"

Bertie had more important things to worry about than fairy cannibalism. The snow had obscured a slight slope to the road, which they only discovered as everything—Ariel, horses, cart—commenced sliding downhill toward the station. "Ariel!"

"I know!" He already had his arms braced across the necks of the mechanical horses. "Grab the reins!"

Shoving the journal into her bodice, Bertie caught up the leather straps, trying to slow them. The horses attempted to obey the command, legs locking stiff and straight as Ariel unleashed matching blue-gray streamers of wind. Head down, he pushed back against the caravan. The muscles in his back worked visibly under his heavy coat, his breath came in crystalline gasps, but the caravan's weight and momentum was too much for him. "I can't . . . stop . . . it."

Terrified, Bertie pulled harder on the reins, all too

easily imagining him crushed under the horses or the wheels. "Get out of the way!"

He looked up at her then, gaze like silver daggers. The winds around them redoubled, freezing this time. The depot's mammoth central spire was not only visible now, but rapidly approaching. Metallic blue ice sparked off the horses' shoes; when Bertie peered over the edge of the caravan, she could see the same was happening to the wheels until, finally, Ariel managed to frost-weld wheels and hoofs to the road, bringing them to a standstill just before the station.

"Are you all right?" Bertie slid down from the driver's seat and straight into his arms.

Far from being exhausted, he glowed like a furnace, as though exhilarated by the exercise. Then his mouth was on hers, the only warm place in this ice-riddled world. The heat spread through her veins, and she heard the hiss of snowflakes evaporating on contact with her skin.

Muffled cries from the carpetbag interrupted the moment with the mewling of an orphaned kitten. "Bertie! Bertie! They ate his feet! How is he supposed to promenade with me if he doesn't have any feet?!"

Ariel sighed against her mouth, a vaguely exasperated noise that turned into a wry smile. "Someday, when we're quite alone, we'll be able to finish what we've started."

The warmth in the promise melted the lump of ice in her middle along with the surrounding snow, and Bertie sank up to her ankles in slush. "I should book us passage on the next train."

Ariel indicated a sign, the same dark gingerbread as the building and framed with scrolled woodwork:

TICKET BOOTH, TIMETABLES, & STATIONMASTER'S OFFICE

"You didn't quite manage 'An Ordinary Station,' though, Bertie." Peaseblossom looked around at the various snowbound curiosities, blinking white flakes from her lashes.

"I don't give a royal fig what kind of station it is, so long as there's hot buttered rum," Moth said. "And I'm not going to drink it, I'm going to take a bath in it!"

"Waschbär, grab them and catch up with us!" Bertie set off at a brisk clip, welcoming the chance to put her thoughts back in order now that Ariel was keeping lips to himself. "We'll need to find passage on something that can also accommodate large freight." She rounded the corner of the building; the sight that greeted her brought a smile to her face.

Under a covered platform, glowing furnaces burned with luminous fire at intervals, and a gleaming row of train cars reflected the glorious rainbow colors of aurorae. Similarly dressed in shades of the northern lights, hundreds of performers clambered into the various ice-painted cars. Silken skirts were bustled back over impossibly long legs, which, in turn, were clad only in white fishnet stockings and lace-frilled garters. Feathers decorated neck ruffs and miniature top hats, even serving as fluttering false eyelashes. Tightrope artists with ice blue eyelids and doll-rouged cheeks minced down nearly invisible wires that led from the station's roof to one of the train cars' windows, tattered lace parasols held aloft, accompanied only by the jingle of the needle-thin icicles dangling from their soft-soled shoes. Up a nearby ramp, tumbling august clowns in whiteface pushed a gilt cage; the cunning prison contained a girl costumed as an exotic bird, avian patterns frosting her skin and a mother-of-pearl beak concealing her lower face and jaw. At the front of the crowd, a sizable gentleman in a pristine white brocade topcoat and tails radiated an air of undeniable authority.

"That must be the man in charge." Despite feeling severely underdressed in her tattered dress and woolen blanket-shawl, Bertie bridged the space between them. Touching his sleeve, her frostbitten fingers still managed to note the heavy weight of the fabric, the delicate fibers that rose from the cloth to wave about like tiny hairs. "Excuse me, sir?"

He turned, and Bertie gasped before she could stop herself. If Waschbär bathed, shaved, and rouged his cheeks, the sneak-thief would be the spitting image of the man who had her by the hand and kissed her knuckles.

"Are you the ringmaster?" she managed to ask.

"Yes, fair damsel." He employed a flourish that outdid even Ariel's most grandiose obeisance. "I am Aleksandr, Leader of the Innamorati, at your service."

"I am Beatrice Shakespeare Smith, the Mistress of Revels."

His eyes grew appreciatively round at the mention of her title, and he groveled a bit lower, if that was possible. "A pleasure to meet you!"

Waschbär, in the meantime, had led the rest of the troupe to join them on the platform. "Greetings to you, Aleksandr!"

"Rapscallion!" the ringmaster cried, enveloping his near-twin in an embrace that involved much good-natured back thumping. "Whatever are you doing here?"

"I've joined the Company," the sneak-thief replied.

"Their gain is certainly our loss," Aleksandr said. "You were the finest Arlecchino ever to grace our transitory stage."

Bertie had a sudden, vivid memory of the Harlequin onstage at the Théâtre, every movement embellished with a dexterous backflip or cartwheel, his eyes twinkling behind his black mask.

Waschbär merely grinned and pointed at the train. "Where are all of you headed?"

"West," Aleksandr said, chest puffing out, "to the Caravanserai."

Adrift in their exchange, Bertie caught hold of Waschbär's sleeve. "How close is this Caravanserai to the White Cliffs?"

The sneak-thief smiled. "Very close indeed. A mere hop, skip, and jump to Fowlsheugh."

"Just what I wanted to hear." She turned back to Aleksandr. "Would you permit me and mine to ride with the Innamorati for a while? We are but a small company, nine in number including the fairies and ferrets, with a caravan and horses that also require passage."

Giving Bertie a look that took in both her person and her entourage, the ringmaster said, "We could easily put all of you in the caboose, with your things fitted in amongst the freight. And I doubt you eat much."

"Appearances can be deceiving," Peaseblossom sniffled. "They just ate most of my beloved."

Aleksandr looked to the boys, who mounted an immediate defense.

"It was snowing."

"We were hungry!"

"That's what people do, in the snow, when they're hungry! They eat each other!"

"We've money—" Bertie reached for the gold disks on her belt before the ringmaster could ask what they meant by that.

"I've no need of coin," Aleksandr said, his eyes suddenly gleaming. "What have you of interest to trade?"

"Not another trade," Ariel said, shaking the remains of an ice crown from his hair.

Mustardseed agreed. "What's with all the bartering?!"

Though she'd never before hesitated to liberally stretch the truth, Bertie wanted no misunderstandings between them, especially if it might mean the difference between safe passage and being thrown off a moving train. "All we have are the caravan and the horses, but neither is in good working order right now."

Waschbär nudged her. "You do have something most valuable."

"Oh, really?" Aleksandr perked up, the way Bertie imagined she did at the scent of freshly ground coffee. "What would that be?"

More puzzled than perky, Bertie looked at the sneak-thief. "I do?"

"You do," the sneak-thief told her, then turned to the ringmaster. "She is a Teller of Tales."

A short intake of breath and another, lower bow; Bertie thought Aleksandr might be eating his bootlaces, but then he asked, "Would you be amenable to a collaboration?

We have need of a Brand-New Play, a lavish production to showcase the many talents of my acrobats and artistes!"

Certain a Brand-New Play would waylay their efforts to get to the Scrimshander—and Nate—Bertie shook her head. "I don't think so."

The ringmaster's expression fell like a trapeze flyer without a net. "You have a grand show already in rehearsal?"

"Not quite," she hedged.

Moth piped up. "*The Montagues and Capulets Are Dead!* is doing quite well!"

"Ariel juggles," Mustardseed tattled. "And Bertie was supposed to tell stories, but she got herself kidnapped instead."

Aleksandr's face was a study in disapproval and disbelief. "The Mistress of Revels should not be reduced to mere chicanery." Before one of the fairies could ask "chiwhatnow?" he pressed the advantage of truth. "It's a grand opportunity, you surely see? An entire troupe of artisans, augusts, and acrobats at your disposal, nay! Your whim! Anything you can imagine, we can perform, in exchange for your passage aboard." He eyed the group as a whole, adding, "Plus a change of vestments, courtesy of the Keeper of the Wardrobe, and the limitless hospitality of the pie car."

"Pie car?!" Four-part harmony. Even Peaseblossom squeaked the words as though someone had trod upon her tiny feet, the promise of pastry perhaps enough to heal her broken heart.

"Naturally," the ringmaster said, his inflections leaving no room for doubt. "Fine dining extraordinaire, compliments of Chef Toroidal and his team of highly trained gourmet gastronomes!"

"I've dreamed of such a thing." The glint in Moth's eyes was that of silverware upon a creaking sideboard. "Lovely imaginings of cherry and apple and mincemeat."

"Lemon meringue," said Cobweb. "Chocolate cream."

"Stop yammering about pie," Bertie told them, all the while knowing there would be no dissuading them now. "Or I'll write your lips shut."

Peaseblossom clapped her hands over her mouth. Irrepressible, even in silence, Moth covered his eyes, Cobweb his ears, and Mustardseed his backside. Bertie gave Mustardseed one of Mrs. Edith's patented Dire Looks, and he shoved his hands deep into his pockets with a grin and an ear wiggle.

"Don't you have an opinion, too?" Bertie turned the same Look on Ariel.

Tendrils of silver hair shifted over his shoulders as he considered the question. "It's not my place to counsel the Mistress of Revels."

"You've a few minutes only to make up your mind," Aleksandr warned. "The Innamorati train will not wait."

There was no helping it. "A play in exchange for our passage."

"AND PIE!" screamed the fairies.

"And pie." Aleksandr spat into his hand. Bertie did likewise, and they shook upon the deal. "Words cannot convey the extent of my delight!"

"I have words enough for everyone." She gestured to the corner of the station. "I'm afraid we experienced a bit of technical difficulty, and we'll need help with our things. They're around the corner."

"Oh, my good Mistress of Revels! My roustabouts will see to the loading of your gilly wagon." When Aleksandr snapped his fingers, a dozen burly, mustachioed men stepped out from behind the ringmaster like a row of muscled paper dolls. With brutal efficiency, they retrieved the mechanical horses and the caravan, now defrosted enough to move as they ought, guiding them up a ramp and into a freight car.

"Oh, my!" Peaseblossom exclaimed. "Look at that!"

One after another, late-arriving hoops rolled out of the station, along the platform, and up the ramp. The fairies goggled after them, though the roustabouts slammed the door shut.

"Those . . . those were made of people!"

"Little girls, holding each other by the ankles!"

"I saw, Mustardseed," Bertie said, "now, all of you, lower your voices, please."

Aleksandr, perhaps taking the fairies' exuberance under consideration, waved a gracious hand at the caboose. "With my compliments. This will afford you a bit of privacy, should you require it, but do feel free to mingle with my merrymakers. They will surely be most humbled and thrilled to meet the Mistress of Revels."

The train's shrill whistle declared its intent to depart.

Mustardseed headed for their guest quarters, the others following him with screams of "Wait for me!" and "Don't hog the custard!"

Bertie pursed her lips, well aware of the wrack and ruin the fairies could wreak upon a hapless buffet table. "Perhaps I should have shoved them in their carpetbag, for safekeeping."

"Dear Beatrice!" Aleksandr looked affronted. "I'm certain they'll be most safe aboard."

"It wasn't *them* I was thinking of."

Aleksandr's laugh was like a lion's roar. "You will feel quite at home soon enough. Now, if you'll excuse me?" With a bow, he disappeared into the swirl of late-boarding passengers, soon lost amidst frothing petticoats, airbrushed unitards, and fabulous candy-colored coiffures.

The steam whistle blasted a second time. Bertie ran for the caboose, almost falling up the stairs in her haste to board, with Ariel and Waschbär close behind her. Stepping inside, she was reminded of an old-fashioned soda parlor or, at least, the Théâtre's version of one: all ribbon-striped cushions, silver paint, etched mirrors, and white wrought-iron benches.

"Nice digs!" crowed Moth as he zipped about the compartment.

"It is that," Waschbär agreed. Pip Pip and Cheerio tumbled from his pockets, pausing occasionally in their gleeful capering to sniff at the air, which smelled faintly of caramelized sugar and vanilla, as though some unseen person was baking waffle cones. Through the tiny windows, the station disappeared like a dream forgotten upon waking, and every turn of the wheels brought her one tiny bit closer to her father.

And to Nate.

When the train lurched, still picking up speed, Ariel caught Bertie by the elbow, preventing a topple face-first into the rosy potbellied stove. "You'll want to consider a costume change, I think."

She looked down at the ruined Mistress of Revels's costume with regret. The flight with the Scrimshander had done the first bit of damage, worsened thereafter by the dousing in the wetlands and the slog through the swamp. The silk bodice and skirts hung in shreds, as limp and bedraggled as she felt. "Mrs. Edith is going to have my head on a pike."

"Mrs. Edith will rejoice if you return to the Théâtre in

one piece." Catching her up, Ariel placed a very gentle kiss on the end of her nose. "And I vow to see to the sanctity of your neck." One hand found its way under her hair, gently stroking the skin there as his voice went low. "I seem to recall your fondness for denim. Perhaps the conductor has a spare pair of coveralls?"

The roustabouts had moved bits of their luggage into the caboose: the smaller of the trunks, the fairies' puppet theater, an assortment of boxes and bags that contained only ridiculous fripperies. The satchel safeguarding Bertie's jeans and sweater was nowhere to be seen, and she wasn't about to wear a frilly nightgown aboard a circus train.

"We're traveling with performers," Peaseblossom pointed out, toasting her little toes next to the stove. "There must be a Wardrobe Mistress tending to the costumes—"

"No!" Bertie refused to let her imagination trip down that path, immediately squeezing her eyes shut and trying to conjure the exact opposite of her guardian. "Aleksandr said there was a Keeper of the Costumes. That sounds like someone you might mistake for Hercules, the Strong Man."

"Perhaps he *is* the Strong Man," Cobweb suggested. "Circus people tend to wear more than one hat."

Moth scratched his head. "There must be trunks of hats somewhere, then."

"Never mind the trunks. I still want pie," Mustardseed whined.

"And how," Cobweb said.

"And ice cream," Moth corrected.

Bertie thought it was too soon to descend upon the un-suspecting Chef Toroidal and his team of gourmet gastro-nomes; highly trained they might be, not even a stampede of elephants could prepare them for four hungry fae on a pie quest. About to protest, her somewhat exposed stomach grumbled, and she reconsidered. "Change of clothes first, ice cream afterward."

With a low whistle, Waschbär coaxed the ferrets back into his pockets. "Follow me!"

"If you take longer than five seconds to get changed," Moth said, "we're going on without you."

Shrugging off the threat, Bertie tried to figure out where to stuff the fairies for safekeeping, only to remem-ber she didn't have pockets, even tattered ones, and the journal took up what little room there was in her bodice.

The boys caught her contemplative glance down her front. "Don't even think about it," Mustardseed warned.

"There's support, and then there's *support*," Moth said.

"And beyond that, there's cruel and unusual punish-ment."

"Maybe you'd like to cross the gap under your own power?" Ariel slid the compartment door open.

"Eep!" The fairies squeaked in alarm at the arctic-laced influx of air and dove for her hair.

"That's what I thought." Ariel indicated Bertie should go in front of him.

Traversing the rickety bit of metal between the caboose and the freight car, she gripped the railings. For added security, Ariel was right behind her every step of the way, both hands firmly on her waist. The snow fell thick and fast even between the cars, enormous flakes that glittered with diamond dust, and the freight car was a safe and quiet haven by comparison.

"Bracing, isn't it?" Waschbär slammed the door shut behind them, his furs so stiff that they crackled.

"That's one word for it." Bertie gave a dramatic shudder, shedding snowflakes in a perfect semicircle around her feet. Going to pat the mechanical horses, she entertained a passing fancy of feeding them clockwork sugar cubes. "Do you think they'll be all right, once they've defrosted?"

Ariel placed his ear against the slender neck of the closest steed, then pulled Bertie close enough to rest her cheek against the cold metal.

Tick, tick, tick . . .

"I do believe you'll survive to bolt again." Smiling, she went to rub its silver-velvet muzzle. The mechanical horse blinked amber eyes at her, albeit very slowly.

"A few more hours out of the weather, a bit of grease, and they should be fine." Waschbär adjusted their heavy woolen blankets.

With one last glance at the horses, the group moved across the next icy walkway. This crossing was just as bracing but less of a shock, allowing all their goggle-eyed wonder to be spent upon the contents of the Baggage Car.

The fairies poked their heads out of Bertie's hair. "Wow, would you check out all this junk?"

"Mr. Hastings would have a field day in here."

Bertie sidled down the aisle between the steamer trunks, each stamped INNAMORATI and various, intriguing things like "The Poplollies" and "Reinikaboo's Rosinbacks" and "Contessa Pollyfox's Sardoodledum." One crate rattled ominously when she passed, and she gave that one as wide a berth as possible. Goodness only knew what it contained, be it an act of warbling frogs or something peeved beyond measure over missing a meal. "Don't touch anything, any of you."

Mustardseed was aggrieved by the admonition. "We haven't moved! How could we touch anything from here?"

"Telekinesis," Peaseblossom said. When the boys didn't answer, she sighed and explained, "Using the powers of your mind to move things."

"Ah, but that's assuming we *have* powers of the mind!" A gale of giggles and then a competition to see who had the least mental capacity, with shouts of "I can move a sesame seed!" and "make way for dust motes!" that occupied them over the third walkway.

This time, Bertie managed to get across without Ariel's solicitous attention, but the sight of the man sitting on an upended wooden barrel prevented her lording her triumph. A sleeveless leather vest covered in ornate tooling showcased the man's impressively bulging arm muscles. Crawling, serpentine tattoos entirely covered his bald pate, a design eerily mirrored by the handlebar mustache perched above his mouth, its curled waxed ends looking sharp enough to poke out an eye. Just as Bertie vowed not to get close enough to put that theory to the test, Ariel and Waschbär crowded into the car behind her and shoved her in the direction of the threatening facial hair.

"Please excuse our abrupt entrance," she managed to say. "You're in charge of Wardrobe, I presume?"

"You presume correctly. I am Valentijn, Strong Man of the Innamorati and Keeper of the Costumes." Though more akin to a blacksmith than a tailor, he nevertheless wielded a needle in dexterous fingers. Gaze upon Bertie, he threaded the thin bit of silver with a microscopic filament. "And who are you?"

"Beatrice Shakespeare Smith." Remembering the effect her title had on Aleksandr, she added, "Mistress of Revels. And Company."

"Mistress of Revels, eh?" The sewing Strong Man

looked her over. "Mistress of Refuse is more like it. You look as though you've been pulled through a hedge backward." Minus the deep timbre of his voice, he sounded exactly like Mrs. Edith. The Wardrobe Mistress wore the same stern gaze, too, though hers was steel while his contained flint.

Seventeen years spent in the company of that good lady meant Bertie could meet his assessment without quailing. "Aleksandr said I should see you about a change of clothes."

"Of that there is no doubt." So deep did Valentijn's stare seem to assess the ruin of her snow-damp clothes that Bertie wondered if he had X-ray vision. "Remove that rag, and we'll see about getting you fitted with something more appropriate to your station." His gaze flickered over the others and landed upon the sneak-thief. "Waschbär."

"Valentijn." Far from the cordial greeting exchanged with the ringmaster, the sneak-thief's nod was curt.

The Strong Man pursed his lips. "I've only just finished a new Harlequin costume, silver-moon embroidery in the Tatterdemalion style, but I fear you've grown considerably about the middle since I saw you last." His gaze slid over to Ariel. "Perhaps new casting is in order?"

"We are not here to perform," the air elemental said firmly.

"Pity," Valentijn said. "You'd make a lovely trickster."

Waschbär headed for the door at the opposite end of the improvised sewing room. "Come. The pie car is just ahead."

"Pie car!" The fairies flitted free of Bertie's hair.

Peaseblossom paused a second, looking conflicted. "Do you want me to stay with you?"

"It's fine. Go ahead." Bertie tried not to look appalled by the idea that she was to be left at the mercy of the Strong Man.

"I don't like to leave you alone." Ariel said, shifting from foot to foot as though caught in the winds whirling outside.

The Keeper of the Costumes shook out the garment in his hand: a chemise of pristine white, embroidered at the neckline and down the flowing sleeves with delicate pastel flowers and vines. "She will be quite safe here, I assure you." Lifting his eyes from the linen, he assessed the air elemental as he might a bolt of cloth, finding every imperfection in the fabric's weft and warp. "Perhaps safer than she would be in your company?"

Ariel flushed at the suggestion and followed Waschbär, pausing only to add, "If you need me, Bertie, I'll be just outside." With a final scowl for the Keeper of the Costumes, he slammed the door shut behind him.

"What made you say that?" Bertie asked after a moment.

"About your safety?" Valentijn stood and held up the chemise, measuring her again with his eyes. "A blind man could see that man would die for you, but that doesn't mean you won't die alongside him."

CHAPTER TEN

Garments of
Changeable Taffeta

Bertie didn't have any desire to linger, dressed in rags or not. "I should catch up with the others. I don't like to be any trouble."

"There's trouble, and there's trouble. And a troublesome young girl without the sense to wear something travel appropriate is only slightly more troublesome than a button come loose." Valentijn gestured to an ancient folding screen tilting drunkenly against a stack of sticker-plastered leather valises. "That will afford you some privacy while I locate something suitable."

With the Keeper of the Costumes between her and the door, Bertie didn't like to test the theory that she'd be faster and more dexterous than the muscle-bound Strong Man.

He could fling me into the nearest open trunk with half a thought.

"Take this with you." Valentijn handed her the embroidered chemise and turned to flick through a freestanding clothing rack.

Moving past the new silver Harlequin costume and the matching golden Columbine, all diamond points and glittering spangles, Bertie ducked behind the thin shield of paper and wood. Setting aside the journal, she easily shucked her ruined vestments without needing to unlace or unbutton, wishing she could strip away Valentijn's premonition as easily.

That doesn't mean you won't die alongside him.

The Strong Man's boxcar was cold; unlike the caboose, it didn't have a visible source of heat, and her breath silvered as she hastened to pull on the chemise. Head emerging from the cloud of immaculate linen, she wished for something more than that between her skin and the frigid air. The appearance of a heavy, medieval-style surcoat of palest lavender wool stemmed the threat of hypothermia.

"This will complement your hair," was the observation from the opposite side of the screen

Bertie examined the proffered overdress, the same color as frost on purple grapes. Having never once voluntarily worn something not black or jewel toned, she immediately lodged her protest. "I'll look like an Easter egg."

"Wear it or go without," was Valentijn's casual dismissal of her concerns. "It makes no difference to me."

Not so much like Mrs. Edith, then.

Her caretaker would never have let her so much as poke her nose out of the Wardrobe without every stitch in its proper place. Deciding that color was less important than warmth, Bertie wriggled into the surcoat and struggled to tie the laces. Her mind wrestled with another issue: the glower the Strong Man had given the sneakthief. "Why don't you like Waschbär?"

"I have no use for one such as he. He never sees anything through to the end." Without warning, Valentijn moved the screen as easily as a lady closing a paper fan. "How's the fit?"

"All right, I suppose."

"May I?" He waited for her nod before deftly adjusting the overdress. "Not bad. Not ideal. Something in green would have been better."

Bertie's thoughts instantly strayed to the many bottles of industrial dye back in the Wardrobe Department. "Green highlights would be interesting, I suppose."

"I meant the dress." Valentijn gestured to a pair of beaded, low-heeled dancing slippers that sat on a nearby trunk. "Fur-lined boots would be more appropriate to the weather, but I haven't any in your size. Those will at least be better than sandals."

Thinking of the tiny acrobats that she'd seen on the platform, Bertie considered her own average-size feet, toes curled under from the cold, and felt very Darling Clementine.

The Strong Man scooped up the shredded remnants of her silks and the belt of gold disks. "As for the cincture . . ." He looped it about her waist, considered its contribution to the ensemble carefully, then nodded at both Bertie and the journal. "There is a pocket hidden in the right-hand seam of that surcoat large enough for your notebook, I think."

Bertie did her best not to snatch it up. "Thank you. I shouldn't like to misplace it."

"Its magic has the strength of flaxen thread, thrice waxed . . . stronger yet than the medallion you wear about your neck with such a casual air." All that remained of the Mistress of Revels's costume disappeared into a velvet sack marked "scraps" in embroidered lettering. "Aleksandr would do well to be wary of you."

"He knows." Bertie strived to sound cavalier, all too easily picturing the emergency whistle sounded and their troupe put off the train in the middle of a barren land during a blizzard. "Waschbär told him I'm a Teller of Tales, but it's nothing to fuss about—"

"'Nothing to fuss about,' pah!" Valentijn forced Bertie to sit so he could attack her tangle of Raven's Wing Black and Egyptian Plum hair, exceptionally vivid against the pastel canvas of the Innamorati's costumes. Once he was done with the comb, he used brilliant-tipped hairpins to create a glittering coronet. "Words are like the delicate stitches in the dress you wear, holding the fabric of the garment together. Without them, the dress and the world are nothing but barren cloth."

"That's a clever turn of phrase." Bertie admired the sparkling halo in the dark crown of her hair. "Perhaps you should be the playwright instead of me."

The Keeper of the Costumes backed away from her. "Mine was never a life meant for such power." His massive arms belied the statement as he settled himself at an ancient sewing machine.

"I'm not sure mine was, either," she said without thinking.

Never taking his eyes from her, Valentijn's foot operated the treadle. "You ought to make your mind up to it, before you snarl the world around you with careless stitches." The Strong Man fed a continuous stream of silk under the machine's metal foot, and a perfectly gathered ruffle, the sort that would line a cancan dancer's skirt, emerged from the other side. "You'll find your party in the next car, no doubt."

It was an unmistakable dismissal, so Bertie hastened to the door with a murmured, "My thanks, good sir, for the change of attire."

A nod. "You are welcome."

Eager to escape Valentijn's disconcerting observations, Bertie hardly noticed the snow as she crossed to the pie car. Opening the door, the scent of butter was one of a dozen assaults upon her senses. This compartment was taller than the others, and longer, so that she could hardly see to the other end for the birdlike ribbon dancers. Wearing only strategically placed feathers and whorls of body paint, they sat perched in filigree-brass swings and screeched gossip at each other like magpies. Innamorati performers sat about in pairs and in larger groups, consuming pastry with vigor, and emitting seal barks of laughter as others practiced in the aisles. No one marked Bertie's arrival in the slightest, so she scanned the crowd for Ariel and the fairies.

"Hup!" hollered a voice in her ear as a man catapulted past her. Blurs of white coalesced into a dozen men and women jumping upon silver teeterboards and tossing themselves backwards and sideways in flip-flaps, walkovers, and cartwheels, sometimes avoiding the ceiling by mere inches. "Allez-oop!"

Bertie dodged the performers as she would snowflakes in a blizzard. There were shouts and cries, clapping and foot stomping and the slap of skin meeting skin as they caught, threw, and landed atop one another. An ill-timed dodge ran Bertie up against a solid wall of nylon-clad chest, though she could look directly into the man's eyes without craning her neck.

"I beg your pardon!" she squeaked.

With several bows and a grin, he made gracious explanations in a wholly foreign language. Bertie, who'd been raised around Players who performed Chekhov in his native Russian, Molière in French, and commedia dell'arte in Italian, couldn't suss out a single word of his speech.

"There you are." Ariel nudged the performer out of the way to reach out to her.

Grasping the lifeline with thanks, Bertie skirted a man juggling ten ramekins of custard and a scantily clad girl, all the while shouting vehemently about something that had nothing to do, Bertie guessed, with either custard or girl. "That last maneuver nearly took off the end of my nose."

"That would be a pity, considering how unutterably fine you look in that dress." He tossed a careless, brilliant smile at her over one shoulder.

Bertie's heart lurched.

I have to tell him I was dreaming about Nate. It isn't fair to let him believe otherwise.

Before she had the chance to say anything, they arrived at the counter. The fairies lay spread-eagle in the ruins of what must have been a coconut cream pie, confirmed when Bertie ran her finger around the edge of the pan, then licked it.

"You only finished one?" The taste reminded her of

the time they'd used a set of sabers to cleave open a purloined shaggy brown tropical fruit on the deserted island set.

I nearly cut off my thumb, and Nate—

When the thick custard stuck in the back of her throat, Bertie nearly gagged. Reaching over them for a thick goblet brimming with ice water, she drank it down before wheezing, "I'm disappointed in you."

"I'm disappointed, too. That chess pie didn't have a single queen or rook in it." Mustardseed belched.

"Chess pie?"

"They started with the Cs." Ariel handed Bertie a menu that listed at least a hundred different variations on the pie theme. "That one between the cherry and the chocolate cream."

"The coconut was their fourth." Waschbär's fingertips skimmed over a Turkish coffee pot, a set of tiny porcelain demitasse cups encrusted with silver. The ornate sugar tongs were shaped like a crane whose beak caught up the cubes like fish from a river. "Would you care for some coffee?"

"Yes, *please.*"

Peaseblossom reached out a hand to stroke the embroidery on the surcoat, then thought better of it, seeing as how she was sticky to the elbows. "Such a lovely dress!"

The caffeine in the Turkish coffee snaked through

Bertie's middle with welcome heat. Her heart gave a tremendous thud of protest, though Ariel's proximity might have had something to do with that. "The encounter with Valentijn was most interesting."

"Rather like seeing Mrs. Edith with a mustache and popping-huge muscles!" Mustardseed said with a giggle that turned into a groan as he clutched his midsection.

"I warned you to leave off the whipped cream," Peaseblossom said. "Serve you right if you explode." Her little eyes filled with tears.

"Cheer up!" Moth told her. "If I explode, you'll get to see your Henry again."

Mustardseed grinned. "Bits of him, anyway!"

"Ah! There you are!" The bellow cut through the haze of smoke and the aroma of coffee as Aleksandr made his way toward them at the front of an impressive procession. He kissed Bertie's knuckles once more and then held her arm up, the better to assess her attire. "Valentijn certainly knows his trade."

Smoothing her free hand over her front, Bertie hoped she hadn't wrinkled the no-doubt costly dress. "I fear I didn't properly express my appreciation of such a fine garment."

"He knows without you telling him." Aleksandr twirled her around to greet his entourage. "May I introduce Salt and Sauce?" The booming introduction was no less theatrical for lack of stage lighting and a larger audience. "The Pachyderm Professors."

The elephant-like men wore wrinkled gray flannel suits with bow ties of pink and pumpkin. With somber deliberation, they ate marshmallow peanuts of palest orange out of striped paper bags.

"A pleasure." When Bertie wondered if she ought to curtsy, the two men simultaneously extended trunks of smoke-stained sterling mesh. She took one in each hand, marveling at the exceedingly fine craftsmanship that had gone into their costumed appendages. She slanted a look at Ariel, curious to know what he made of it.

But while he still hovered in the vicinity of her elbow, the air elemental's attention was wholly preoccupied with the giraffe-girl standing adjacent to Salt and Sauce. A necklace of hammered gold and amber emphasized her elongated neck, while her freckles were flecks of iridescent cream in milk. Long lashes framed huge brown eyes, and her slightly pointed ears twitched a bit as the train rollicked on the tracks. Gait wobbly, she moved to the counter in search of sustenance.

Bertie wasn't permitted to gawk any longer, as Aleksandr steered her into the nearest leather-upholstered booth. "Come, good Mistress of Revels! We have a Spectacle to plan!"

"A Spectacle, indeed." She had the distinct feeling

ld be surprised by if not appreciative of the
uantity of spectacle she could produce with
"What sort of Brand-New Play did you

The Innamorati ringmaster slid onto the bench across from her, wisely leaving the place next to Bertie free for Ariel. "Let us storm your brain in search of ideas."

"Hold on, hold on!" Peaseblossom waved her little hands to and fro. "We need different outfits for brainstorming!" The fairies began shedding layers, stripping down to black unitards.

"Oh, good grief." Though Bertie had no opinions on proper brainstorming attire, she was fairly certain it shouldn't involve skintight anything.

Waschbär poured out more of the thick, strong coffee and passed the tiny cups around the table. "Maybe the story of a journey?"

"How original," was Ariel's dry observance, but the fairies shushed him violently.

"How can she create with all your negative energy?"

"Yeah, man. You're bringing us down."

"This is about as low as it gets," Ariel said. "Where did you get those ridiculous black berets?"

Moth adjusted his recently donned beatnik attire. "This is what the hip cats wear, daddy-o."

"Can you dig it?" Cobweb stroked a few wisps of fake

chin hair, while the others nodded and snapped their fingers.

Aleksandr had gone pink around his cheeks and nose, either from imbibing the very strong coffee or in anticipation of grand production plans. When he held up his hand, a girl wearing only strategic sequins and body paint produced a leather portfolio, its contents dog-eared and travel worn. "Perhaps this will spark something."

Bertie turned it over to reveal the ornately lettered title:

The Big Pop-up Book of Scenery

"What is that?" Moth asked with a heaping helping of suspicion.

"This, my inquisitive fae friend, is a compilation of the set pieces traveling with us, a compendium, if you will, of landscapes, cityscapes, and dwellings of all sorts."

"I thought they'd be bigger," Mustardseed sniffed, unimpressed.

"This is merely the travel edition." Aleksandr flipped through the folder, irritated, perhaps, at their lack of appreciation.

Bertie caught glimpses of cunning, three-dimensional designs as the ringmaster turned the pages: a winding road surrounded by meadows; a quaint village of thatched-roofed cottages; a miniature version of the train station.

"Well, Mistress?" From the very air Aleksandr seemed to pull a sheaf of parchment and a three-foot-long feather pen, its plumage a scarlet exclamation point. Offering both the writing paraphernalia and his contagious enthusiasm, he asked, "Where will you begin?"

Experiencing a moment of pure panic, Bertie cast about for inspiration. Out the tiny window, snow still obscured the sky.

Sky. Day and night. Celestial bodies.

"It's the story," she said with convincing fervor, "of the sun and the moon."

"Perfection," Aleksandr breathed. "One performer dressed in palest gold, the other silver, performing with skipping ropes. Forward throws and somersaults."

Bolstered by the approving noises of the Innamorati, Bertie continued, "Only one can own the sky at a time. The winter days and nights pass on the tundra, the ground covered in snow." She closed her eyes and tried to picture the scene. Her left hand closed over the scrimshaw with a flare of pain, but when she began to write, it was pleasant, almost relaxing, to watch her handwriting fill the paper, edge to edge, without the fear that something might land on her head.

(Lights up on THE SUN, standing Center Stage. THE MOON enters, regal and haughty.)

THE SUN
The day is my domain. You do not belong here.

THE MOON
I am an admirer, milady. (He circles her with light steps.) Would that you belonged to me.

THE SUN
Be gone with you. The sky is mine. (She rises on a platform into the sky.) And so the day triumphs over the night.

THE MOON
(When THE SUN travels in an arc overhead) But not for long. As you set, so shall I rise.

While Bertie crafted the dialogue, Aleksandr kept the fairies amused by flipping through *The Big Pop-up Book of Scenery*. One wire-rigged contraption immediately captured their fancy.

"What is that?" Moth demanded.

Aleksandr spoke with great reverence. "The Wheels of Death."

"Death my arse," said Mustardseed. "That looks like two hamster wheels on a taffy puller."

"Wheels would be perfect." Nay, Bertie had just been

entertaining notions of such staging, and the coincidence surprised her. "Maybe we need to add more Players? Two seems hardly enough."

Sitting on her left side, Ariel looped an arm behind her. "Perhaps a musical number?"

When he began to toy with her hair, Bertie's stomach imitated the maneuver she'd witnessed the acrobats performing earlier. "Stop that. It's distracting."

"The aerial silk-dancers would make excellent Ice on either side of the stage." Aleksandr's eyes skimmed the crowd, potential acrobats already filtering forward. "Never fear, good Mistress of Revels, I can add in a variety of specialty numbers once you've crafted the storyline."

It made sense, really. "Enter the Chorus it is, then."

(Near the front of the stage, ICE
descends on pale blue ribbons.)

THE MOON
This is no longer your world. I cast a long silver
shadow, and the very air freezes.

"He's aggravated because he loves her." Ariel's soft observation raised the tiny hairs on the nape of Bertie's neck. "A circumstance to which I can relate."

"It's very *Romeo and Juliet*," Peaseblossom observed. "Minus all the stabbing."

"Stabbing?" Aleksandr asked, his puzzled expression bordering on concern.

"Don't worry," Moth hastened to reassure him. "Only Juliet stabbed herself."

"She sounds like a most troubled person," the ringmaster said. "And I don't think we require any of that in this piece."

Bertie rubbed her thumb over the smooth surface of the medallion, the cut on her palm burning under its handkerchief bandage. Inspired, she pictured a transition from running upon metal wheels to walking along the knife edge of a narrow passageway. "So the Sun and the Moon fall in love, though it is forbidden, and they run away together."

THE SUN
This is the place that cuts the day from night. If we cross it, we can be together.

THE MOON
I shall go first.

THE SUN
You are waning. Let me light the way.

"But of course they succeed, though they should be set upon by many trials." Aleksandr waited until her pen stopped moving before he continued. "And we finish with the lovers being married. It is a good play that ends with a wedding!"

Bertie, drafting the lines as fast as her hand would permit, could hardly think for the excited laughter and clamoring of the circus performers.

"Oh, yes! A wedding."

"With music and dancing!"

"A trampoline act that portrays the tossing of rose petals—"

"Hand balancing," one of the acrobats called. "To symbolize the handfasting!"

About to pen "and they all lived happily ever after," Bertie paused. The knot on her handkerchief-bandage had worked loose during all her frantic scribbling. "Handfasting?"

The giraffe-girl blinked her long lashes. "The bride and groom cut each other's palms. The blood is mingled, the hands bound at the wrist with a ribbon, vows are spoken."

Something in her throat made it difficult for Bertie to swallow. "You don't say."

"It's one of the oldest of wedding ceremonies," the giraffe-girl hastened to add as she was swept away by the enthusiastic performers.

"Chef Toroidal, a nuptial cake, if you please, one full of plums and ginger, soaked in brandy!" Aleksandr closed *The Big Pop-up Book of Scenery* with a bang and leapt up. "Casting and rehearsals commence this second, and we must have sustenance!"

The Innamorati cheered. Fiddle music accompanied the ensuing organized chaos as the ringmaster sorted his acrobats from his animal-people, preparing to block out scenes and rehearse transitions. The fairies rushed back to the counter to order another pie.

"What kind of pie starts with the letter *D*?"

"Let's skip ahead to the lemon meringue!"

Bertie didn't move, paralyzed by the idea that she'd married Nate without meaning to. Worse yet, that not even a ceremony like that, unintentional or not, had had the power to pull him through.

We have to get to Sedna. No more mucking around with vows and word-spells and—

An electric current of pain ran up her arm, and she squeaked.

Ariel jerked his hand away from her, whatever attempt he'd been making upon her person thwarted. "Is that wound paining you?"

Pulling her hand into her chest, Bertie shook her head. "It's not."

"It won't help matters any if it's infected." He tried to

coax it from her, fingers teasing, smile lighthearted even as his eyes narrowed with a familiar determined expression. "One small look—"

"Leave it be!" Bertie caught up everything on the table—the quill pen, the remaining blank pages, *The Big Pop-up Book of Scenery*—and fled. Pushing and shoving her way through the auditions already in progress, she stifled a cry when one of the acrobats roughly jostled her hand. Opening the door to the compartment, she ran over the narrow walkway as the winds roared around her, "Married? Married? Married?" Each direction shift brought a new condemnation: *Thoughtless child* came from the North Wind and *treacherous betrayal* from the South. East and West agreed she was *not to be trusted* as they chased her into Valentijn's boxcar. The Keeper of the Wardrobe was in absentia, the costumes hanging from the racks and pegs swaying like ghosts as Ariel caught her around the waist.

"Why are you running?" He held her as easily as he would a kitten by the scruff of the neck.

Bertie spit and swore, fighting to get away from him. "I have to write this stupid train to the Caravanserai. We have to get to Nate before—"

"Before what?" Ariel's grip on her faltered.

"Before he's . . . I mean . . ." She strained against the circle of his arms, but it was a secret that broke free.

"I pulled his soul from his body. He's not going to last much longer, separated like that."

With a subtle shifting of muscle, Ariel turned her around to face him. "When did this happen?"

Clamped between them, *The Big Pop-up Book of Scenery* dug into Bertie's chest, though Ariel's gaze went deeper than that. "That first night, when I wrote that he entered."

The air elemental's fingers clamped down on her left wrist, unwrapped the handkerchief, and brought her wounded palm inexorably up to the light. "And this." The words were blue-black diamonds hacked off some unseen ice block with a razor-sharp pick. "Tell me again how this came to be."

No matter how much she wanted to voice a lie, she couldn't. "I thought the blood would help pull him through. All of him."

The air elemental studied the ragged line as a scholar would an ancient text, one of his fingers air-tracing the wound. "A blood pact."

Though he didn't touch it, Bertie could feel the intent behind the gesture along with the tiniest bit of wind he let slip across the healing furrow. "Yes."

"You married him."

"No!" Still held prisoner, her hand spasmed. "That's ridiculous!"

"Is it now?" Ariel's voice had gone gentler still, and

it was more frightening than the loudest of shouts, the harshest of winds. "This mark says otherwise, if he gave it to you. What vows did you exchange? Did he promise to protect you with his sword? His body? To honor and cherish you, for a year and a day, for a lifetime, for eternity?"

"None of those things!" Bertie jerked from Ariel's grasp, nearly falling in her haste to get away from him, from his questions that pricked like needles. He wanted to write the story on her skin, like a tattoo, except he had the wrong story, and she wasn't about to let him mark her with his version of things. "I need to think. Leave me be."

He made a noise like he was being strangled from the inside out. "Or what? You'll write me out of existence? Or maybe you could trade me to Sedna for your precious *husband*—"

The door to the compartment slammed open and the Keeper of the Costumes entered, burly arms filled to overflowing with silks and satins. Looking from Bertie to Ariel, Valentijn dumped the fabric on a steamer trunk and set his fists on his hips. "Can I help you?"

"No!" Bertie surged through the open door, across the walkway.

"We're not done!" came Ariel's shout behind her, followed by another stern query voiced by the Strong Man, but Bertie didn't slow, didn't care. She ran past the mechanical horses, who rested with their necks bent, heads hanging low, eyes closed, over the next walkway. Back in the caboose, there was nowhere to go now but out the back door, onto the tiny balcony—

To heave myself off.

But Ariel was right behind her, step for step. "Where do you think you're going?"

Bertie flung everything she was carrying at him. Papers scattered across the compartment, the quill skittered under a bench, and *The Big Pop-up Book of Scenery* slid across the floor, coming to rest next to the fairies' puppet theater. "Where I'm going, now or any other time of the day or night is no business of yours!"

"*You* are my business!"

"Where did you get *that* misguided notion?"

"You told me you loved me!"

Bertie's mouth worked as Ariel advanced on her, but nothing came out. His stride faltered, and she saw the precise moment when he realized those words had not been meant for him.

"I see." Though he'd been three inches away from sweeping her into his arms, he stopped short, hands clenched at his sides. "I've been ten sorts of fool."

CHAPTER ELEVEN

Such Stuff as Dreams Are Made On

Y̶ou could write a most enthralling duel scene, milady playwright: the humble swashbuckler and the Lothario, each willing to die for the hand of the fair maiden." Pushing past her, Ariel opened the back door to the train car. The currents that rushed in were bleak, drawn from midwinter's longest night, and he spoke to those winds. "I shouldn't have returned to the theater."

"Don't say that—" The cold ripped the words from Bertie's lips, and she couldn't finish the sentence.

"I thought I had a chance to win your heart, but there's no way to compete against the idea of a man, something you've built up into a terrible fancy in that imagination of yours."

"This has n-n-nothing to do with imagination." Bertie's teeth were chattering so hard that she feared they'd crumble to dust. "S-s-stop being ridiculous, and come in out of the c-c-cold, you idiot."

"I don't think so." Ariel considered the blank canvas of the landscape and took a deep, cleansing breath, the sort that sounded like he was letting something go. "Tell me you love me, at least as much as you love him."

Bertie's good hand closed around the medallion, and she saw herself trapped between them: a woman draped in moss, cedar-still. Her feet were rooted in loam. Her features were carved of stubborn wood: cheekbones of burl and a nose that was a snub wood knot. Twisted-branch arms scattered leaves like sheets of journal paper.

Above her, brilliant red butterflies led straight to Ariel. Held aloft by coiling wisps of smoke, he swayed to an unheard tune, eyes closed. The translucent beauty of his ethereal self stole the very breath from Bertie's lungs, and the air spilled over her lips in a cloud-colored ribbon that dragged her toward him.

But he was not the only one calling to her. Far below, the tide pulled Bertie out to sea with gentle blue-green hands. Nate's face was coral-carved, his clothes moving in the water like the sails of a sinking pirate ship.

Caught between the water and the sky, Bertie tried to stay grounded.

The water and the wind will wear the wood down, until only water and wind remain.

She grew obstinate, unyielding to either wind or water. A forest took root around her, protecting her from the other elements, the trees ancient and far-reaching into the earth. Between the massive trunks, Bertie caught a glimpse of a clearing.

"What is mine, and mine alone?" She let go of the medallion to push back a curtain of moss, seeking that place of twilight, a between-place. "Neither my days nor my nights."

"I will give your days back to you, then." The words seemed to come from a great distance, except Ariel's hand closed around the medallion. With a swift jerk, he pulled it from her neck. "And your nights as well."

The forest disappeared instantly, lost to snow and ice. Bertie stared at Ariel in horror as he leapt atop the railing and let the scrimshaw dangle over the edge. It spun wildly on the end of the leather string Nate had once worn in his hair.

Bertie lunged at him. "Give it back, I need it."

"You don't." He pretended to drop it, letting the scrimshaw swing like a pendulum.

Everything shifted. Unbalanced, Bertie fell over one of the wrought-iron benches, trying to reach him, reach the necklace. When she landed on her wounded hand, a chrysanthemum-burst of fireworks cascaded up her arm to ignite hot fountains of sparks in her elbow and shoulder. The handfasting scar began to bleed in earnest. "Ariel—"

"Say please."

Lulled as she'd been by his manners and charm the last few days, Bertie had almost forgotten his quicksilver side: mercurial, selfish, and cruel. "Please."

"Like you mean it."

"Please." Gathering her strength like so many dying vines, Bertie forced herself to stand again.

He considered the plea for a moment, before deciding. "No. I shall keep it, as a souvenir of our brief and bitter time together."

"You can't mean to leave—"

"Ask me to stay." His eyes pleaded with her, too.

Adrift in a stark realm of blackest night and whitest snow, all her words were bits of caged color, and Bertie could not free them.

"I thought as much." The expression on his face stabbed her to the heart. "Farewell, milady. Parting is such sweet sorrow." Making her a lovely, sweeping bow, he stepped off the back of the train, immediately lost to the blizzard.

A final blast of wind knocked her backward, where she lay panting on the cold floor of the caboose, the wooden planks like frozen steel. Tears trickled from her eyes, forming icicles on her cheeks. Snow swirled in the open door. Reality fell away from Bertie in jagged-edged chunks even as she wrestled the journal from her pocket. The fountain pen had gone missing somewhere between Wardrobe and pie car; sleeve crackling with ice, Bertie's sound hand closed around Aleksandr's ridiculous quill and managed to scratch out the word,

Truth

The floor under her cheek slanted a bit, tilting the stage of the fairies' puppet theater toward her. Montagues, Capulets . . . It was only fitting to repeat the line.

"Parting is such sweet sorrow." Except Ariel's bitter departure and his theft of the medallion might just be her undoing. Another tear slid down her cheek; this one did not freeze, though, falling instead in an onyx droplet to the floor and cracking like an egg on impact.

Out danced a tiny figure that moved like a marionette, though she was without strings when she gestured at Bertie. "O! what a noble mind is here o'erthrown!"

Squinting at the not-puppet, Bertie recalled Alice's Wonderland "Drink Me" bottle back in the Properties Department, imbibing its contents, and fearing she would shrink down to nothing. The memory cued a costume and scene change, both; her spine was the crease on a piece of paper, her bones no more than diagonal folds on a bit of origami. The caboose, the snow, the cold, all faded into the blackout. For a moment, she could see nothing, could feel nothing beyond the rustle of her vellum limbs.

A gentle amber spotlight came up, tightly focused on the marionette without strings. With screwed joints at knee and elbow, and hinge lines now visible at the corners of her mouth, she bent over in cheerful greeting. "Hallo!"

Bertie sat up with difficulty. "What are you doing here, Ophelia?"

The spotlight's radiance diffused outward, and Bertie found herself sitting on the edge of *The Big Pop-up Book of Scenery*. Open to its version of the Théâtre Illuminata, it rendered the velvet curtains in paper, the gilt with metallic gold paint.

"The next line," the curious marionette said, "is yours."

Bertie could taste the words in her mouth, like crimson lip rouge. "My mother was a star, an ingénue on the rise, a society darling."

"Not really." Puppet-Ophelia string-danced to her dressing table and sat down upon a chair. "The performances night after night, the make-up and the costuming and the curtain calls . . . all of it was weary, stale, flat, and unprofitable. I got sick of being Polonius's daughter and Laertes's sister and Hamlet's girlfriend. I wanted, for just a while, to be only myself. That's when *he* arrived."

A deep-timbred voice spoke from the shadows offstage. "I haunted the cliffs and shores, waiting for the day when my lost love would take pity upon me and open the gateway to her underworld. Then word came via travelers to the Caravanserai about a place where the Sea Witch ruled."

Bertie shifted, trying to catch a glimpse of him, and nearly fell off the edge of the book. When the Mysterious Stranger entered a few seconds later, he walked with a stiff-legged gait to Center Stage. The hood of his gray cloak fell back, revealing the papier-mâché mask of a bird, complete with feathers and a yellow bill. His lower, decidedly human jaw was left free to speak.

"I came to this place, this theater, looking for her."

Ophelia twisted around in her chair. "What are you doing in here? Get out, before I call the Stage Manager—"

"You are not a mermaid." The bird-creature lifted two handfuls of Ophelia's hair and brought them to his face. "Yet you smell faintly of the ocean."

"That would be the seaweed." She twitched free of his impertinent grasp. "And no, I am not a mermaid. They're just beginning Act One, if you've come to see the play."

"I'm in the wrong place," the bird-creature answered. "I apologize for the interruption, but I was passing by, and thought I recognized your scent . . . that is to say . . ."

"I should summon one of the stagehands before you defile the floor." Ophelia pursed her lips. "Why are you backstage? You aren't one of the Players. I have no idea who you are, Stranger, or even *what* you are."

"I am a fulmar," he said, then added, "the bird of the storm."

"Just who do you seek?" Tilting her head to one side, she regarded him with a full measure of sudden curiosity.

"There was another who smelt of the sea. I have searched for her everywhere, but she is not to be found." The bird-creature rustled uneasy feathers. "You are obviously not her, so I will make my apologies and leave."

"Leave?" Ophelia repeated the word as though it had just occurred to her. Then she said it once more, this time with inflections of salted caramel candy. "Leave."

Considering her with those jet-black eyes, the bird-creature asked, "Do you also wish to leave?"

"I do!" She spoke with enough vehemence to ruffle his feathers. "I am trapped here, performing the same play night after night, unless . . ."

"Unless?"

Ophelia's smile was brighter than the stage lights. "Unless I pull my lines, my story, from The Book. It will be like I never existed at all." Clapping her hands, she went to brush past him, but the bird-creature filled the doorway, standing stiff and still for a long moment.

"For the sake of another who wished herself away, I will take you with me, if you like."

"Are you certain?" Ophelia asked, looking up at him through her lashes. "I shouldn't like to be any trouble."

The bird-creature shook his head. "I do get the feeling that trouble might be a specialty of yours."

Ophelia stood on tiptoe to look directly into the glossy surface of his eyes. "The moment you tire of my company, we'll part ways."

The couple disappeared into the wings of the stage as two black-clad stagehands lifted the edge of the enormous page. Bertie slid off just in time, her hasty retreat accompanied by the faint cry of the Call Boy, "Ophelia to the stage, please." The Théâtre set folded in upon itself as the cliffs rose. Ophelia's costume changed as well, to gray velvet with shadowed trim that helped her disappear time and again into the shifting lights.

"I was the first to figure out how to free myself from the theater," puppet-Ophelia said as they crossed to Stage Right. "I took my page with me to the seaside, and it was there that I fell rather unexpectedly in love."

"It surprised both of us," the bird-creature said softly. "There was no slipper, nor spinning wheel, nor true love's first kiss. This was not a fairy tale with a happily ever after."

The scene shifted again with the crackle of cardboard so that Bertie's puppet-parents stood inside a cave. Warm stone walls curved in at the top, while bits of leaf and twig lay scattered on the floor. From behind the set, something did a decent job mimicking the roar and moan of the ocean. Bertie clambered back into *The Big Pop-up Book of Scenery*, afraid to speak for fear they would stop telling her story.

"You must admit," Ophelia said with a laugh as she made a nest Center Stage, "that there was something between us right from the beginning."

"There was yearning, I will admit, and a loneliness inside me." Though the bird-creature's words were for Ophelia, his eyes were on Bertie until he turned and entered the scene. "And you were lovely, and young, and full of life. I hardly knew what to make of you."

"For the first time in centuries, I felt as if I could breathe." Ophelia's smile was only for him. "Though I was surrounded by water, I had no desire to throw myself in."

The bird-creature circled her; as he moved, the lights lowered, and there was the suggestion of a thunderstorm outside. In the flashes of light, Bertie could see his feathers drift to the floor. Soft bits of down swirled and settled until he knelt before Ophelia, more man than bird. "Yes, there was something between us." He brought her hand to his mouth for a single kiss.

Bertie could not think of him as her father yet, but he was no longer a Mysterious Stranger, either.

What part is he playing for me?

Watching Ophelia nestle against the man's broad chest with a happy sigh, Bertie found it hard to breathe, hard to swallow. "What ruined it? Was it me?"

"Never think that—" the man started to say, but black-clad stagehands rushed into the cave set, wrapping the two figures onstage in long, twisted strips of sparkling aquamarine. Torn apart and coiled in separate cocoons, Ophelia reached for him, while the Scrimshander thrashed his arms and legs. The water was a winding sheet, though neither was dead yet.

"No!" Bertie cried when their motions slowed and finally stilled. The fabric settled into sloppy-wet pools. Ophelia lay in a heap, her swollen belly straining at the sodden green fabric of her dress.

The man crawled to her, his hand seeking the fullness of her middle before sliding up to her throat. He shook her gently. "Breathe, my love."

A pale blue lighting special washed over her cheeks, but Ophelia obeyed him. She turned her head to one side and spat silver glitter onto the stage. "It's all right. I'm used to it."

Gathering her to his chest, the man cast about the cave. "It's not safe in this place."

Ophelia clutched him. "What are you saying?"

"We have to go back to the theater."

"You're supposed to be my handsome prince," Ophelia cried. "This is supposed to be my happily ever after."

"Calm yourself." He gathered her in his arms. "I'm not leaving you. Not now. Not ever."

"But you did," Bertie whispered.

"Hush," he said as the set shifted around them, a scrim curtain running across the stage with the blur of motion, the rush of air that suggested flight. When it came to a standstill, Bertie could see it was painted with the Théâtre's façade. The marquee dangled from invisible-thin wires, Hamlet's name spelled out in lights.

The bird-creature set Ophelia on the stage, feathers once more obscuring his features. "The journey came at a great cost. Summoning my almost-forgotten flight-magic awakened the wild creature I'd once been."

Ophelia turned to him, grasping his face in her hands. "Don't you dare leave."

His every muscle trembled with the effort of holding on to her. "Don't let go, whatever you do." A haunting melody began to play: whale song, the call of the gulls. The bird-creature shuddered. "She's calling to me. She claims she'll open the portal."

"Lies." Ophelia wrapped herself around him like a starfish clinging to a rock. "Stay with me."

"I love you." His words were a croak.

"And I you," Ophelia cried. "Do you doubt that?"

Bertie stiffened at the words.

Do you doubt that?

The line echoed all around them as a golden sheet of paper—*her page from The Book*—fluttered free of Ophelia's pocket and then disappeared. The water-maiden immediately faded around the edges.

That . . . that . . . that . . .

"Your opening line," Bertie said.

The performance taking place that night . . . an understudy onstage perhaps . . .

Someone said Ophelia's first line, acted her page back into The Book, pulled her back into the theater.

Unbidden, the Theater Manager's face swam before Bertie as the stage tumbled into a blackout.

"No!" both women screamed in unison.

When the lights rose to half, Ophelia was trapped behind the scrim curtain. Only thin gauze separated her from the Scrimshander, who had fallen to his knees, but it was enough to keep them apart. He trembled, hands pressed against the stage floor, shoulders shaking. Without her to tether him, he began to transform.

Ophelia pounded on the painted door; though the scrim was no more substantial than a whisper, she could not broach it. "My love!"

His keening cry cut through the space, the humanity

fading from it, and there was nothing of the man left to recognize her. The bird shook, settling every feather into place before he launched himself into the sky. The scrim curtains slithered offstage, their task performed, and Ophelia fell as though her strings had been cut. Bertie ran to her mother, past the stagehands who flipped the pages of *The Big Pop-up Book of Scenery* to the Théâtre's Lobby with the swift crackle of stiff paper.

"Ophelia." Bertie lifted the woman's limp form into her arms.

"He promised he wouldn't leave." Her puppet-mother stared up, eyes wide and unseeing.

Bertie choked, wishing there was something she could do, except this was a mere recitation of events long since past. Two of the faceless, black-clad stagehands rushed in and pried her off Ophelia.

"You must let her finish."

"The play is not yet done."

"I don't want to see anymore!" Bertie twisted in their grasp.

Stage Left, another stagehand pulled a tab so that a two-dimensional cutout of Mrs. Edith glided across the stage. As the Wardrobe Mistress passed before Ophelia, the stagehand pushed the tab back into the book. The figure flipped about, and the new version of Mrs. Edith held a swaddled bundle in her arms.

Ophelia sat upon the page, the salt water of her tears reclaiming her. "We must be patient: but I cannot choose but weep."

The Theater Manager's voice echoed all around them. "I think it would be best for everyone if you took the child away from the Théâtre."

Mrs. Edith's rejoinder was stern. "What does Ophelia think of your plan?"

"Not a thing," he said. "She remembers nothing of the outside world, nothing about the child."

Ophelia put her fists to her eyes, crying out. Accompanied by the croon of a single violin, a series of ghostly projections waltzed across the stage: dark silhouettes of her first meeting with the fulmar, their journey to the sea, their time spent together in the Aerie. The lighting darkened, the shadow-recollections showing their return to the theater. Ophelia clutching the Scrimshander. Panting in childbirth. Cradling a newborn baby. Then the projector clicked off and took the memories with it.

Rising, Ophelia gave Bertie that calm yet vague smile that had been her signature expression for years. "The curtain is coming down, don't you see? You ought to be off."

The blackout that followed was swift and certain. With the performance finished, a single, bare lightbulb flickered to life, dangling from a wire overhead. Spots danced through Bertie's vision as her eyes struggled to adjust. Left alone once again, she swallowed and swallowed, refusing to cry.

For any of them.

CHAPTER TWELVE

Of His Bones Are Coral Made

"Ophelia didn't forget me . . . her memories were taken from her." Bertie's fingers closed around a single feather the Scrimshander had left behind; it was cold, like the kiss of great icebergs passing through arctic waters. Frost slid through her, salt-spangled and tasting of the sea. "And my father didn't abandon her. He was trying to stay."

Not only that, but—

She's calling to me. She claims she'll open the portal.

Another crossing-over place. One that would lead her to Nate—

A whistle blast cut through the darkness, shattering the single lightbulb. Bertie ducked her head to avoid the glittering shower of glass.

"Bertie!" The cry seemed to come from the end of a train tunnel. "Bertie!" Getting closer.

She refocused her eyes upon four tiny perturbed faces only half illuminated by the tiny coal-burning stove.

"How long have you been like this?" Peaseblossom wanted to know, except her features were sculpted from marzipan.

"Insane?" Bertie levered herself upright, every muscle protesting. "All my life, I think."

The boys had been carved from milk chocolate, dark chocolate, and what appeared to be peanut nougat. "Were you asleep?"

"Not exactly." The very idea jabbed at her vitals with rusty nails, because if she had indeed been asleep, then why had she not dreamed of the grove, of Nate—

Unless I'm too late to rescue him?

Between them, the boys managed to get the door to the rear balcony closed, though they had to shove part of a snowdrift out with it. Beyond the windows, the landscape was a midnight canvas, and Bertie concentrated very hard until the fairies' candy coating disappeared.

"Where's Ariel?" Peaseblossom asked, adjusting the wick on the nearest lamp. Now the light sparked with a tiny cascades of red and orange glitter, sifting down the length of the walls to decorate the surface of the re-maining snow.

"He left." Trying to rein in her panic over the prospect that Nate might have unraveled just as reality was now coming apart along the seams, Bertie allowed her head to rest against the wall. "And I don't think he's coming back."

Mustardseed gaped at her. "Why would he do such a thing?"

"Jealousy," Waschbär said from the doorway. "Something to do with the cut on your hand, I imagine." As he approached her, Bertie wondered if he'd always so closely resembled an upright raccoon, or if the absence of the medallion played such merry havoc with her senses. He knelt next to her and held out a paw. "Let me see the wound." When she unfurled her fingers, the feather fluttered out. The sneak-thief raised it to his nose, already aquiver. "This is a fulmar's feather."

"You were right," Bertie said. "My father is a seabird."

The end of the sneak-thief's nose twitched again. "Your hand smells of infection." He placed his wrist against her forehead. "You've a fever, there's no doubt about that."

"Does my fever smell of strawberries?" Holding up her good hand, Bertie tried to imagine it full of fruit. "Hot strawberries? Boiling strawberry jam?"

"Keep talking," Moth said before she could manifest any sort of preserves. Laying on his back, his arms and legs carved the suggestion of wings into the snow left inside the train car. "And don't forget the hot buttered toast."

Peaseblossom was already wrestling one of the railroad blankets off the luggage rack. "We need to cover her up." The boys helped her tug the length of scratchy wool into place, then the fairy marched up Bertie's chest and wagged a finger under her nose. "You're to rest, do you hear? Waschbär, fetch a hot lemonade from the pie car and tell them to go easy on the whiskey."

For a second, Peaseblossom looked like a tiny pink frosted cupcake, and Bertie shook her head, feeling her brain jiggle inside her skull. "I don't want a hot lemonade. I need coffee, and lots of it."

"No more coffee!" The pink cupcake shivered sprinkles all over Bertie's collarbones.

"I can't fall asleep." The dreamlands beckoned with the promise of the ancient trees. Desperately wanting to step beyond the moss-curtain to check on Nate, Bertie feared that if she traveled again to that place of solace and safety, she might never come back, might never wake up. "We have to get to the Scrimshander. He knows where the portal is."

"We're on our way." Moth solicitously tucked the blanket under Bertie's chin. "You can't speed up a speeding train."

The others hastened to shout, "Don't even think about it, Bertie!"

"I don't want to die in a horrible, fiery train wreck!"

Bertie located the journal on the floor but the fountain pen was still nowhere to be found. The medallion's absence weighed upon her more heavily than a suit of armor—something she knew for certain, because she'd once tried one on in the Properties Department—and her movements grew more sluggish with each passing moment.

Concentrate. There will be no one to save Nate if you slip into a dream coma.

"I'm not going to speed up the train," she said, trying to reassure the fairies. "I'm just going to skip us ahead."

"Like skipping a rock on a pond?" Moth had his forehead all wrinkled up, but he'd latched onto the perfect imagery.

"Just like that." Bertie held up the feather. "I'll use this to get us to the Scrimshander."

"Many wearing rapiers are afraid of goose quills," Moth muttered.

"Her dad's not a goose!"

The sort of topsy-turvy delicious nonsense that appeared in Gilbert & Sullivan's musicals fuddled Bertie's thoughts. She hummed a few bars under her breath, then sang,

"The feather of my father is
The weapon with which I must write;
Though swords may poke through all the blokes
They cannot do the job just right. . . ."

The fairies looked at her, appalled.

Peaseblossom shoved Aleksandr's plumed pen at her. "This will work better than a feather without ink, I believe. And no more rhyming for you."

"Someone gag her with the blanket," Cobweb added, "before she composes an entire operetta, and a troupe of rosy-cheeked maidens appears to sing a rousing chorus about their dashing lads in knee breeches!"

"I refuse to warble lines in a falsetto!"

"That will be the straw that not only breaks the camel's back, but jumps up and down on its corpse and then hacks its head off!"

"With me in the starring role as the camel, I should think. Camels are nice, aren't they?" Struggling to focus, Bertie commenced skipping the rock across the landscape. "Have you ever seen the Caravanserai, Waschbär?"

"Tens upon hundreds of times." The sneak-thief crouched next to her, expression wary. "It's the grandest of the Thirteen Outposts of Beyond, with an amphitheater large enough for entertaining an empress. You will never forget the first moment you set eyes upon it, rising out of the desert like a sand castle."

Bertie tucked the Scrimshander's feather behind her ear, opened the journal, and wrote,

They arrive, rather sooner than expected, at the Caravanserai.

Then, fearing they would miss it, she pushed the blanket off and struggled to her feet.

"What are you doing?" Peaseblossom looked alarmed. "You need to rest!"

"We've reached our stop, whether the good conductor knows it or not." Bertie reached for the red-painted metal handle marked EMERGENCY BRAKE, and pulled upon it with her remaining strength.

Half a second for the bell to ring the engine, another half second for the conductor to react, followed by the terrible squeal of metal meeting metal. Ever nimble, Waschbär rocked back on his feet, hooking one arm around Bertie when she stumbled past him. The fairies, unprepared for the sudden cessation of forward momentum, smacked into the wall like particularly juicy mosquitoes hitting a windscreen.

"Ow, my spleen." Moth, face pressed to the wood

paneling, left a dribble of drool in his wake as he slid to the floor.

"I think my innards are now my outtards."

"Why in the blue blazes would you do that, Bertie?"

"Because we're here." Dangling like a limp dishrag from the sneak-thief's arm, Bertie caught a flicker of torchlight through the caboose's window. One step closer to the Scrimshander, one step closer to Nate; she could feel it in her bones. "See?"

Waschbär half carried her to the door. "We should have had at least a night's journey before us."

Nevertheless, they'd arrived at a station and beyond that, the Caravanserai rose from the landscape, a massive golden sand castle against the night's dark curtains. Pennants flapped atop the ramparts, caught in a wind that carried with it the suggestion of starfish and seaweed. All that had been snow before was now softly glittering stone. Burning at intervals, hundreds of torches illuminated the curving path to the gateway, where other travelers and pilgrims entered and exited despite the late hour. Indeed, distant cries from the marketplace, faint strains of music, the trumpet of a perturbed elephant all indicated that the Caravanserai was the sort of place that never slept.

The Innamorati disgorged from the train, marveling at the speed of the journey. The scene on the platform was organized chaos, with performers and roustabouts moving in a dozen directions at once and yet somehow managing to assemble themselves in preparation for a grand parade. Either they'd traded their muted costumes for ones of teal and turquoise, the deepest plum and brightest yellow, or Bertie's fevered brain saw their true colors, no longer snow-filtered. Right in the thick of it, Valentijn's vivid purple cape flashed with amethyst light, and when Aleksandr arrived on the scene, his ringmaster's crimson and black livery were elaborately trimmed out with massive quantities of gilt cording and rope. An enormous emerald was affixed to the top of his walking stick, and he rubbed jeweled hands together with flashes of ruby, topaz, and star sapphire.

"We've reached the outpost sooner than expected," he said.

Bertie, held upright only by the grace of Waschbär's arm, was saved answering by the blare of the Innamorati's trumpets. The elephant-men led a massive procession up a winding road of warm beige brick. The bird-girls rode upon their swings atop golden, flowering floats, while jewel-adorned acrobats walked miniature tightropes from one rolling platform to another. A massive tipsy calliope blasted music and steam from teetering brass pipes, with the Keeper of the Costumes sitting on its bench and pressing the keys as deftly as he operated the treadle sewing machine.

Waschbär settled Bertie atop the Mistress of Revels's caravan, then took the reins to guide the mechanical horses into place. They rattled up the road at the end of the parade, an afterthought, an uninvited guest sneaking into a masquerade ball. Inscriptions spread along the walls in every imaginable language, though Bertie wondered if the missing scrimshaw was responsible for her inability to read them. Her throat felt naked without the medallion's reassuring weight, exposing her to other sorts of pain.

Curse you thrice, Ariel: once for not giving me the chance to explain; another for taking what was mine; and the third for leaving.

"What do the words say?" Bertie asked.

"Welcome," the sneak-thief replied with a brilliant smile. "May all who enter here find that which they seek."

"What is it you seek, Waschbär?"

The sneak-thief stiffened next to her. "What do you mean?"

"You left the Brigands, you left the Innamorati. Are you chasing a wandering star? A dream? A woman? An idea?"

"Careful, now. Those words have more meaning than you know." He threaded the reins through uneasy hands.

"How long before you leave the troupe?" Bertie persisted. "That's inevitable, isn't it? Valentijn told me you never see anything through to the end."

"Oh, he did, did he?" Waschbär's mouth tightened as they passed under the archway and entered the courtyard.

Even an Opening Night at the Théâtre was no match for this marketplace. Light came from torches, paper lanterns, and brass braziers, and the Caravanserai was a kaleidoscope that fragmented every color Bertie had ever seen into a myriad of new shades. Within arm's length, there were trousers of midnight, a shirt the color of the sky at dawn, and a flowing dress that matched the spiked, yellow-throated irises for sale on a nearby table.

The Innamorati parade garnered quite a lot of attention as, calliope blaring, they progressed by inches. One girl walked forward, body encased in a hundred thin silver hoops that she kept in perpetual motion with gentle undulations of the hips and arms. The acrobats they'd seen rehearsing in the pie car performed a human juggling act. Dressed in peacock blue trimmed in silver fringe, they flung one another over stalls and carriages with raucous bird cries of "hup!" and "allez-oop!"

The color and chaos surrounding them reminded Bertie of an "All Players to the Stage" call at the theater, and she couldn't help but search the crowd for a wayward air elemental.

Will Ariel's winds tell him we've arrived at this strange place?

She thought, for a moment, that she could smell cool silk under the hot grease, exotic incense, and tropical flowers, but the suggestion of him was fleeting, and Bertie told herself that she had no time to spare for his games. "Which way to the White Cliffs?"

Waschbär, enjoying himself hugely and waving to the crowd, took a moment to answer. "The only way to the shore is through the marketplace."

That's all she needed to hear. With little thought to her limbs or recent jelly legs, Bertie slid down the side of the still-moving caravan, missing the cart's wheels by mere inches. The fairies careened after her as the sneak-thief shouted to her and the horses both.

"Whoa! Where do you think you're going?!"

Peering down the various stone-walled corridors, Bertie thought she spotted an exit portal. "Through the eye of a needle!"

He tossed the reins to the nearest roustabout. "Take that with you to the performers' courtyard!" When Bertie quirked an eyebrow at him, Waschbär added, "They will take the parade all the way down the easternmost passageway, which leads to the amphitheater."

Bertie tried to get her bearings as bells jangled and voices called and livestock protested over breezes that carried suggestions of yeast, simmering meat, dried spices, and hay. The fairies flew about her, practically sparkling with excitement, and Waschbär moved alongside her, his bulk an effective shield against the jostling crowd.

Looking up at him, Bertie spared a moment to smile before setting off down the nearest aisle. "Why do you feel the need to act the guardian?"

"I haven't the foggiest notion. It's most perturbing." Disconcerted or not, Waschbär kept pace with her.

"Someday, I'll be able to take three steps without having a shadow. Or four tiny ones." Bertie cut through a corner stall, only to have a horse—real, not clockwork—snap at her with clacking teeth. Hurriedly, she backed into a different horse, this one thankfully happier to make her acquaintance. It nudged her pockets with a velvet nose and whickered at the fairies, who scattered with tiny screams and the sudden brandishing of swords.

"Get back here," Bertie hissed at them. "And put those things away. Do you want to start a riot?"

The fairies sheathed their weapons, toothpicks purloined from the pie car, just as they passed a mountain of a man swallowing two feet of tempered steel.

"Golly," said Mustardseed.

"Don't get any ideas," Bertie said. "You'd split yourself open from the inside out, and I'm not giving you mouth-to-mouth."

"What about snakes?" Of course Moth was staring at a snake charmer, coaxing a length of gleaming-scaled serpent from a woven basket.

"No snakes!" Bertie said. "Remember the asp problem?"

"Asps?" Waschbär asked.

"Malfunction during a *Hamlet* rehearsal. Suffice it to say I'm not a huge fan of snakes." Bertie tried to duck through the crowd, but everyone around her seemed determined to thwart her progress, especially the jester capering in front of them, holding a tambourine in one hand and a dripping dill pickle in the other.

"Hail and well met!" He bowed to Bertie with much jingling of his bells. "Would the lady care for a taste of my gherkin?"

"She would *not*," Mustardseed said, no doubt thoroughly offended by the stranger beating him to a vulgar suggestion. "Apologize at once, or feel the wrath of my toothpick."

"Ooh, he is a rude one, isn't he?" Delighted, the jester stuffed his pickle into the depths of an unseen pocket. "You are searching for a new gown, perhaps?" He reached out to hook a finger under a wooden hanger over which flowed a garment of scarlet loveliness.

Bertie scowled at her assailant. "Kindly get out of my way."

Instead, he turned the hanger around, and the red dress faded to a creamy confection of ribbons-through-lace.

Spiders dangled from the delicate cobwebbing, still knitting the sleeves and collar. "Something more appropriate for a summer wedding?"

Recoiling, Bertie shook her head. "Absolutely not!"

"What sort of lady cannot be tempted with finery?" The jester capered in place.

"The sort that is going to have your arms removed if you don't get out of her way." Bertie signaled to the sneak-thief, and Waschbär snarled, displaying all his teeth.

Under his gaudy makeup, the street performer paled. "My humblest of apologies!" He tripped over his own feet as well as a nearby tent pole, trying to back away and bow and beg her pardon until he disappeared from view with a last muttered, "I hope I didn't offend thee!"

"An offense to mine eyes as well as mine ears," Bertie said, leaning against the nearest stall to gather her strength. Silk streamers decorated a hundred wooden dowels, and the occasional breeze tugged at the miniature maypoles. She stared at the ribbons until they bled into a watercolor river that cascaded to the ground in paint spatters, speckling her shoes. The stall owner cried out her dismay, trying to catch her wares in copper pots.

The sneak-thief skirted the puddle of color to put a hand on her arm. "Bertie?"

"Hmm?" She blinked, which did nothing to dispel

either the ribbon-river or the nimbuses of light surrounding the fairies hovering nearby.

Peaseblossom waved a hand before Bertie's face. "You look awful."

Waschbär, too, looked concerned. "We need someone to look at your wound. Your fever is escalating, and you're changing things without meaning to."

"It's not just the cut on my palm." Bertie rubbed a hand across her eyes, trying to get them to focus on the here and now. "The scrimshaw used to show me what was real, even if what was real wasn't the part that was real." Though the sneak-thief steered her true, she stumbled, banging her knee against the corner of the stall. A miniature burst of fireworks accompanied the pain with a sudden flare of light and color. "Did you see that?"

"I did." Waschbär slid an arm around her waist as the fairies danced among the falling sparks. "That medallion of yours was acting as a stopper between your imagination and reality, I think. You used it to focus, yes?"

"I used it to see to the heart of things."

"Now that it is gone, you are seeing multiple truths. Possibilities are manifesting as realities." Waschbär glanced sidelong at the milling crowd, who couldn't help but notice the changes taking place around them.

"Good lady!"

"Perhaps you'd care for these—"

A dozen hands plucked at Bertie's sleeves, tempting her with wares ranging from twisted gold earrings to honeyed desserts. The first offering transformed into tiny gilded eggs, the latter into a miniature dragon whose copper talons scrabbled at the striped awnings before he disappeared into the sky with a roar.

"Bertie, you must stop." Waschbär indicated the nearest stall. Its sun-bleached curtains shifted to reveal rows of green bottles and crystal flasks. "We'll find what we need in here." He added a potent glare at the fairies. "Don't touch anything."

Coiled up on an enormous floor cushion, legs impossibly tucked underneath her, a woman looked up as they entered. Her skin was covered in mother-of-pearl scales, luminous with rainbows held captive. "Greetings to you, sneak-thief. Fair warning: There are no unwanted things here."

"I would never dare pilfer from your stall, Serefina." Waschbär unfurled his fingers to reveal they were empty. "I might wake up a toad on the morrow."

"What is needed today? Unguents for rashes, or liniments for aches? Powders, pills, the old herbal cures?"

"This young lady has a wound—" Waschbär started to say.

"Ah, yes, the walls have already whispered of this one

to me." When the woman licked her sun-parched lips, she did so with a forked tongue. "Show me, child."

Without entertaining the notion that she could disobey, Bertie held out her injured hand. She tried to not look at the ugly, ragged edges of her skin, the streaks of red radiating from the cut, the ooze of thick white fluid, for the sight of it made her stomach lurch.

"Ooh, Bertie," Peaseblossom breathed, "that looks terrible."

"You don't have to tell me, I know—" Pain strangled Bertie's words, choking them off when the herb woman pressed her thumbs hard on either side of the ragged furrow. Spots of mirrored light swirled in lovely patterns over every surface as *click, click, click* went Serefina's tongue against the roof of her mouth

"A ceremonial knife made this cut, oh, yes." The herb woman reached for a silver-lidded pot of liniment. "You didn't know what your lad was doing, did you? That's why the cut's gone bad."

"I knew. Sort of." Bertie tried to pull her hand away, but Serefina didn't relax her grip.

"Blood-magic is powerful magic."

"Tosh," Bertie found the spirit to say. "If that were true . . ."

I should have been able to rescue Nate.

"Don't argue with me, child." The woman reached out,

and though Bertie flinched back, she still managed to tap the empty spot between Bertie's collarbones. "That sort of magic is almost as powerful as bone-magic, and I think you know something about that."

Color flared on Bertie's cheeks. "What do you mean?" A low chuckle was the herb woman's only response, but a gentle draft stirred the stall's curtains, and then Bertie knew. "You've seen Ariel."

Serefina tied a bit of clean linen around Bertie's hand. "The rest of you, stay here. The girl will come with me."

CHAPTER THIRTEEN

The Memory Be Green

Without another word to anyone, Serefina ducked through the back curtains of the stall, disappearing into the gloom of its innermost recesses.

Four sets of little hands grabbed hold of Bertie's hair and clothes. "You're not going with her!"

"No, I'm not." Except the spot where the herb woman had touched her skin ached. Bertie looked to Waschbär for reassurance, but the sneak-thief had his nose lifted to the air. "Was Ariel here?" After a moment, he nodded. "Did he have my medallion with him?"

With furtive steps, Waschbär moved nearer the back curtains. "Yes."

"I have to get it back." Bertie wobbled a bit, though the throbbing in her hand was greatly reduced; indeed, a blissful numbness had encapsulated her arm and pre-vented her from pointing at the fairies. "You four stay here with Waschbär."

A chorus of wails, but Bertie was already shuffling down a long corridor. Following the herb woman, she climbed a narrow set of twisting stairs, moving deeper into the mammoth, mica-flecked stone structure of the Cara-vanserai itself.

"Come along this way, girl." Just ahead of her, Serefina turned right into a small alcove.

Doors of various shapes and sizes lined the walls, each fitted with a padlock and each padlock depicting a different brass-wrought animal. The larger doors were locked with lions, wolves, or bears, while lizards and rabbits safeguarded the smaller portals. Bertie blamed her fever when the ani-mals peered back at her, blinking their metal-shuttered eyes, twitching their lustrous ears and noses. A panther hissed a warning when she strayed too near, a cache obvi-ously in use, as the key had been removed from that lock.

"What fits in something so tiny?" She touched a finger to a door no larger than a paper clip, admiring the mini-scule hammered-metal butterfly that fluttered its wings upon it. The number 169 was inscribed on its ivory plate in a series of ornate flourishes.

Serefina spared it a glance. "Secrets. Hearts' desires. Perhaps something else, but it's none of my never-mind."

An enormous elephant's head protected the largest of the doors, ears extended and trunk encircling the central mouth-lock. Bertie didn't think she could pull the mammoth key out, much less carry it without help. "Convenient, if Bluebeard strolls through and wants to tuck away a troublesome wife or three."

"Bluebeard knows better than to return to my establishment after the commotion he caused last time!" From somewhere on her person, Serefina produced a brass key, looped through with a heavy chain and an ivory plate marked with the number 572. "The air creature traded something with me."

The cubbyhole that matched the number on the key was, unsurprisingly, fitted with a lock in the shape of a bird. Bertie wanted more than anything to leap at it, but she resisted the urge in order to meet the herb woman's gaze. "It was not his to give."

"So I surmised," Serefina said. "The question is now: What will you trade to get it back?"

"There are the coins on my belt, but I doubt very much that's what you mean." Bertie knew this game well by now. "What is it you want?"

From her pocket, Serefina drew a crystal flask and held it up to the light so that Bertie could see it was empty. "Fill this."

"With what?"

"With words."

Bertie would have scoffed, except she remembered the changes she'd wrought in the marketplace: rivulets of ribbon-color, golden earrings transformed into eggs. "Just words?"

"It's never just words," the herb woman said with a knowing smile. "Is it?"

"No, it's not." For a moment, Bertie contemplated refusing.

The words are all I have right now.

When the lock-mouths began to whisper to her in dozens of different animal languages, Bertie knew she would never make it through the Caravanserai and to the Scrimshander without the scrimshaw. She began to pull words out of the furthest recesses of her still-cloudy brain, with *rareripe* streaming out of her mouth alongside *horbgorble, moonglade* followed by *curliewurlie.*

Though Serefina sought to catch only the most meaningful, inevitably some nonsense also slid inside the crystal flask, which she capped off with a cork stopper. "This will want sealing wax, I think."

Unwilling to wait a moment longer, Bertie interrupted. "The key, please?"

The herb woman paused long enough in her appreciative petting of the flask, its contents rainbow-sparking with power, to complete their trade. The key's weight settled into the center of Bertie's palm as she fit it into the lock and twisted. Inside the tiny niche lay a black velvet bag. Everything seemed to slow as Bertie pulled it out, untied the drawstring, and tipped the contents into her hand, but the moment the scrimshaw touched her skin, the world came into sharp focus and the animals ceased their whispering.

"He replaced the chain." The first one she'd broken before their fateful tango; the new one was a singularly fine series of interlocking gold rings, and Bertie traced it with her fingers before clasping it around her neck. The medallion settled between her collarbones. "What did he trade it for?"

"A flask from my stall, one that would banish memories." Serefina took Bertie by the hand, leading her away from the alcove and down yet another set of stairs. "He wanted something to dull the pain of a broken heart."

The numbness from the salve seemed to have spread to Bertie's own chest.

He's going to kill the parts of him that knew me. Loved me.

Serefina opened a door and gestured to a narrow alleyway. "This is where you leave me," the herb woman said. "May you find what you seek beyond these walls."

Bertie stumbled out into the tiny street, intending to make her way back to the marketplace, to Waschbär and the fairies. Thankfully, with the medallion in its rightful place, she had no more waking dreams. Instead, just before her, a small archway revealed a glimpse of another world. Beyond the shifting curtain of moss, Bertie could see trees: not the palm trees of the desert, but her trees.

She shook her head and wrapped her hand around the scrimshaw. "I don't have time for that place. Not now."

The curtain dissolved with the hiss of falling sand, joining the shimmering metallic dunes outside the Caravanserai. The shore that would lead to the White Cliffs. To the Scrimshander.

To Sedna's kingdom.

No time to double back to Serefina's stall, no time to fetch the sneak-thief and her miscreant companions, not with her father so close. Bertie jerked the nearest torch off the wall and struck out across the beach, only to realize within seconds that it was tricky slogging along. The scrimshaw hummed against her skin as she walked.

Peaseblossom would tell me this was a very bad idea.

Such an odd feeling, being without her tiny conscience. Even the boys would say it was unwise for Bertie to head off on her own, with no one to know where she'd gone. Her fears chased her, misshapen imps that tugged at her clothes and pulled her hair:

Nate, sucked under by Sedna's waters.

Ariel, drinking the contents of a flask just to be free of her.

Her father, flying far and fast away from her and Ophelia both.

When Bertie swung the torch at them, they danced into the shadows but were not dissolved.

"I cannot think of such things," she muttered, cresting the next dune. "I can only move forward."

Before her, the sand curved around the dinner-plate shoreline and the ocean filled the earth's cup until it brimmed over the horizon. Light from the moon washed the towering cliffs of Fowlsheugh silver before clouds entered the scene. Everything began fading to black, just as it did back at the Théâtre, with a slow hand on the dimmer.

Hardly able to see where the sand left off and the sea began, Bertie crossed her fingers and made a wish that went down to her toes: that a portal would yawn open like a feeding whale's mouth, that stepping stones would surface to lead her down into Sedna's world. Everything wavered; she felt the moist air shift, waited for salt-laden scrim curtains to slide past her . . .

Instead, high up in the side of the cliff, a faint pinprick of light hinted where the Scrimshander's hearth fire now burned.

Bertie uncrossed her fingers. Only now, staring up at his home, did she understand her real wish had been for something, anything, that would save her the necessity of confronting her father again, of trying to pry or cajole the way to Sedna's kingdom from his stubborn bird-brain.

Then her mind opened to the idea that this was where he'd brought Ophelia—

This was where my story began.

—and suddenly, a thousand other tales wanted to be told. The sand sucked at her feet, every grain a separate story. The cliffs rose before her, a tale too old, too large to fit inside her skull. A vein in Bertie's forehead throbbed.

It's too much.

But if she wanted to rescue Nate, she had to hold it inside her, had to carry it with her as she climbed the shallow steps carved into the cliff side. The footing was precarious, and there was no railing. The crashing waves below called to her to jump in Nate's lilt.

"Lass."

Spurred by the sound of his voice, she ran, with the winds pulling at the lavender gown, tugging her close to the edge and speaking with Ariel's inflections.

"Jump. I'll catch you."

A gust of wind extinguished her torch. Bertie clutched the useless stick of wood, forcing herself to climb the last ten steps to the low entrance. Ducking her head with a sob of gratitude, she entered the Scrimshander's Aerie.

Her first reaction was sympathy for Jonah. Whalebones soared overhead, curving alongside the inner walls and meeting tip to tip at the ceiling's highest point. Light from a tiny hearth illuminated the countless carvings decorating every exposed inch of the ivory beams: ships tossed at sea or armed for battle; sirens luring sailors to their rocky doom; every seafaring mammal and salt-blooming plant imaginable.

"You shouldn't have followed me here."

Startled, Bertie dropped the now-useless torch as she turned toward the voice. The bird-creature, no more than a dark shadow, huddled under the vast expanse of carvings. Trembling with exhaustion and the effort required to speak in a human tongue, he might have commanded sympathy.

But only from someone, Bertie thought, who had not chased him over half the countryside and through a snowstorm. "And you shouldn't have dropped me."

In the puppet theater, she'd seen his transformation from bird-creature to man and back again. Still, it didn't prepare her for the violent shedding of feathers as he unfolded from the floor, for the swirling tattoos that decorated the patches of visible flesh. No longer confined by the caravan's low cciling, the Scrimshander towered over her, spindly through the legs but thickly muscled in the chest and arms. His face was, once again, the one he'd shown Ophelia in their short time together. "You need to leave."

Bertie searched his features—elongated nose, strong chin, high cheekbones—trying to catch a glimmer of herself there. It was hard to tell for certain, in the uneven light from the hearth. "I will, just as soon as you tell me how to reach Sedna's kingdom."

"Little One, I don't—"

"I *know* there's a portal. Sedna promised to open it for you." Bertie paused to catch hold of her temper and tears, both threatening to escape, before she added, "It's no use lying to me. I've seen your story."

The Scrimshander turned on his heel, as though he found it easier to address the hearth than her. "Then you know it was not my choice to leave." Golden radiance filled one lamp, then a second before he moved farther into the cavern, carrying a burning rushlight.

"Yes." She chased him with her argument. "But it's your decision whether you help me now or you force me to pull the knowledge from you like a fat worm from the grass—"

Her voice faltered when he lit the final lamp at the far back of the Aerie. Illumination poured over a massive bone slab that rested against the wall. Upon it, the Scrimshander's carvings were a hundred variations on one study: Bertie's own face, as she might have looked at age three or four. Against her will, she reached out a hand, fingertips tracing the tiny, stippled holes.

His voice was feather soft. "You came here, once. Do you not remember?"

The silence that followed was underscored by the distant call of the sea, and she recalled the scene in Mrs. Edith's part of *How Bertie Came to the Theater* when Young Bertie put her toes over the edge of a towering cliff, held her arms out wide . . .

I wonder if I can fly.

It was like falling again, to listen to him speak.

"I saw you jump." With every word, the Scrimshander's voice evened. Feathers drifted loose, swirling like inky leaves on the floor of the cave, leaving more of his skin visible. "Such a strange little bird, in your silken skirts and kerchief. I caught sight of your face as you plummeted: eyes wide-open, expression joyful. You reveled in the wind that tore at your clothes and hair." His own eyes were closed, perhaps to picture the breathtaking plunge. "You hit the water and sank like a stone. It's a mercy you survived the fall, a greater mercy still that I found you. The water was dark, and you were tangled in the kelp. Your eyes were closed then, but you had starfish perched in your hair and the crabs hastened to cut you free. I dragged you to shore, where you spat water from your lungs and complained that I'd spoiled your swim. By the time the Mistress of Revels reached us, I was glad to hand you back into her keeping."

This bit of the story was another piece in the puzzle, albeit an unexpected one, all ragged edges and hard corners. Had it been real, Bertie would have pressed it to the flesh of her inner arm, just to see if something could hurt more than the ache in her heart. "Did she tell you who I was?"

He nodded, a stiff jerk of his head that belied the grace of his talented hands. "She gave me your name, yes."

"But did you know *who I was*?"

The Scrimshander faltered then, as though some wave broke upon his shore and knocked down all the careful walls he'd constructed over the years. "She didn't have to. I would have recognized those eyes anywhere." He paused before adding the inevitable, "You have your mother's eyes."

"You knew who I was, but you let her take me back to the theater?" This fresh betrayal cut as deep as the wound on Bertie's palm. "Why didn't you tell her you were my father? Why—" she choked on the accusation, barely able to finish asking, "why didn't you keep me with you?"

"The flood destroyed the nest." As he looked about him, the room seemed to fill once again with water. "In my absence, sea creatures had crawled in here to die."

The memory of unseen things wrapped themselves about Bertie's bare ankles, oil-slick with a razor's edge that cut. Ribbon-tendrils of her blood snaked through the water, luring other creatures, blind and hungry creatures, out of their hiding places. Then, with hisses and thrashing, the water evaporated, and flesh melted from bone until only their bones remained. "The mess would have made no difference to me."

"This was no place to bring a child, to raise a family. I was only half alive anyway, and entirely wild—"

"And you'd conveniently forgotten me." Bertie balled her hands up into fists, wishing she could hit someone, something.

The Scrimshander didn't deny the accusation. "It was only when I looked into your eyes that I remembered there was a mother, or a child." His gaze shifted toward the desk, where knives and needles lay in neat, glinting rows between bits of bone. "Only when you turned up here did I realize that something had happened to Ophelia, that things hadn't gone the way I'd intended."

"Really?" Bertie managed to shove a lifetime of thwarted sarcasm into a single word.

"The Mistress of Revels promised you'd both go straight back to the theater, and I thought it would give me time to remember what it was like . . . to be human." He reached out, fingers closing around one of the tiny tools. "I took to gouging bits of bone with my fingernails, thumbnails. Rough markings only—"

She made a rude noise through her nose, one worthy of the fairies. "And how did that work out for you?"

"It was harder than I could have ever imagined. I know I lost days, weeks. Maybe years. Trying to recall your face." His fingertips grazed the hundreds of portraits, skimmed in search of the right place to begin. Finding a tiny space free of other marks, the blade of his knife met the slab in a running series of scratches and scrapings. "Trying to remember your name. Then I found a special piece of bone in the deepest cavern of the Aerie: a bit of Sedna's finger, lost to her for so many years."

"Also brought here by the flood." Bertie scanned the ivory beams, and beyond the full-rigged schooners and lounging mermaids, she found what she sought: a rowboat tossed by waves, a princess cast overboard by her father. "He cut her fingers off, didn't he?"

"Yes."

"Because she was clinging to the side of the boat, and you were coming for her."

"Yes." The fire crackled countless condemnations before he spoke again. "I began to carve the Théâtre's façade upon it. As long as I stared at the bone, the tools, I managed to stay human. If I acknowledged anything else—the position of the sun in the sky, the direction of the winds outside the cave, my own hunger—that which is bird would take over. I'd lose myself to those instincts, to the winds, to the hunt, only able to recall my humanity when I returned to this place and to the work." The Scrimshander rubbed a bit of pigment into the etching he'd created of Bertie's seventeen-year-old self as though rubbing salt into his unseen wounds. "When the medallion was complete, Ophelia's face stared back at me from every one of the theater's statues. I remembered fully what had passed between us, what I had lost when I could not hold on to my humanity, and I hated the scrimshaw—every line, every bit of lampblack—almost as much as I hated myself." His voice dropped to a whisper. "I threaded the medallion upon an old metal chain and left it on my workbench, wishing it would disappear, wishing I'd never have to again lay eyes upon it. In the morning, it was gone."

"An unwanted thing." Bertie understood how Waschbär had come into possession of it now. Though the ivory walls radiated heat, the smooth stone of the floor was both damp and cold, and she shivered.

"How thoughtless of me. You aren't dressed for this rough setting." Striding back to the hearth, the Scrimshander added sticks of driftwood to the fire. Within seconds, the conflagration burned phosphorescent blue and green with tinges of violet around the edges, more glorious than any of the pyrotechnics they'd used at the Théâtre. A moment passed, marked only by the salt hiss and crackle. "This is a fool's errand. I can't imagine your Nate would have you risk your life for the sake of his—"

"Make no mistake, I am going." Bertie wondered if

he'd grab her by the elbow and lock her in a cage, or a bedroom, or wherever bird-fathers confined recalcitrant teenagers. "If you ever loved my mother, tell me how to get to Sedna's kingdom. She promised to open the portal to you."

"It was a lie." He remained kneeling, though he looked at her and not the hearth.

Summoning shades of the snake charmer in the Caravanserai, Bertie fixed her glittering gaze upon him, uttering words in a way meant to mesmerize. "Show me where it is."

The Scrimshander could not look away. "I won't."

"You can tell me." Not just the snake charmer now, but Serefina, her commands not to be denied. The herb woman's inflections were joined by Mrs. Edith's tempered steel. "You must." The Theater Manager's way of Settling The Matter. "You will."

Trembling with the effort, the Scrimshander rose, breaking free from her spell. "I've no idea how many you have twisted about your finger, how many you have tried to charm or coax or badger into giving you what it is you want, but I am your father, and I am telling you no."

The finality of his words was like a slap. "Then I'll find it myself! There must be some hint here … directions. A map." When he took a step toward her, she pointed a finger at him. "If you will not speak, then neither will you move. You have failed at every turn, twice as a husband, again as a father. Let your failures bind you."

Her fury drove the word-spell home, nails through his soul that pinned him to the wall of the Aerie. There he remained, unmoving, unable to dissuade her from flinging quills, trinkets, and bits of food every which way. Half-eaten biscuits, half-rotted fish, rocks, sticks, tattered clothing, reeking bits of rag . . .

"Even the fairies would think this place is disgusting, and that's saying quite a lot." Trying to tamp down her rising panic, Bertie went to his desk, rummaging through the bits of parchment, empty ink bottles, net mending needles, thumbnail sketches of various landmarks and ships. "No wonder Sedna left you. I cannot believe Ophelia lived in this sty."

He spoke with great difficulty. "Your mother would not wish this for you."

"You haven't the foggiest notion what my mother would wish for me!" Bertie picked up a small skull off the desk and hurled it at him with a passing hysterical thought of *alas, poor Yorick!* As her grip on her temper loosened, so did her hold upon him.

"It is not failing you to see you safe from harm." He managed to duck when she threw a rough clay mug, struggled forward as she flung a small stone tablet. "You will calm yourself." Blocking the various projectiles, he grasped her by the wrists. Bertie twisted and kicked, but he held her out from him as though she were no more than a tiny fish hooked on a line. "An unseemly display. I see you inherited Ophelia's temper as well."

Panting, Bertie realized how great a fool she'd been. "I don't need you to tell me." Jerking away from him, she wrapped her fingers around the scrimshaw, thinking of Nate, of Sedna, of the cavern. "I will find the portal myself." Her heartbeat hammered in her ears as one second passed, then another. The walls around her pulsed with the earth's heartbeat followed by the thrum of blood in ancient veins. Everything contracted, a muscle clenched before settling back into place.

Behind the bone slab, a tattered leather curtain fluttered. The Scrimshander lunged for it, but Bertie was faster, ripping it from its ivory hooks, pulling it atop herself. Tangled, smothered, she fought her way free only to stare, blankly, at the descending stairway it had been concealing.

"It's down there, isn't it?" Grabbing a fat wax candle from the floor, Bertie paused only long enough to light it. A smaller animal's ribs formed the rafters of the narrow passage, the darkness beyond leading to the waiting belly of the earth. Upon the first bit of bone, her father had scrimmed Sedna's lair: her throne surrounded by cavern walls and water. Schools of fish swam past seals, and whales dove deep to worship the Goddess of the Sea. Yes, there she was, with her cold features and her mutilated hands, ruling over them all. "This is the map."

"It's not a map," was his faint reply as the passageway narrowed, the ceiling dipped yet lower. He followed, albeit at a distance, as though he could neither bear the thought of being so enclosed, nor the notion that Bertie would disappear from sight. "They're only the markers of the journey."

"You must have been there." Bertie moved down one step, then another, the flickering candlelight illuminated the next engraving: some sort of massive Hall, with sky-reaching columns and an ice-tiled floor. "You must have seen it."

"In my mind's eye, only," he said. "The bones whispered to me. They showed me the way."

But he was not the only one to whom the bones had whispered, for beyond the Hall was a picture of a knife-thin passageway over a Cauldron, then a set of interlocking circles labeled THE ICE WHEELS.

The scrimshaw hummed against Bertie's skin with the pleasure of recognition.

It showed me the journey to Sedna's lair as I wrote the Innamorati's play.

"It is a wise child who knows her own father." The words of the inverted quote echoed, matching the vibration of the medallion, which grew stronger and louder with every descending step. When the stairs finished, Bertie stood in a tiny rotunda with no exit save the way she'd come in. The only bones here were a set of massive tusks half buried in the curving stone wall. Even if the resultant archway had not borne years' worth of elaborate carvings, she would have sensed what it was.

The portal.

Hand to the wall, Bertie willed the stone to move. "How do I get through?"

At first, only silence greeted the question.

"Bertie." Her name on the Scrimshander's lips was a plea. "Sedna's is goddess-magic. Do you really think you're a match for her, Little One?"

She couldn't second-guess herself now, not unless she wanted to end up a quivering mass of jelly on the cold floor. "I'll have to be. Now tell me how to open this."

"I don't know!"

Rounding upon him, rage filled Bertie with fire, the accusation exploding from her mouth with a cascade of sparks. "Liar!"

"I speak the truth!" And to prove it, he rushed at the stone. "I died innumerable deaths of the heart, of the soul, trying to get through!"

Bertie retreated a few steps, sickened by the repeated crunch of flesh and bone meeting unyielding stone.

Forgetting that she hated him, Bertie grabbed the Scrimshander by his newly feathered arms and dragged him back. "Don't—"

He tore from her grasp with a bird-shriek, preparing to fly once more at the wall, but a mighty wind knocked both of them down. A wordless call came from a distance. Wax spattered over Bertie's skin in burning droplets as her candle guttered then fell to the floor. At the top of the stairwell, the light from the hearth blazed up, casting chimera shadows down the walls before it dwindled to the barest red glow.

In the resultant darkness, the Scrimshander moved between Bertie and the unseen threat, his voice a croak. "Get behind me."

"Your concern is adorable." There was another cry, this one closer, and calling her by name. "But I am perfectly capable of protecting myself, especially since I recognize the voice." Pulse thudding in her ears, Bertie shoved past him.

Ariel couldn't have taken the potion, unless that was the noise of a man casting his memories to the wind.

As she ran up the stairs, her emotions were a giant cauldron over which the witches from That Scottish Play cackled, stirring her soul with a stick.

I should have told him I loved him. It's true enough, isn't it?

Except I can't love someone I don't trust with my whole heart.

When Bertie stumbled, her father grasped her by the arm. He sounded aggrieved even as he pulled her to her feet and kept her from falling again. "No doubt your ire keeps you better protected from random attacks than one might expect."

"I wish I was still angry." She sidled past the bone slab and peered around the Aerie. "When I'm angry, I forget to be afraid."

"That's just the trouble." With an expression so dark that she could barely make him out, Ariel stood in the mouth of the cave. "When you forget to be afraid, you forget to worry about the sanctity of your limbs."

Halfway across the room, Bertie staggered to a halt, held at bay by the cold fury in his words. The Scrimshander's arms twitched, as though he would still like to wrap them about her, or fly at the intruder.

"Don't attack him. Not yet, anyway." Bertie turned back to Ariel, almost afraid to voice the question. "What are you doing here?"

"A marvelous question, and one you might ask yourself." He strode across the room, his anger reaching for her with barbed tendrils. "What were you thinking, coming here alone?"

Bertie located her spine, more than a bit bruised by her tumble onto the floor, and straightened it. "Says the man who jumped off the back of a moving train!"

With the hissing flare of a match, the Scrimshander relit the lantern nearest him. "I assume this is a friend of yours?"

"Of sorts," Bertie said. "Ariel, meet the Scrimshander. My father."

"Charmed," Ariel said, looking anything but.

"The feeling," the Scrimshander returned, "is mutual."

Each of the men took the full measure of the other, after which Ariel assumed an infinitesimally more polite tone. "My apologies for the abrupt entrance, but I feared for her safety, sir."

"There seems to be a lot of that going around tonight." Kneeling, the Scrimshander began to build up the fire with a careful arrangement of sticks and tiny scraps of paper.

Not requiring even false privacy, Bertie didn't bother to lower her voice. "What are you doing here, Ariel? I would have thought you'd be halfway to Timbuktu."

There was nothing of the tender lover about him now, hair and clothes twitching like a cat's tail. "I tried, gods help me. I flew as hard and as fast as I could, but it was as though I was tethered to you, a chain pulled taut the farther I flew."

"That chain was of your own making, Ariel. I had nothing to do with it."

"You had *everything* to do with it. I am no more free in

this world than I was in the Théâtre. I could not turn my back on you." Ariel reached out and traced the medallion's chain with his finger. "I could not break free of you."

"Don't you ever touch it—or me—again." Bertie took half a step back. "Not after you stole it. Not after you *sold* it."

"I did," he said. "I figured that, for all the trouble it's caused me since you started wearing it, it was at least half mine to pawn."

"You thought wrong." She threw words at him, rather than a punch. "Such a pity the draught didn't work."

Everything about Ariel—hair, clothes, expression— went still as he looked at her. "It didn't have the chance to work. I poured it into the sand."

It was easier to guard her heart when he was angry, for his fury fueled her own and acted like a shield. When their mutual rage dwindled, she was vulnerable to whatever arrow he might let fly, and so her words were a whisper. "I cannot imagine what would have stopped you. You who cherish freedom above all things? You could have been free of me. Isn't that what you wanted?"

No answer for a moment save the crackle of the fire. "When everything else crumbles to dust, all we have left are the memories. I thought of Ophelia, wandering the theater, mind half gone . . . Never shall I cut from memory my sweet love's beauty."

After everything that had happened, she didn't want to believe him.

Vows are but breath, and breath a vapour is.

Ariel took pity on them both then and acknowledged their audience. "Did your father have anything insightful to say about rescuing Nate?"

In response, the Scrimshander ruffled feathers-unseen. "Is he worth it? This soul she wants to go down there to save?"

"Worth her risking her life?" One of Ariel's mirthless laughs. "I think not. But he is her husband."

CHAPTER FOURTEEN

This Green Plot
Shall Be Our Stage

A terrible squawking noise from the Scrim-shander. "Her *what?*"

"Leave it to you to tell tales, Ariel." Bertie grasped the last of the relit lanterns from her father's curved, talonlike fingers. "And inaccurate ones, at that."

Conversationally, Ariel addressed the Scrimshander. "Have you ever heard of handfasting? She has a mark on her palm that binds her to the pirate."

"Do you?" Expression fierce, the Scrimshander's brow furrowed like the sand-ripples Bertie had seen on the shoreline.

"I do." Her gaze traveled over her linen-bound hand, and she realized what sort of magic it might take to open the portal. With the revelation came a new surge of worry that it might not work, that she might be too late.

Ariel's righteous annoyance gave way to concern as she ran for the back of the Aerie. "Wait . . . where are you going?"

Without answering, Bertie took the stairs three at a time, ignoring the very real possibility of stumbling and falling arse over tea kettle, unable to slow down. At the bottom, she set the lantern upon the ground and ripped the bandage off the handfasting wound. Scraping it against the stone, she left a wet red smear across the barrier. "Blood-magic will help." She wrapped her uninjured hand over the medallion. "And bone-magic."

When it came, the slow thud of the earth's heartbeat rocked her back on her feet. Bracing herself against it, she waited for the next sign of life. And waited. The earth marked the passing of time by the slow run of sap in the springtime, the shifting of mountain ranges, the melting of glaciers. In contrast, Bertie's own pulse hammered in her ears, a lively mazurka atop a stately waltz. She tried to control her breathing, to bring her own flow of blood in time with that of the earth, but still she skimmed across the surface of a frozen lake, not deceiving the ice.

Her heartbeat was the key. Only when it slowed to meet that of the earth would she pass through the portal.

"Little One—" the Scrimshander started to protest, coming down the stairs behind her, but Bertie would hear none of it.

She counted off the beats as her heart began to slow. "One for bad news, two for mirth."

The words were part of an old rhyme Mrs. Edith had taught her, one they'd sung when doling out pins and buttons in the Wardrobe Department. A counting song, meant to tally magpies, with their number signifying what was to come. Theater people had many superstitions, but this one Mrs. Edith must have brought in with her, from a place where birds roamed the skies.

And suddenly there was a double meaning in every word.

"Three is a wedding." The cut on her hand thudded in time with her slowing pulse. "Four is a birth." Echoes of Ophelia's laughter rippled through the stone. "Five is for riches, six is a thief."

Though Waschbär isn't anywhere near.

"Seven, a journey, eight is for grief."

Ariel, standing alongside her, put a hand to his own chest in surprise. "What are you doing?"

"Shifting." The palm of her hand sank an inch into the stone. The floor heaved underfoot as the layers of the earth adjusted to let Bertie through. "Nine is a secret, ten is for sorrow."

Ariel's hand slammed over the top of hers, driving both of them farther through the barrier. His fingers slid between hers and clamped down. "Don't you dare let go." When the rock sucked them in, his face contorted with panic.

The Scrimshander tried to pull her back, but Bertie's flesh dissolved to flecks of mica under his grasping fingers.

"Eleven is for love, twelve, joy for tomorrow." Encapsulated, she knew only the rightness of granite. Tiny opalescent orbs bubbled to the surface of her skin, each one containing a different recollection: a thousand desserts stolen from the Green Room, notes pinned to the Call Board, laughter shared with the fairies as they raced down the hallways and onto the stage. Mrs. Edith, Ophelia, Nate, Ariel . . . the stone scrubbed her skin clean, and the memory-bubbles popped. Soul scraped bare, like bark flayed from a tree trunk, what was left but the pale inner flesh?

That's when Bertie saw the trees.

Hand outstretched, she caught hold of leaves. Branches enfolded her in tender welcome, and Bertie rooted herself to the ground with ivy tendrils that clung to earth and dust and rock. Tiny scuttling spiders spun floss to keep her tethered there, and she thanked them with a silent smile. In this place without wind—

Unless I summon a breeze.

Without water—

Unless I want it to rain. I am mistress here.

"This place is mine and mine alone."

A low chuckle in her ear, as though someone heard the thought and was amused. Bertie turned, glancing over her shoulder at the largest of the trees.

"Who's there?"

Another bit of soft laughter, like the brush of fur against bare skin. She took a step toward the nearest tree, her fingertips traveling the rough whorls of bark and fancying a face peering out of dense foliage. Vines sprouted from the places where nose, mouth, nostrils would be.

She brushed the worst of the overgrowth away. "Who are you?"

Puck, Pan, or Green Man, he could not answer, trapped as he was deep in the heart of the wood. Bertie knew without trying that she could reach in for him, past the rings of years-imprisoned, past sap sticky as blood, and break the binding spell as easily as another would have snapped a twig. There was something about his face she trusted, leaves or no, but—

"This place is mine and mine alone," she said, taking a step back. The tree rustled, perhaps in protest, but she turned her back on the promise of company and moved with purpose into a clearing ringed with ferns. Upon a moss-bedecked tree stump she emptied the pockets of her verdant green gown; glittering flecks of sand and tiny bits of stone rushed through her fingers. Dipping her hand into the mound, she realized each one was a memory of this place, brought with her through the stone as gifts from the children of the earth.

Atop the pile sat an emerald. Holding it up to one eye, she could see a green jungle bowed under monsoon rains. Ripe fruit dripped from the canopy above, and the padding footsteps of large felines echoed the thud of her heartbeat. Bertie could hear bare feet slapping against pounded dirt, bodies launched off felled trees and limbs brushing under low-dipping vines.

The emerald cracked, shedding granular tendrils until it was reborn as a ruby, large and flawless. Through the red jewel's filter, she saw a place of desert trees, thick with fronds. A puff of wind shifted the sand over her feet.

"I remember pyramids, sand, rich turquoise lighting . . . and a Danish Prince?" Bertie frowned. "That cannot be right."

Then the ruby was transformed into a wreath of daisies intertwined with crimson ribbons. Through it, she could see a very different sort of landscape: rolling hills, dotted with bonfires. Brows wreathed with hawthorn and primrose, many gathered to celebrate the wedding of the god and goddess.

"Beltane," she whispered. "May Day, the Jack-in-the-Green's celebration."

Upon the hill, a horned god fed marigold custard and oatmeal cakes to a woman white-clad to celebrate the Light Half of the Year. The red and white ribbons of a maypole fluttered overhead. Hand in hand, shadow-couples leapt one bonfire after another, faster and faster still, until the flames were the only streak of color against the night's canvas.

A butterfly brushed against Bertie's cheek, but she dismissed it with a laugh. The ferns circling her trembled as she knelt, cupping her hand to lift the sands. A sparkling cascade of shimmering quartz slipped through her fingers. "Where is my forest, my realm?"

Her hand closed around a chunk of plaster, gold painted: a bit of statuary, the same face that had peered from the tree. For a moment, she was surrounded by darkness, the blur of red velvet, the flash of gilt. Now the visage was part of a building's edifice, carved in stone, trapped in time.

"I know this place," she whispered.

A light came up behind a curtain of moss to reveal a scene most familiar: a four-poster bed, an armoire, a dresser. Each piece of pale wood was carved in the sweeping flourishes of the art nouveau style. Rugs of mint and crushed green grass were scattered on the forest floor.

"My room." Delighted, Bertie circled it, touching things she knew to be hers: a small armchair of woven golden saplings, a jewelry box inlaid with mother-of-pearl, a stack of well-worn books in which each page was a pressed leaf.

A sanctuary, fit for a Forest Queen.

"Am I a queen?" The thought pleased her, and she felt as at home wearing it as she would a dress of wheat-gold. Turning, she spotted a hart invading her realm, paused on the edge of the clearing. With a hiss, she took up a long-bow that rested against the armoire. "You have no place here. This is mine and mine alone."

She selected an arrow. Three fingers held the bow-string, drawing it back until her thumb touched her jaw-bone. Her index finger kissed the corner of her mouth. Every muscle in her shoulder and back stretched with the string. She held her breath as she let the arrow fly—

But something prompted her to close her eyes the moment it hit home. When Bertie opened them, both hart and arrow were gone.

A fanfare of trumpets sounded as a knight entered the clearing, riding astride a brilliant white horse. He raised his hand in a salute, colors rippling in an unbidden breeze. Much of the knight was hidden from view by his silver-chased armor; mouth and nose were indistinct, and the eyes that met hers with an unwavering gaze could have been those of either friend or enemy.

"Who are you?" Bertie still held the longbow, and

over her dress she summoned a breastplate and arm guards of verdigris.

"Your Majesty, if it pleases you, I would take you away from this place," the knight said. His horse shifted, as restless as he, and pawed at the ground. "You must return to your quest, milady."

Milady.

"Do not presume to call me that." With a look, Bertie summoned vines to bind him. Cords of variegated green dragged him from his horse, towing him through bracken and fern, bringing him to rest at the tips of her slippers. "I am no lady of yours."

"You've forgotten the wind—"

"We have no need of wind here," she told him, and meant it.

"You've forgotten the water." A note of pleading now in the knight's voice as her vines dragged off his helmet, loosing his silver hair, his silver gaze. "And the ocean."

Bent to her will, the helmet became a hair comb. A knack, a toy, a trinket. "The ocean?"

The knight's voice faded. "Have you forgotten him?"

"Nate." When Bertie breathed his name, a saltwater wave slammed into her chest. She sank into the loam underfoot as though towed by an anchor. Falling through the darkness, she thought she could once again feel Ariel's fingers interlocked with hers.

She stepped free from the granite into an explosion of a thousand stars. When the sparks cleared, Bertie and Ariel stood in enormous version of *The Big Pop-up Book of Scenery*. Bertie was dressed in the golden skirts of Columbine, while Ariel's silver-patched Harlequin costume reflected the pale green light shining down upon them.

He kept his fingers laced through hers as he towed her Center Stage. "We're not alone."

Putting a hand up to cut the glare, Bertie could see rows of sandstone benches that curved around the edges of the book. A gathered crowd murmured in the universal undertone of an expectant audience, but every face in the amphitheater wore a pale, blank mask. Men, women, even the smaller figures of children were indiscernible from one another.

A ringmaster appeared atop a marble pillar, his face quivering gold-flesh and his eyes two gaping keyholes. "Ladies and Gentlemen! You are about to witness an act so extraordinary, it has never before been attempted in any otherworldly arena!"

When Bertie squinted hard and peered past the footlights, the masks were no longer void of expression. Heavy eyebrows were raised like query marks, foreheads had puckered, and mouths were rounded in anticipatory Os.

The stage plunged into a blackout, then twin spotlights came up behind them on a contraption that reminded her of a pair of fantastic opera glasses. A massive steel arm, like a propeller, was fixed upon a center shaft. At either end, enormous matching circles served as counterbalances. Only when they began to turn could she see the black-clad stagehands, one inside each hoop. Both facing Stage Right, they walked, spinning the mesh wheels counter-clockwise. Someone in the audience clapped once, twice, not applause, but setting a rhythm that slowly increased. Soon the stagehands ran, the wheels spinning full tilt, each arcing around the other, both held forever captive by the center axis.

"It's like *The Big Pop-up Book of Scenery*'s Wheels of Death." Bertie stared up at it, doubly appalled when the stagehands decreased their pace. Counteracting their momentum by slowing the circles, they brought them into perfect balance, the silver at twelve o'clock and the gold at six.

"The Sun and the Moon, Ladies and Gentlemen!" the ringmaster cried.

The crinoline under Bertie's massive skirts swayed as she tried to back away. "The scrimshaw whispered the journey to me, and I put it in the Innamorati's play: the Ice Wheels, the Cauldron, the Hall. It's how we'll get to Nate. This is the way to Sedna's kingdom."

"How is that even possible?" Ariel sounded as dismayed as she felt. "You wrote it on ordinary paper with that ridiculous quill pen. . . . I sat there and watched you."

"How else do you explain this?" She held out her day-brilliant skirts. "Or that?!" She pointed at the mesh wheels, the silver one in the sky and the gold nearest the floor. "The sun and the moon. Only one can be in the sky at a time. That's what I wrote."

"Winter days and nights, you also said." As though he'd cued the special effect, snow began to fall in earnest, swirling about the stage floor and shoving them with fingers of ice toward the edge of the book. Crystals cascaded into a nonexistent orchestra pit, lost to a vast nothing that separated the stage from the audience. Ariel raised his arms; Bertie expected a wind to push back at the snow, but nothing happened.

"Ah, ah, ah," the ringmaster chortled. "No cheating. You left your winds in the other world, air elemental."

Ariel lowered hands that were now fists. Every muscle tensed, but that was the only movement he wrought with the effort. "He's right, Bertie, I can't fly."

The ringmaster capered atop his marble column. "It's true, it's true, and our dear Beatrice is without her enchanted pages!"

Bertie knew he spoke the truth; there were no pockets in the Columbine's tightly cinched bodice. Her hands reached for her throat, reassured to find the medallion still hanging there, even after their costume change. "Which way are we supposed to go?"

Overhead, light poured through a brilliantly lit square, and a few feet of rope ladder unfurled. "Into the light with you. It is the first leg of your journey."

Ariel made a hissing noise as he looked up at the trap-door. "I don't know how you managed to do this, Bertie, but when the curtain falls on this demented production, let's have a long conversation about the power of your words, all right?"

"You won't say anything I don't already know." She'd have to use the wheel to reach the ladder. Thankful she wore ballet flats and not chorus girl high heels or, worse yet, pointe shoes, Bertie stepped inside the circle of gold.

The first black-clad stagehand grasped the edges of her circular cage and pushed it off the ground. Her stomach leapt as the wheel rose to the top of the arc. The moment it reached its zenith, Bertie could see its silver twin precisely underneath her. Above her, the light from the trap-door taunted; the rope ladder swung lazily, too far to reach from inside the hoop.

The audience sounded their appreciation—or impatience—with a lion's roar of applause. Arms aloft, Ariel bowed Stage Right, then ran to the opposite side to drink in their adulation. Aghast that he would take time to work the crowd, Bertie started to ask, "What are you doing?" when, against her will, she struck a self-assured pose, like one of the Innamorati bird-girls in a gilded cage, arms gracefully outstretched and toes pointed.

The show must go on.

Acknowledge the audience. Wave. Smile. Bow.

I wonder if I can fly. . . .

Clutching the side of her wheel, Bertie peered down at Ariel, not as afraid of heights as she was of falling, not as afraid of falling as she was of smashing into the floor. She cursed the irony of being her father's daughter, of having spent her childhood in the catwalks of the theater only to get vertigo now. Wishing she was the one prancing about on the ground level, she managed to shout, "Now what?!"

The snow waited for Ariel to take yet another bow before it gleefully shoved at him. He skidded several feet, falling to his knees. The sugared grains skittered over the edge of the stage, trying to drag Ariel with them.

"Can you reach the rope ladder?" His words were half garbled, and it appeared to cost Ariel something to utter a line she had not written.

Bertie shook her head. "Not from the inside of the wheel."

"Give me a moment to think."

Her first line spilled from Bertie alongside her panic. "The day is my domain. You do not belong here."

Don't look down, don't look down. . . .

"I am an admirer, milady." Ariel struggled against the snow, trying to make his way back to Center Stage. "Would that you belonged to me."

"Be gone with you. The sky is mine—" The line ended in a shriek as an inadvertent shift in her weight caused the sun's wheel to fall back toward the stage. Bertie nearly tripped as she swung past him. "Ariel!"

He gestured frantically. "You have to run!"

More than that, she practically had to fly. Somehow, Bertie managed to orient herself; feet skimming metal, she chased her own shadow. The medallion thumped between her collarbones with every step, matched only by the jarring thud of Ariel catching hold of the opposite wheel. She could barely make him out, a silver-blur against the lights pouring over them in shades of amber, purple, magenta. Light on his feet, even without his winds, Ariel probably could have skipped rope atop the other spinning circle, run blindfolded, turned somersaults.

Then the temperature onstage dropped, and Bertie's breath formed sparkling crystals in the air. Hundreds of pale blue ribbons fell from unseen rafters, manned by frost-bedecked acrobats. With faces and hands carved from ice, they hung in perfect stasis for a moment, fabric twined about them like the silk ribbons on a dancer's pointe shoes. Then, by some unspoken cue, they pirouetted through the air in downward death spirals.

"This is no longer your world," Ariel called out, his words following the same arc as the wheels. "I cast a long silver shadow, and the very air freezes."

Stopping inches from the stage, backs arched, bare toes pointed, the ice-faced acrobats elicited gasps from the spellbound audience. Hoarfrost slicked the inside of Bertie's wheel. Slipping, she fell against the frozen metal, face pressed to the bitterly cold mesh when the sun arced back into the sky. Spun sickeningly up and over, she fell back when the arm began its descent . . .

"Bertie!"

. . . and landed, somehow, on her feet. Sliding, sliding . . .

Mustardseed was right. We're trapped in hamster wheels!

She looked up in time to see Ariel leaping from the top of the moon. Airborne, silhouetted against the stage lights, he hung in time and space for a moment. Crashing cymbals urged him to fall as he caught hold of the rope ladder's bottom rung. Though it swayed, Ariel managed to hook one leg through it, then the other.

Flipping backward, he hung from his knees and held out his hands. "I'll catch you!"

Even upside down, he was as she'd always pictured him: arms outstretched, luring her over the edge. "I can't!"

An enormous rumble from below, and trapdoors began to open all over the stage. Snow cascaded through, leaving darkness in its wake. The ribbon dancers scampered up, only to have an unseen hand cut their silks. They fell like severed icicles, the emptiness swallowing their screams, a few smashing into the stage and shattering into a thousand pieces. Bertie's wheel passed Ariel again.

"You have to jump the next time!" Another shudder below, and the entire contraption began to descend by inches. Ariel shouted to be heard over the drum roll, "It's your last chance! You have to trust me!"

The wheel arced up, carried her over, right arm outstretched—

He caught her by the wrist, and Bertie dangled over the wheel as it spun on without her, disappearing below the stage with the muffled roar of glacial ice falling into the sea.

"Don't you dare drop me, Ariel!" Her other hand shot up to catch his other arm, and she kicked her feet as though she could gain purchase on the air.

"Stop struggling, you're making it worse!" His face had gone bright red with the effort of holding her, and Bertie realized just how much of the time he'd rested on the laurels of his winds, allowing them to transport him around the theater, tend to his hair and his clothes. . . .

Do his heavy lifting.

She flailed harder.

"Bertie, so help me, you are going to kill us both. Look at me. *Look at me.*"

She stared up at him, eyes gone wide, panting from her exertions on the wheel. Cold sweat trickled along both sides of her face, in rivulets between her shoulder blades and her breasts. Her hands, similarly slick, slid a quarter of an inch down his wrists. A tight spotlight appeared on them. An unseen orchestra cued up the mocking strains of "The Man on the Flying Trapeze."

"Hold on to me," Ariel whispered. "The show must go on."

"The show must go on." She sounded like a pirate's parrot, but the mantra somehow helped. Bertie tightened her grip on Ariel's wrists, forcing the rest of her muscles to relax.

"We have to make it through the scene change."

As they swung gently, Bertie summoned a brilliant smile. "The show must go on."

Far below them, the black-clad stagehands turned over the page in *The Big Pop-up Book of Scenery*, and swaths of star-lit paper rustled across the stage. The new set appeared with the creak of wood and steel: two platforms, the closest just out of reach of her feet.

"You have to swing us over there," Ariel said.

Bertie recalled the Innamorati acrobats, heaving themselves around the pie car. "Arch my back. Point my toes."

She kicked her feet, with purpose this time. "No different from sitting in a rope swing."

"Of course not," Ariel said with a groan. "Even if the rope swing's arms are about to fall off."

Glaring at him through the lace of her cap, Bertie said, "I know you are not choosing, at this critical juncture, to suggest I weigh one ounce more than I should."

"I wouldn't dream of it." With a grunt and a heave, he let her go.

There wasn't time enough to scream before Bertie landed atop the platform. Twisting about, she watched as Ariel levered himself upright. He leapt from the rope ladder, landing with less grace than usual.

Far below them, the stagehands pulled the tabs along the edge, and silk net bubbles rose and fell on the surface of the page. Steam drifted over the paper floorboards.

"I get the tightrope act," Ariel said, "but we're over a cauldron of *what,* exactly?"

Bertie watched the vapor uncoil like the Caterpillar's hookah smoke. "Boiling ice."

"A physical impossibility," Ariel said.

More concerned with the "knife-thin" passage, Bertie peered at the glinting obsidian edge of the supposed tightrope. She could feel her heartbeat thudding in the wound on her palm as she raised her voice so the audience could hear. "This is the place that cuts the day from night. If we cross it, we can be together."

"I'll go first." But his face was ashen.

"You are waning. Let me light the way." The moment she was done speaking the line, Bertie looked at the cutting-edge of the crossing and screamed, "Why did I write that I would go first?!"

CHAPTER FIFTEEN

A Mote Will Turn the Balance

The light shifted, and Bertie now held a ribbon-striped pole. Needles of ice had rent a dozen holes in the Columbine costume. Her tights hung in golden tatters. Looking at the ragged, obsidian edge of the would-be high-wire, she could only be thankful her shoes remained intact.

"It's in the script," Ariel muttered. "Just don't look down."

Of course she did. Far below them, demons and imps frolicked and cavorted. Twisted of purpose, they wore lurid costumes and leering masks. The boldest among them leapt from bubble to bubble until their odd trampolines burst and they were burnt to ash in an instant. "I think falling would be a very bad idea."

"I concur."

Careful to balance her weight with the pole before she took the first step, Bertie moved out onto the edge of the knife, her existence reduced to the soles of her feet. Using a gentle singsong voice, she coaxed herself along, as though speaking to a small child. "I'm like one of the puppets in the hatbox theater. I have a string that runs aaaaall the way down my back." Her posture became very good indeed. "Someone is holding my strings. Someone with talented fingers . . . Waschbär! Waschbär lifts my right foot, then my left, placing them one in front of the other. Come on, Ariel."

His spotlight eclipsed by her growing bravery, Ariel shook his head. "I can't."

She'd never expected him to hesitate, never imagined him as fearful. "Look how far ahead of you I am. Twelve steps, one for each hour." The balance pole bobbed. Instinctively she compensated, one foot in the air, toes pointed. Imaginary puppeteer still holding her strings, Bertie twisted around to look for her partner.

Ariel remained on the platform, eyes haunted.

Panic surged up the back of Bertie's throat, thicker than bile. Knowing that shouting might unbalance her, knowing that the audience watched them, knowing that the show must go on, she tried not to betray the anger boiling inside her like the ice far below them. "You're afraid?"

"Damn right, I am!"

"Because you can fall. It's not so easy, is it?" Demons of her own prodded the taunts from her, though she masked them with a brilliant smile. "'Jump, I'll catch you!' he says. Do you understand now what you were asking of me?"

Imps the size of rotten apples manifested on either end of her balancing pole, jumping up and down, more demented than the fairies at their worst. Misshapen of face and limb, the imps cartwheeled and gestured, doing their utmost best to unbalance her. But years spent in the company of Cobweb, Moth, and Mustardseed made it easy for Bertie to deal with them. Rolling the pole over in her hands, she dumped the worst of the vile things back into the Cauldron. The survivors leapt onto her shoulders, screaming their ire as Bertie took a step backward on the knife's edge.

"Step toward me, Ariel."

"I can't."

Another step back. The imps fed cruel words into her ears that spilled out of her mouth without her permission. "I guess we know which boy wins the fair maiden's heart, then, don't we?" Bertie bit down on her tongue, trying to stop the taunt, but too late.

The lines cast by the imps' words pulled Ariel out onto the knife. "You won't reach Nate without me."

"Oh, but I will." Using her voice, her smile, the imps

dragged him forward another step. "And the reunion will be sweet."

The next step Ariel took was of his own volition. He'd forgotten his balance pole, so he held his arms out to either side. "Remind me, if we live, to throttle you."

While she couldn't claim to be enjoying herself, the imps certainly were, including the ones who twisted her ears and forced her to ask, "Why did the chicken cross the road?"

"You're calling me a coward now?" He was taking two steps for every one of hers, catching up swiftly.

"I am." Her own words this time; glancing over her shoulder, she saw that with only a few steps more, they'd be safe.

The demons decided this wouldn't do. Possessing all the power of flight that Ariel had lost, they surged up from the depths of the Cauldron to grab hold of ankles, skirts, the ends of Bertie's balance pole. So close to the ledge, she could have jumped for it.

But Ariel will never make it.

She dropped the pole, watching it spiral back down into the Cauldron, and kicked the nearest cackling demon as hard as she could. Imps had Ariel by the elbows and knees, trying to throw him off balance. He stumbled forward, falling, his knee smashing into the dull edge of the obsidian knife with the sickening crunch of bone. Blood spurted from the wound.

The ringmaster cackled. "So he can bleed, like any other man!"

The audience roared, this time with bloodlust. Demons leapt for her ankles as Bertie ran back for Ariel. She bobbled, caught herself, arms pinwheeling, as the demons dragged the air elemental's wounded leg over the side. He cried out—

But it was Bertie who miscalculated her fleet-footed steps. It was Bertie who fell, just as she had from the White Cliffs, the same sort of plummet as when the Scrimshander had dropped her. Wind buffeted her from all sides, filling her frilly skirts one second and sucking the air from her lungs the next.

"Little One."

Any moment now, she would smash into the surface of the stage.

"Remember who you are."

Child Bertie whispered to her:

I wonder if we can fly.

A cry of protest, the call of a gull. Tattered bits of lace fell into the boiling ice and were lost. Golden slippers danced into the darkness. What had been skin was feathers, and the free fall ended with a dizzying circle out over the audience.

Everything shifted, then the world clicked back into place.

The bird wheeled around, catching hold of the demons that surged up from the depths of the Cauldron. It plucked out their eyes with a sharp beak, rending and scattering limbs, but they were not her prey. The lights transitioned to a single spotlight that illuminated a pale worm, writhing on a hook.

She soared out of the dark to catch hold of him just as he would have fallen, sharp talons digging into his protesting flesh. Wings beating, she flew up, dragging him to her perch, dropping him into the nest.

Another harsh cry, this one of triumph, as she landed alongside him.

The creature spoke. "Bertie?"

She tilted her head at the noise. The word was foreign, but it echoed between her ears.

The creature reached for her, and she snapped at him, beak closing down upon his pale fingers and drawing blood. Crimson droplets fell on her white feathers, dotting the plumage with rubies.

"Bertie."

She shuddered, and the feathers marked with his blood fell out.

"You're in there, aren't you?"

The creature's words made no sense at all, but his voice . . . his beautiful voice . . . called to her with all the winds she'd never flown. He reached for her again, pulling aside the beak that was now a mother-of-pearl mask.

"Air," she squawked, trying to remember what it was like to be human. "Ariel."

Another swirl of feathers and down drifted away when he slid his hands along her face. "You flew." The wonder in his voice echoed in her head, then his lips were on hers, pressing the words into her mouth.

"I flew." She held on to him, his touch leading her back to humanity. "Like my father. Like . . . like you."

"You are like me." He enfolded her in his arms, the next words whispered into her hair. "I knew it."

Bertie could feel the scene changing around her, the platform lowering them in a spiral path back to the stage level, the Cauldron disappearing along with the demons and imps. The brush of air over her newly naked flesh was painful. She felt the loss of her feathers keenly, the sharp edge of a knife scraping lightly over her skin.

"Hold still." Ariel covered her with the tattered remnants of his own silk shirt, and the weight of it made her cry out.

"The Lovers' Pas de Deux," a voice announced as the lights faded to a soft spotlight upon them.

Wearing just the tightly fitted pants of the Harlequin, Ariel was only slightly more dressed than she. The cut made by the knife-passage exposed his injured knee: a bloody gash in his pale flesh that forced him to favor that leg when he rose. "We've done this before."

But it was nothing like the tango, which had been castanet-bound, a race between guitar and bandoneón. Bowstrings met violins, and Ariel caught her under the knees, cradling her as one would rock a child to sleep. Arm looped around his neck, Bertie pressed her cheek to his bare chest, the drums replacing the thud of his heartbeat as he held her.

No lines, now, but the dance told his story: *I have waited forever to have you.*

When he slid down to the stage, she sat a moment upon his good leg, then flowed away, running. *You haven't tamed me yet.*

He rushed to catch up with her, but she pivoted, changing direction, mocking him with the laughter of flutes. They played hide-and-seek around the columns, like children, but with greater joy.

The music shifted, and he was scornful, a series of jumps telling her he would not be bound. *You toy with my affections.*

A knack, a toy, a trick. Dancing solo, she was confident performing in her own spotlight until the music changed again.

He was back, hands upon her waist, lifting her high in the air once more, unable to free himself from the dance, the music, from her. *Though I be damned for it, I must have you.*

It ended in a pose Center Stage, kneeling, arms wrapped around each other. The scenery shifted again, and fear sidled through Bertie.

"I didn't write anything after the knife-passage, Ariel. Aleksandr just assumed it would end 'happily ever after.'"

With great effort, Bertie raised her head from his shoulder and found herself nose to nose with someone quite odd. Dressed in silver robes that shifted in and out of reality like star-shine on a cloudy night, the creature also wore a glass death mask under which smoke coiled and unfurled. Two glittering sapphires winked at Bertie from the eyeholes.

Its voice was thunder in a bottle. "She was once the Sun."

The second creature's breath smelled of salt and kelp. "The other was the Moon, now turned mortal. Such a trick to play. Do you think we ought to return them to the sky?"

Bertie tilted her head up, her mind trying to make sense of the distant ceiling. Pale blue ice formed a massive dome beyond which water moved in sunlit currents. A mosaic of marble, silver-glass paste, and mother-of-pearl covered the walls, forming never-ending galleries that extended Stage Right and Stage Left.

"Which way?" The whisper came as Ariel unfolded himself just enough to take in their surroundings.

Exposed, there was no place to hide save behind the massive white marble columns, nowhere to run save up a grand, white staircase topped with an enormous set of double doors. "There."

"Stand," the first creature commanded. "Explain yourselves."

"I can't, because I'm not quite myself today." Unbidden, Alice's line leapt from Bertie's mouth as they rose from the floor. A hundred sorts of fish were frozen in the ice tiles; under that, darker water eddied and flowed. "And what are you?"

Twin blinks. "Guardians."

Of what? she started to ask, but the first Guardian voiced his question first.

"What would you have us do with you?"

Ariel stiffened, raised his chin. "Marry us, so that we might spend eternity together."

It is a good play that ends with a wedding.

Aleksandr's words came back to haunt her as the Guardians raised their arms.

"Very well," the first said. "Summon the guests." Immediately, a curious parade entered Stage Right. Half human, half animal, all masked, they carried with them vestments of white.

"I can't!" Bertie's hand throbbed. "I'm—"

Already married? Not about to do this as long as there's breath in my lungs?

A clucking group of bird-creatures pulled her away from Ariel, alternately carrying and dragging Bertie behind a column. They stripped off the remnants of Ariel's silk shirt and cinched her into a bodice of swan's down. "A perfect match, a lovely match, he's strong and handsome."

Grasping the pillar, Bertie leaned out far enough to spot her "lovely match." The Gentlemen's Chorus was dressing him in a shirt of white linen, embroidered at collar and sleeve, and a severely cut frock coat.

"A fine match, an easy match, she's your equal in every way," they intoned.

"Ariel, we *can't*," she tried to protest, but the Ladies' Chorus drowned her out with song and silk stockings.

"A wreath of blossoms for your hair. A veil to cover the eyes." The two groups joined together to sing, "Though she will forever see to the very heart of you."

Guarding it from strangers' gazes, Bertie kept her hand closed over the medallion, the same hand Nate had cut with Waschbär's knife. It burned with new fire as she tucked the scrimshaw down the bodice of the wedding dress, doubly guarded once an icy veil settled over her face and neck.

"Come. It is time." The spirit-animals urged her down

an aisle, newly strewn with white petals. The joyous cries of birds, of seals, of tusked creatures echoed over the ice. The feathers on the bridal dress rustled, summoning memories of flight and her father.

Another trapped between two loves.

I am more like him than I thought.

Every step brought her closer to Ariel: impossibly beautiful, expression unreadable, and standing under an archway of carved ice.

"Ariel, we can't—"

"You're supposed to wait to object," he said. "I do believe the cue will be, 'Speak now, or forever hold your peace.'"

"You know what I mean, Ariel. I might already be . . . I mean, I've already . . ."

"What took place between you and Nate happened in a dream."

"A place no less real than this one." Bertie wanted to bolt, but her bare feet were frozen to the ice tiles.

Now Ariel looked down at her. "You told him you loved him, but did you vow to take him, forever and always? In sickness and in health?" When she didn't answer, he took her unmarked hand in his. "I didn't think so. A marriage without vows isn't binding."

The Guardians moved to stand before them. "We are gathered on this day," the first said, "to witness the joining of this couple."

Snowflakes fell, whiter than rose petals or rice.

"It isn't the vows, but the intention behind them," Bertie said, hardly able to see Ariel for the snow. "I said I loved him."

The Guardian's words flowed around them. "Do you promise to share the pain of the other and seek to ease it? To share their laughter and their dreams? Will you honor the other?"

Ariel looked down at her. "Do you love him still?"

Bertie gave the smallest of nods, afraid to do more than that. "Yes."

The first Guardian turned to Ariel. "And you, sir?"

"Wait, what?" The ice-lace of her veil began to melt as Bertie's temper flared. "No! Ariel, tell him—"

He nodded. "I do as well."

"Damn it, that's not what I meant!"

"Join their hands," the first Guardian said. Its twin bound her to Ariel, wrist to wrist, with a long crimson ribbon.

Bertie struggled against it, but the animal-spirits only laughed. "The bride, she blushes!"

Another knot tied in the ribbon. "Ariel, tell them this is a mistake!"

"I will not. You are as much mine as you are his."

Unbidden, she thought of the ancient grove of trees.

What is mine, and mine alone.

"Blood is drawn, to seal the covenant." A blur of smoke and sapphire; so fast did the Guardians move that Bertie didn't see what sort of instrument they used. Her right hand this time, but the fire of the cut was the same. Drops of blood decorated the front of her gown with crimson beading.

"You may now kiss the bride," the Guardians pronounced as Ariel turned back her veil.

The scrimshaw had worked its way free from her bodice, and Bertie's free hand clamped down upon it.

The first Guardian grasped her arm with frostbitten fingers. "What is that?"

The second Guardian caught sight of the scrimshaw. "Bone!"

"Bone, bone, bone!" The echo came fast, furious, and from all sides.

"Not just bone," the Guardians said in horror, in wonder, "but Bone of Her Bone."

The spirit-animals wailed until Bertie thought she might bleed from the ears. With hisses and screams, they diffused, spraying glittering crystals in every direction. Coalescing several yards ahead of Ariel and Bertie, they formed a ragged-edged half circle on the ice tiles, and every one of them screeched, "Kill them!" They rushed to tip over the archway, which broke into ragged chunks of ice on impact. "Lay their heads upon the block in sacrifice to Her!"

The Guardians seized Bertie and Ariel, still bound at the wrist, dragging them forward. "It must be done."

"Like hell, it must!" Bertie twisted about, struggled to concentrate on her captor's glass mask, its sparkling sapphire eyes. "I see what you really are." The scrimshaw showed her what was in its heart of hearts: no more than captured smoke and bits of mirror, a spirit held prisoner by Sedna's whims. "Sound and fury, signifying nothing."

The first Guardian shrieked and clapped its hands over the mask, but too late. The glass fragmented. Blue-white smoke escaped dome-ward. Empty, its robes puddled on the floor, sapphire eyes rolling across the ice tiles with a noise like marbles. The Second Guardian released Ariel as it fell to its knees. Toppling forward, its glass mask smashed against the ice tiles.

"Come on!" Ariel led the charge up the stairs with a thousand specters of the sea at their heels. The set of double doors opened before them, a yawning mouth. Together, they fell through the entryway and slammed the doors shut upon the reaching hands and claws.

Sedna's voice crawled out of the darkness. "That was quite the entrance."

Sand underfoot now, as though they'd skated off the ice tiles and onto a beach. Light began to trickle toward them in waves: wavering green and eerie, to match the waves that lapped at their toes and broke against the base of the Sea Goddess's throne. The chair of onyx and obsidian sat some distance out, marking where the waters of the world began and ended. The tips of Sedna's seaweed hair floated atop the foam at her feet, tethering the limp and lifeless form of a drowned mariner.

Now Bertie was the hart, her vitals pierced by the hunter's arrow. "Nate."

CHAPTER SIXTEEN

Hold Fast the Mortal Sword

"Is this what you came for?" Sea green plaits of Sedna's hair lifted Nate by his neck and arms.

Bound as she was to Ariel by the crimson ribbon at their wrists, Bertie nevertheless took step forward. "Monster."

"Reckless child," Sedna countered, smiling with row upon row of shark's teeth. "You broke my Guardians."

"It's your own fault for taking something that did not belong to you—"

"I will have to fashion new masks, recapture their souls," the Sea Goddess continued as though she had not been interrupted. "You are proving a most troublesome little snip, Beatrice Shakespeare Smith."

"I get that a lot." Bertie slanted a look at Ariel, whose smile was reassuring if fleeting.

"Such a lovely ceremony. A pity your pirate lad was not there to give the bride away."

"I am not his to give away." Bertie met Sedna's full gaze, wishing she could wrap her hands, wounded or not, around the Sea Goddess's throat. "I belong to myself and no one else."

"The cuts on your hands say otherwise." Sedna shifted her attention to Ariel. "What say you, air spirit? Do you consider yourself bound to this girl?"

"She is mine to protect, if not mine to love or hold." Ariel met the full force of the Sea Goddess's gaze without flinching.

Salt spray unraveled the knots in the crimson ribbon, and Bertie's hand was once again her own as Sedna unfurled her starfish fingers, beckoning Ariel forward. "She doesn't begin to comprehend the sacrifices you've made for her, but I do. I, too, was betrayed by a lover. What I lost, because of him . . ." The Sea Goddess paused to smile at him. "You have a nice look about you, air spirit. Would you care to take the Guardians' place, to fly between the worlds and retrieve the souls of the dearly departed?"

"Perhaps some other time." Except Ariel stepped forward, grimacing when he placed his weight on his injured leg.

"It's a different wind to ride." Sedna flung temptation in the form of emeralds at him. "Unlike any you've ever known before, I'd wager. What would you give to have such a thing at your command? What would you trade? A cockle or a walnut shell; a knack, a toy, a trick?"

"We're not here to barter for a wind," Ariel said, the words coming only with great effort.

Sedna's precious stones dotted his arms, each one larger than the last and filled with green-fire dreams. In their facets, Bertie could see him riding astride a wind of brilliant cold. Frost decorated his silver hair and clung to his eyelashes.

"No!" Bertie grasped the largest of the emeralds and tried to pry it off, but it clung to his skin. She twisted and pulled until it came loose, leaving a trickle of blood behind.

"There's no need for that." Cast by Sedna, another stone landed upon Bertie's arm. It scuttled sideways on spindly hermit-crab legs and sank pincers deep into the flesh of her arm.

Before she could yelp at the sharp sting of it, Bertie saw herself riding the wind behind Ariel, felt her arms wrapped about his chest, her frozen cheek pressed against his broad back.

"You could spend eternity like that," Sedna offered. "You don't have to leave. The three of you can stay here forever in this paradise that knows no passage of time. Young forever. In love, forever."

"You know nothing of love." It felt as if some part of Bertie died when she dug her fingernails under the terrible, lovely dream-thing and threw it with all the strength in her arm, though her voice didn't waver. "Take back your false visions. I don't want them."

"Perhaps not yet," Sedna said, "but that will change."

"Ariel." Bertie tore the enchanted stones from his flesh. "Wake up!" When he didn't respond, she slapped him across the face as hard as she could. The blow rocked him backward, knocking him out of the reverie that threatened to drag him under with shackles of seaweed hair. Bertie grabbed him by the shoulders to shake the last wisps of the dream away. "Lies, lies; her words are nothing but sound and fury, signifying nothing."

"Yes." The dream-bites had raised red welts all along his arms, but his eyes were his own again, and they were angry.

"Well done, Beatrice Shakespeare Smith." Sedna used Bertie's name as though she were reining in a skittish horse. "But if he does not want emeralds today, perhaps he will take rubies tomorrow or sapphires the day after that. Everyone has a price. I found Nate's. I will find Ariel's. And yours."

"You'll rot like a hooked fish before you find mine," Bertie said just before she slapped Ariel as insurance.

"All right!" he said with an uncharacteristic yelp. "I'm fine! You can stop doing that!"

"I'll stop as soon as you get that dippy, mooning look off your damn face. And I owe you more than a slap for the handfasting!" Truth be told, it reassured her to see the color on his cheek, even if the red patch was in the shape of her hand. "Now, if I can just get Nate to wake up, too . . ."

Sedna rustled through the water and the dim, green light. "There is nowhere to go, no escape. I could flood this cavern any time of my choosing, but you're not worth the trouble."

Bertie remembered she wasn't entirely without weapons. "Like you tried to drown my father?"

The Sea Goddess hissed. "What do you know of that?"

"You tried to kill him, didn't you? You discovered his Aerie, and you wanted him back, but you were too proud to ask." Guesses all, but they hit their mark like harpoons.

Advancing, Sedna's face contorted. Her long tresses towed Nate to shore as her bare feet met the sand. "I will summon the crabs to cut the tongue from your mouth."

"I am no little mermaid, and I will not be silenced." Bertie tried not to look at Nate. "Do you still love him? My father?"

Foam like spittle-lace sloshed over Bertie and Ariel when the Sea Goddess spat out her disgust. "The memory of him is no more than a grain of sand against my skin."

"I'm not certain I believe you. I think you took Nate so that you wouldn't be alone."

"I took the pirate lad because a price was owed to me for the stolen bone of my bone." Sedna's weed-hair caressed Nate's face, and her skirts were currents of dark water that hissed and roiled around them. "My knowledge of Man, forced upon me by my father and yours . . ."

"Take me instead," Bertie said without meaning to.

Ariel clamped his arms around her neck as if to choke the words from her. "No!"

"You? The filthy, blood-tainted, bastard child of my once-upon-a-time love!" Sedna screeched. "Hardly a fair trade. The pirate is mine until I say he can go. Only then may he return to the surface." The Sea Goddess's horrible laugh raked sharp fingernails over Bertie's skin. "If he ever wakes. If he remembers how to swim. If he remembers there is a surface, or a Beatrice."

Bertie set her jaw. "I won't leave him here."

"He is no longer any concern of yours!"

"This man's heart belongs to me. I will have it back."

"Cut the heart from his chest, if it's yours," Sedna said. Bertie couldn't think of an answer to that, and the Sea Goddess laughed again. "Pardon my amusement, won't you? It's been so long since I had such pleasant diversion."

"It's not really that interesting a game, is it? You hold all the cards."

Sedna dragged Nate forward and dropped him in a heap on the sand. "Rouse him, if you can. Then we shall see what sort of game we are playing."

Bertie reached for him, drawn to Nate like the Sleeping Princess to the spinning wheel. Arms sliding down to her shoulders, Ariel refused to let her take a step.

"She's toying with you."

Sedna's laughter was the sort of noise that sank ships and dragged drowning mariners from the rocks. "I am that."

Bertie shuddered, turning to whisper because she had no desire for the Sea Goddess to overhear. "You should have let me come alone, Ariel. This wasn't your fight."

"Your fights are my fights." His arm slid down to her waist, fingers digging into the swan's down of her bridal dress.

"I have to try to save him." She pulled Ariel's hands from her skirts and took a step away from him.

"You don't." His face worked as though he wanted to say more.

Bertie kept her gaze upon him as she took another step back; it was the knife-passage all over again, except this time, she didn't want him to follow. "If it was me, would you be able to turn around? To walk away without trying to save me?"

"Must you always fight dirty?"

"Yes!" Picking up her skirts, Bertie pivoted on her heel and ran, certain that waves would catch her up and slam her into the sand at any second. But the Sea Goddess did not interfere as Bertie fell to her knees next to Nate. Dragging him into her lap, she was horrified by the way his head lolled, a puppet with his strings cut. His flesh was pale where once it had been bronze, and his eyes were as vacant as two pebbles. She traced the planes of his familiar and longed-for face with her hands.

"Call to him," Sedna commanded. "See if he answers your summons."

"Nate." Bertie held him tighter, as though she could transfer his memories of her, of the Théâtre, through his skin and skull. "You have to wake up. Say something, please."

Ariel reached for her with his words. "He's too far gone, Bertie—"

If there's anything left of his soul, it will be in the forest.

Unfocusing her eyes, Bertie let all the colors of the cave swim around her. This time, sinking into the dreamlands was like sliding through the surface of a soap bubble without popping it. For a fleeting second, she could still see the cavern, Sedna's face twisted in silent laughter, Ariel running, trying to reach her. Distorted by the opalescent surface of the bubble, they wavered, then faded along with the lights. Black velvet curtains slid into place, muffling Ariel's shout.

Alone in the dark, Bertie put a finger to her lips.

Quiet, please. No talking backstage.

The palest green light faded up, the promise of safety, of solace beckoning with a moss-tipped finger; the Forest Queen woke from her slumber, crowding into Bertie's heart and mind. There was hardly room for both of them, and Bertie marveled anew at Peaseblossom's schizophrenic portrayal of Juliet, Lady Capulet, and the Nurse.

But this is no mere performance, and when I was the Forest Queen, I didn't care about rescuing Nate. I didn't even remember there was a Nate.

With a thought, Bertie transformed the gentle green border of ferns into a circle of massive blocks of cold granite. Sun warmed and moon dappled, the henge would protect the blood and bones of those within its confines. The Forest Queen forced her to prowl the inner boundary, her steps soundless despite the whirl of leaves that appeared underfoot.

"Please permit me to go," she pleaded with Bertie's lips, yearning for her trees. "My place is there—"

"We have to save Nate." In the dreamlands, he'd always appeared with the light; perhaps she'd arrived too late. Bertie tasted bile in the back of her throat when she whispered, "Where is he?"

"Are you a fool? A watery hearth is no home for us." The Forest Queen clenched Bertie's hands into fists, causing the handfasting wounds to burn. "Leave him to the Sea Goddess. It is she who called to him in his sleep, she whom he could worship for all time."

Bertie couldn't believe that was the truth, or the stones would crumble to dust. "Sedna's not his goddess, she's his kidnapper. Nate wants me to rescue him."

"The way a hart longs for the arrow?" The Forest Queen swept aside her skirts, the animal they'd shot appearing at her feet. An arrow winged with horn protruded from just under its heart. "A true ruler cannot grieve the animals she brings down in the Hunt. Their blood and bones are hers for the taking."

As Bertie stared at it, fur trembled and dissolved to sand, shivering off the flesh of a wounded man.

"Lass?"

She dropped beside him for the second time in as many minutes. "I'm here."

He reached for her with a salt-scarred hand. "I think I dreamed of you."

Blood burbled around the arrow lodged in his side. "Nate, hold still. It's not real . . . you're dreaming."

His hand touched the shaft of the arrow and he blanched. "Don't worry, lass. 'Tis but a Cupid's dart you fired long ago."

I never.

But the denial stuck in her throat, unable to cross lips

that remembered every one of the pirate's kisses. "Hold still." Without waiting for his permission, Bertie drew the arrow from his flesh.

Nate's scream filled the rock circle. He dug his heels into the soft earth in protest, kicking over one of the stones that surrounded them. The circle broke, the soap bubble popped. The Forest Queen disappeared with a howl of protest, and with her the promise of the trees. Both Bertie and Nate sat in the damp sand of Sedna's cavern, and when the pirate blinked the dreams out of his eyes, his face crumpled in horror.

"I told ye not t' come here! What in th' name o' all that's holy are ye doin'?!"

"I came to rescue you." The shift had happened too fast. Ears popping, Bertie tried to dispel the dizziness and the feeling that her skin didn't quite fit her properly anymore.

"Get th' hell out!" Nate shoved at her, as though he could banish her back to the surface with wishful thinking. Blood burbled from the wound just under his heart; he'd carried it with him from the dreamlands, though here he clapped a hand over it before Bertie could see the extent of the damage. "Are ye insane?"

"Quite likely." Ariel appeared on Bertie's other side and didn't wither under the pirate's fierce gaze. "Don't blame me, swashbuckler. This was all the lady's doing."

"Ye should ha' kept her out o' here! What were th' two o' ye thinkin'?!"

Water battered the far walls as Sedna scowled and the sea followed suit. Her eyes were narrow slits in her pale green face. "Come to me, my pirate lad."

Nate's body jerked, but he didn't move toward her. "Go t' hell, ye sea-spangled bitch."

Unadulterated rage poured out of the Sea Goddess. "I gave you everything."

Nate rose, shaking with the effort of standing, of resisting her. "Ye gave me nothing. Ye took everythin' from me an' called it love."

"She would do the same!" Sedna screeched, pointing a starfish finger at Bertie.

"That's my choice an' hers. Ye've nothin' t' do wi' it."

"Such foolishness." A piece of golden paper appeared in the Sea Goddess's hand. "You were drowned, but now you will live just so I may have the pleasure of watching you die again." Sedna slowly crumpled Nate's page from The Book.

He leaned over, retching from his lungs all the water he'd sucked in at the Théâtre. Bertie held on to his shoulders, trying to keep him from falling back to his knees.

"We have to get you out of here." She thought of Serefina, of the many-faceted jars and bottles in the herb woman's stall. "Get you to a healer."

"He does appear to need attention, doesn't he?" Sedna laughed. "Would you like to take him back to the surface?"

"Yes." Bertie licked her lips and tasted salt.

"But what of your gallant air elemental? You cannot think to leave here with both these handsome lads." Before Bertie could interrupt, Sedna's eyes widened in mock surprise. "I know. For the sake of a love lost, I will make you a bargain. You will lay your soul and your heart bare to my gaze. The one you love most will return to the surface with you, and the one you love least will remain behind with me."

"I will leave no one behind!" The matching wounds on Bertie's palms burned with salt and sand.

"You have no choice in the matter. This is my kingdom, and my will rules here."

An enormous wave slammed over the three of them, tearing Bertie away from the others. She heard Nate shout, felt Ariel reach for her, but it was Sedna who caught her up and made her kneel in the frothing waters. Insistent currents grasped Bertie's wrists, tugged at her bridal skirt as Sedna's moist breath trickled along the sides of a neck forcibly bowed.

"Count to three," the goddess said. "Open your heart to me."

The rushing sound again, but is it wind or water?

"One." Starfish hands crawled over Bertie's face and covered her eyes. "Two."

What would be worse? To open my eyes and find myself on the shore with Ariel, or with Nate?

"Three."

Bertie's heart opened, and the ocean poured in. The medallion burned into her chest when Sedna peered deep inside her.

"Who do you love most, Beatrice Shakespeare Smith?"

Sedna must have found Nate deep inside Bertie's heart. Surely the Sea Goddess saw for herself the thousands of smiles exchanged in swordfights and rough play. She saw, as Bertie saw, the wink of white teeth in tanned skin, the muscles that lifted her as easily as they heaved coils of rope. She saw the man who would trade his life to keep a girl-child safe.

When Sedna twisted about in Bertie's heart, she found Ariel's voice, his songs, his temper. The games they'd played when she was small, the hours spent leapfrogging the scenery until Mrs. Edith decided it was best to keep them apart. Sedna saw, within every one of Bertie's memories, the heartbreaking loveliness of his face the day he returned to the Théâtre, and to her.

Sedna saw, the moment that Bertie did, that if love could be measured out in brass weights, in gold coins, in grains of sand, that the scales balanced. She realized, just as Bertie did, that Bertie loved them in equal measure.

Triumphant and terrified, Bertie shoved Sedna out of

that intimate place and opened her eyes, but the shore she found herself upon was the one of green and gloom in Sedna's lair. Nate and Ariel stood on either side of her, each man clasping one of her wounded hands. For another three-count, this one marked by Bertie's earth-slowed heartbeats, she and Sedna locked fierce stares. She saw at once the Sea Goddess was furious about this turn of events.

But some part of me has always known the truth of it.

"Very well, then." A terrible sort of calm settled over the cavern: that moment before a maelstrom sucks ships under. Sedna swept her skirts aside and sat upon her throne, summoning a scepter into existence. Dream-emeralds studded the coral length of it, and she used it to stir the waters lapping at the base of her chair. "It's only fair to offer a similar bargain to your men."

"What d' ye mean by that?" Nate still pressed a hand over his wound, trying to staunch the bleeding.

Sedna held the scepter above the water. Bertie could see its reflection shimmering atop the waves, even as it transformed into a sword. The Sea Goddess reached down and plucked the reflection from the water. "One for each of you, my lads. To the death. I shall let whoever wins return to the world's surface with the fair Beatrice."

Two flashes of silver spun through the air and landed in the sand at their feet with twin *thunks!*

"Don't touch them," Bertie whispered. "It's a trick."

Sedna spoke not to her, but to Ariel, still standing on Bertie's right-hand side. "You warned her about rescuing the pirate lad, but did she listen?"

"No, she did not." Ariel had his eyes fixed upon the weapon closest to him.

"Not an uncommon occurrence, I would wager," the Sea Goddess purred.

Still he stared at the sword, eyes glazing over with its silver-lure. "A wager you would win."

Bertie tried to kick it out of his reach, half burying it in the sand. "Don't, Ariel—"

"Pick up the sword, air spirit." Sedna drowned her out with the command. "Or all three of you shall die."

Ariel's hand closed around the grip, and that which had been bland and featureless transformed into a rapier with an elaborate hilt, thickly decorated from crosspiece to pommel. He smiled at the pirate, deceptively careless. "And what will you have?"

Nate's eyes were also lit by the sword's light, and he came up holding the cutlass he'd worn every day at the theater: a short, broad saber, gently curved along the cutting edge, a weapon so much part of him that it was an extension of his arm.

"Don't do this." Caught between the two men, the two blades, Bertie refused to move, refused to give them a clear path to kill each other.

"Get out o' th' way, Bertie."

"I will not, you idiot. You're both hurt—"

"Is he now?" Nate's gaze skimmed over Ariel until he saw the blood-rose that bloomed at the knee of the air elemental's wedding trousers. "That's good t' know."

"Your own weak spot is bleeding," Ariel pointed out with jovial good humor. "What happened there, my friend?"

Nate's glance flickered down to the wound under his heart. "None o' yer damn business." By far the more experienced with the sword, he normally fought with a stance fluid as the water, body relaxed to permit quick movement. Now, shirt hanging in tatters, every muscle was bunched in anger. "Get her out o' th' way, Sedna, if ye want this t' happen."

"With pleasure." In place of henchmen, Sedna sent another wave to capture Bertie. Foam and sand filled her mouth when she tried to protest, seaweed coiling around her ankles and dragging her into the shallow water at the base of the throne. Spitting and coughing, she scrabbled at her bonds even as the men circled each other, shades of Montague and Capulet.

Ariel spoke Tybalt's line, " 'Have at thee, coward.' "

"Save yer breath for a pretty death rattle."

Their weapons met with the metal-clash that would not end with curtains falling, bows, applause, but with the fury of a wounded beast smashing against a wall of wind.

Nate hacked and slashed the way he would at an enemy who'd boarded his ship. Lightning quick, Ariel dodged and spun, dipping in to land swift cuts when he could before dancing back, only slightly favoring the leg hurt on the obsidian knife-crossing.

Tugging at the seaweed, managing to pry loose the first of a dozen slime-slick ropes, Bertie would have screamed at both of them to stop, but she could see there was no use. This never would have come to pass at the Théâtre, each of them bound by formalities, restrained by the parts written for them. Sedna's bitter hatred had filled them the moment they picked up the weapons, a magic more powerful than Serefina's draught for making them forget Bertie was not a prize to be won with violence.

When their swords locked, Nate pulled his head back and smashed it into Ariel's nose. Blood poured down the air elemental's upper lip and dripped into the sand as he backed away, looking far more wary—and furious—than before.

"I told ye once I was glad t' see ye bleed like any other man," Nate said. "Now I'll see ye dead like any other man."

The crimson droplets that spattered on the sand turned into rubies that scuttled through the water toward Sedna. She winked down at Bertie. "Such a merry tournament, is it not?"

"What would he say, if my father could see the changes in you?" The churning water hid the fact that Bertie had loosened her bonds enough to start pulling one foot free.

Sedna reached down. Starfish hands crawled over Bertie's neck, grasped her hair, pushed her face into the shallow water to grind it into the harsh black sands. After a moment, Sedna pulled Bertie back up to hiss, "You will be silent and watch them die, then I shall claim them both."

With a shout that echoed in the cavern, Ariel swung at Nate's sword arm. The pirate blocked, then backhanded the air elemental into the sand, immediately swinging the cutlass in a downward arc. Ariel brought up his sword in both hands, using Nate's momentum to turn the cutlass aside before ramming the rapier's pommel into the pirate's ribs. Nate wheezed with pain and stumbled back, the hole left by the arrow bleeding freely.

Sedna loosed Bertie to clap her delight, and Bertie launched herself from the water to intercept Nate. They collided, the pirate swearing in three languages and Bertie only one.

"You have to stop." She scrabbled at his sword hand, but he would have none of it.

"I'll see this finished." He caught her around the waist

and slung her out of the way, propelling her into the cavern wall.

Bertie's head collided with the volcanic rock. She fell to her knees, stars cascading through her vision, a lightning bolt traveling from behind her eyes down the length of her arms and into the sand. Air and water trapped there exploded with the heat of her pain, her fear, expanding to form a dagger of glass, the milky white twin of the obsidian knife.

The fight continued behind her, with grunts of pain as Sedna's weapons did their work. The Sea Goddess coaxed them to further violence with empty promises and gleeful laughter. "Lovely, my handsome knights. But your work isn't done. Only one can claim the maiden fair."

Bertie shoved blood-sticky strands of hair out of her eyes in time to see Nate duck under a wild swing of Ariel's sword, rapier sliding along cutlass. With a twist, a grunt, a heave, Nate cast aside both swords, sending them flying in twin parabolas to land in the water. Grappling now, he grasped the elemental by the shirt and his silver hair, bringing his knee up over and over again into Ariel's stomach. The air elemental's weak leg buckled under him, but he returned the kicks, favor for favor, landing punches wherever he could and then jamming his thumb into Nate's arrow wound.

Dizzy, stomach twisted at the sight of them, goddess-goaded, trying to kill each other, Bertie drew the still-warm weapon from the sand. When she stood, blood wended a warm and sticky trail from her temple to her chin.

"Stop," she said, "or this happy dagger will have a new sheath."

CHAPTER SEVENTEEN

The Sea, All Water

So like Juliet's words, they rang through the cavern with the power of a death knell. Ariel and Nate hesitated, the clouds chased from their eyes as they registered the threat.

Bertie dug the tip of the knife into her skin just above her heart until blood welled up around the glass. "Would Romeo have stopped her, if he could?"

"Yes." Hoarse whispers from both men.

Sedna rose from her throne, face contorted with thwarted bloodlust. "I command you two to fight!"

Bertie issued a command of her own. "Move away from each other."

Each man fell back a few steps.

"I tire of this game." The Sea Goddess snarled,

displaying all her jagged teeth as water began to pour in from unseen channels. "I will kill the three of you and be done with this."

Bertie looked at Ariel and Nate, seeing they were hardly able to stand after the damage they'd done to each other and understanding they certainly wouldn't be able to swim for long.

Say ye love me. Even if it's not true, let me take th' words back wi' me.

The wounds on her palms blazed hot and bright, twin reminders of two ceremonies, two sets of promises exchanged. She scraped the glass dagger over both wounds, opening the handfasting scars until the blood ran free.

Tell me you love me, at least as much as you love him.

Blood-magic and bone-magic, earth-magic and word-magic; Bertie prayed that together they would be enough. She closed her bleeding hands around the medallion and willed the sands of the shore to enfold both men with the arms of the earth. "Get thee gone."

Black glittering bits of rock crawled over Nate and Ariel, swarming up their legs, sealing their wounds. Their faces contorted first with panic, then horror as they realized what she was doing.

"Bertie, no!" Their cries of protest echoed off the cavern's walls.

She imagined them in another place: a beach covered

in sand as white and pure as the cliffs that rose high above the shore. Gripping the medallion, blood oozing between her fingers, Bertie banished them. "Get thee gone."

Sedna uncoiled from her throne with a screech. "What are you doing?"

"The waters may be yours to command," Bertie answered, "but the rocks are mine. The sands are mine."

"Don't—" Ariel managed to say when the rock reached his chest.

She wouldn't stop. "The blood is mine. The words are mine."

"Lass!" Nate cried out before his features were granite-written.

The Sea Goddess sent wave after wave at the men, smashing water into the still figures, but they melted like sand carvings as she screamed her displeasure.

Swaying, utterly drained, Bertie watched the statues dissolve. "I couldn't let you kill them. They are mine, and mine alone."

"You have used up all your magic." Sedna's gaze sliced through Bertie's skin, nicking her heart. "I didn't think you'd be the sacrificial sort."

Bertie tried to twist away. By now, the rising tide had reached her waist. "You're just jealous because I can love two men in equal measure and you couldn't even manage to love one properly."

Dark bubbles boiled around Sedna, her face convulsing with fury. "I am going to enjoy watching you die." The water still poured in all around them; before long it would reach Bertie's chest, her neck. "I will fill your lungs and watch you drown. Once you are dead, I will rouse the waves to a suitable funeral procession so as to deliver your corpse to your father." Sedna paused for effect. "You can picture it, I think?"

Yes, Bertie could imagine the Aerie filling with water, the same as it had when the puppets danced in the hatbox theater. Except this time the ocean wasn't fabric streamers carried by stagehands, and the broken, bloated body the Scrimshander cradled wasn't Ophelia. Bertie slogged to the double doors and tugged upon them.

Sedna's expression shifted with currents of malice and cruel satisfaction. "There is no way out of this place."

Buoyant now, Bertie kicked her feet feebly. She wanted to summon the sands to her, wanted to escape through the same earth-portal, except there was too much water, and she was too weak. The Sea Goddess's seaweed hair snaked around Bertie's waist and neck in sodden ropes so she could heave Bertie up, as though examining a fan or a comb in the marketplace, twisting her this way and that to get a better look.

"You are alone, truly alone, perhaps for the very first

time. So I ask you, Beatrice Shakespeare Smith, who will really miss you? Who will mourn your passing?"

Against her will, Bertie imagined the Company ranged along the shore, staring at the water, waiting for her to return.

"Think of them," Sedna crooned.

The fairies will cry, won't they? Peaseblossom's prone to heartfelt tears, and the boys might sniff when they think no one is looking.

"The one who stood alongside you."

Hard to imagine tears suiting Ariel's lovely face.

"The one you hoped to save."

Nate will rage. Yes, he will mourn.

"The ones who await your return."

Bertie thought of Waschbär's merry black eyes, of Mrs. Edith, with her stern looks and years of affection freely given, and Ophelia, the mother she'd hardly known.

"And your precious father." Sedna towed Bertie through the dark, rushing water. "They have all abandoned you."

"I don't need anyone to save me." But she couldn't summon the sands to her, couldn't concentrate with Sedna's tentacle grip squeezing the air from her lungs. Bertie could taste nothing but ocean when the water closed over her head. Just as it had when Sedna invaded the theater, everything churned with foam and bubbles. Through stinging eyes, she saw the Sea Goddess, a creature of purple ink and glittering emerald scales. The medallion floated up around Bertie's neck. Water poured into her lungs. Her body jerked in protest. Her heart beat an erratic tattoo, and she could hear her pulse slowing in her ears again.

But it did not stop.

Through the dark eddies, Sedna gazed at her in horrified fascination. "This is no bird magic," she whispered, words audible even through the salt water. "Who was your mother?"

A week ago, Bertie couldn't have answered that question. But now the knowledge was hers, as well as the triumph. "Ophelia, the ever-drowned." The water moved in and out of her lungs, heavy and thick, like the sugar syrup the fairies used for stage blood.

"I will remove all that is your cursed mother from you, like cutting the soft bruises from the flesh of an apple." The Sea Goddess wrapped her starfish hands about Bertie's throat and squeezed. "If you will not die for me, I will kill you myself."

Everything shifted: What had been water and salt, emeralds and onyx and obsidian, was now only dreamy dark.

Sedna tightened her grip. "You are alone now, and you are mine."

I am alone, but I am not yours.

Power surged through Bertie, drawn from the ancient trees rooted in her heart of hearts. It sizzled through her limbs and poured through her hands as Bertie pried Sedna's starfish fingers from her throat. "I belong only to myself."

Sedna lunged at Bertie again. "You will die alone!"

"That is your fear, not mine." Bertie's words shoved the Sea Goddess against the far wall. The cavern shuddered and shifted.

If the ceiling caves in, we'll be trapped together, forever, in an underwater cairn.

Sedna gave Bertie a slow, horrible smile that twisted her pale green lips. She curled her fingers in to form tremendous fists.

"Don't!" Bertie cried, but the Sea Goddess threw her arms wide to smash the wall behind her. Fissures spread like spiderwebs, radiating outward in the promise of impending collapse. Bertie didn't mean to panic, but it was hard not to, what with the bone-rattling shudders that traveled up from the ocean floor. "You trap me, you trap yourself!"

Sedna shook her head. "I am the sea, and all that I am will escape in bits and pieces. My arms will be eels, my torso seahorses, the rest mud dragons and jaw worms and anemones. I will drift on the foam until I gather enough strength from the tide pools and coves to assume this shape again." Her low chuckle triggered the first avalanche; it echoed in Bertie's ears as the roof fell in on them and the walls crumbled. "This is your living grave. Curse your mother's name, when you wish you could have drowned."

A heavy weight smashed into Bertie's back and crushed her against the rock in front of her. She struggled against it, managing to shift just a bit to the side before another boulder pinned her flat. Sedna's laughter fragmented all around her. Though Bertie could not see the transformation, she could well imagine the plethora of sea creatures worming their way free of the rubble.

"Damn you," she whispered, the words as rough as the rocks that grated against her lips.

"No," said a thousand voices that were all the Sea Goddess. "Damn *you*."

Sedna escaped with the fizzle of soda poured in a tall glass, then Bertie heard nothing more, not even the popping of tiny bubbles or the shifting of sand. She fought against the weight that held her captive even as she suppressed waves of panic and claustrophobia.

"Calm down. Concentrate."

Somehow, talking aloud helped, despite the grit and water that swirled in her mouth and up her nose. Something scuttled around her ankles, and undiluted panic edged out every bit of clarity and reason. Bertie jerked as though she'd stuck a finger in one of the many faulty electrical outlets back at the Théâtre, the effort accompanied by a stream of curse words and futile wriggling. One particularly sharp rock dug into her forehead, another into the small of her back. The utter absence of sound filled her ears, and Bertie realized she was light-headed.

"Ophelia's magic can't save me from bleeding to death."

Her heart waited for a cue that would not come. The blood settled in her veins to burn like acid.

There's no way to mark the passing minutes. Has it been one? Three? Five? Am I unconscious yet? Brain-dead? Not while I'm still thinking, I guess. But is it colder now?

Bertie would have shivered, but there wasn't even room for that.

So tired.

"To sleep, perchance to dream." The shore, the White Cliffs. The words she mouthed were like a magic spell. "Scene change."

The jagged weight against her back disappeared, as though lifted by unseen stagehands. The cavern rocks shifted.

"Our Queen," they murmured.

"Don't call me that again." Bertie realized with a start that Nate called her "lass" to imply she was young, and Ariel used "milady" to claim possession; "My Queen" was just another label, another costume to wear, another weight upon her shoulders.

There is a Beatrice who exists beyond the obligations of a daughter, outside the object of man's affections.

She took one step, then another. As she moved through rock and soil and sand, bits of loam kissed her upturned face.

"Seek out the company of those who will never ask you to jump," the earth advised.

Bertie remembered the rush of feathers as she soared above the audience. "I can catch myself."

"Of those whose love will never fill your lungs with water—" the earth argued.

"But it did not kill me."

"There should be more to love," said the earth, "than 'it did not kill me.' More than 'I survived it.'"

The wounds in her palms ached, the pain traveling up her arms to settle between her collarbones alongside the medallion. Bertie recalled the many things Sedna had seen when she peered into her heart: the hours of play, the laughter and games. "I want things to be as they were."

"Before love?" The earth laughed at her. "That's impossible. Old as we are, we cannot remember a time before love. Stay safe here, in our heart. Return to your forest—"

"I can't," Bertie said. "'Our revels now are ended. These our actors, as I foretold you, were all spirits and are melted into air, into thin air.'"

Massive tree roots gathered about her ankles and wrists, helping her to climb up, up . . .

"'And, like the baseless fabric of this vision, the cloud-capp'd towers, the gorgeous palaces, the solemn temples, the great globe itself, ye all which it inherit, shall dissolve.'"

Everything went hazy around the edges, curtains of green and brown and amber parting to let her pass. The earth decorated her ragged skirts with diamonds and ore; Bertie held aloft the largest bit of gold, using its light to hold the darkness at bay.

"'And, like this insubstantial pageant faded, leave not a rack behind.'"

It was harder to move now, but Bertie pressed forward, through the darkness, through earth and air and water, refusing to succumb to the dull ache of fatigue that settled into her bones.

"'We are such stuff as dreams are made on,'" she gasped, pushing up like a new green shoot, "'and our little life is rounded with a sleep.'"

CHAPTER EIGHTEEN

A Tangled Chain, All Disordered

Bertie brought the water with her, if nothing else: a parting gift from the Sea Goddess. For several minutes, her entire existence consisted of a violent bout of hands-and-knees, yak-water-out-of-her-lungs contractions until frothy, blood-tinged foam decorated the sand between her palms. Several helpful people clapped her on the back. Yet more babbled a stream of questions and concerns that, to her addled ears, almost hurt more than the coughing.

"I'm fine!" she wheezed between desperate breaths. Unfortunately it came out sounding more akin to "ugggggg fiiiiih!" Her throat hurt, as though she'd swallowed a swordfish sideways.

"Again between the shoulder blades, Moth!" The tiny

voice belonged to Peaseblossom. The boys obeyed, each giving Bertie a solid blow so that the last of the water was expelled from her lungs.

"We need to get her closer to the fire," Waschbär added, sounding remarkably calm, given the circumstances.

Two sets of arms, neither of which was hairy enough to belong to the sneak-thief, hauled Bertie upright faster than strictly necessary. The world teetered precariously, righted itself, then went wibble-wobbly around the edges again. She blinked the salt from her eyes until she could see the beach, the morning-streaked White Cliffs, and the four highly concerned fairies that hovered three inches away from her face.

"She's alive!" Mustardseed crowed.

"Of course she's still alive," Moth said.

"Never doubted it for a second," Cobweb added.

"She's blue," Peaseblossom fretted as she tugged wet strands of hair out of Bertie's eyes.

"Drowning tends to do that to people." Ariel was on her right.

Glancing to her left, Bertie realized she might have survived a run-in with the Sea Goddess only to perish under Nate's blistering gaze.

"Ye daft wench! Whate'er were ye thinkin', comin' down there?"

"Saved you, didn't I?" She lifted a hand to his cheek,

needing to confirm he really was there. Time and weather would tan his skin again, but Bertie knew it would take longer to scrub his sojourn with Sedna from his soul.

"Always have t' have th' last word, don't ye?"

"Yes." She noticed both men had located a change of clothes in the caravan's luggage. They were battle scarred, with bruises blooming like flowers and cuts in various stages of clotting. Nate had his left arm tucked over the chest wound, and Ariel's weight shifted to accommodate his bandaged leg. They stood on either side of her, invisible swords still at the ready, but some sort of truce had been called in her absence, and she hoped it lasted. Then maybe, for a little while, she could hug close her joy that they were both here and safe, without having to think about matters beyond that.

The Scrimshander cleared his throat. By the thin morning light, Bertie could see that whomever she'd gotten her nose from, it hadn't been her father. He rubbed the beaked appendage with the tip of one finger like a nervous cockatiel grooming himself. "How are you feeling, Little One?"

"Little One," Nate muttered as he and Ariel settled Bertie near the fire. "Little, my arse."

"It hurts to breathe," Bertie noted. Not only that, but her heart was leapfrogging around her chest cavity like a demented toad. She had a newfound respect for Ophelia's fortitude, especially when her teeth started chattering.

Nate and Ariel remained glued to her sides, neither willing to step away first. Ariel went so far as to try to claim her right hand, but found it was already occupied.

"What do you have there?"

Bertie unfurled her palm, expecting to find a chunk of loam-encrusted gold, but startled to see that she'd brought Nate's page from The Book with her. "A souvenir."

Moth rushed in to take a look. "Aw, I thought it would be a snow globe!"

Bertie tucked the paper into the tattered bodice of her gown. "It's better than a snow globe."

Appalled by such a statement, the fairies went on to compile a list of the many souvenirs Bertie should have brought them from the underworld, starting with apparel that read "Bertie Went to the Underworld and All I Got Was This Stupid T-Shirt" and ending with nesting Sedna dolls.

Remembering the twisted circus acts, the demons latching on to her ankles, the scuttling sea creatures, Bertie's skin crawled. "You're lucky we didn't bring anything else back with us."

The Scrimshander shifted his weight from one foot to the other. Unspoken questions flitted across his features in avian-shaped shadows until he cleared his throat to ask, "Is she . . . that is, what I mean to say—"

"Yes, Sedna's still angry with you," Bertie said.

"I was afraid of that." He looked out at the listless surface of the ocean, expression inscrutable. "But she let you go. That's a good sign, at least."

"Not quite," Bertie corrected.

He tensed. "Not quite what?"

"It was more like she failed to kill me. Twice." She paused to consider. "Yes, there was the drowning and then the cave-in. Three times, if you add that she tried to strangle me."

Moth whistled appreciatively. "The Stage Manager would be jealous."

That startled a laugh from Ariel. "True. Many is the time he'd have liked to wrap his hands around Bertie's throat."

"Maybe," Mustardseed suggested, "he could send Sedna a nice thank-you note."

"That would be difficult." Bertie reached for the medallion and realized it barely warmed to her touch. "She broke apart to escape the rocks. The ocean is probably seething with all the bits of her."

"I didn't fancy a swim, in any case," Ariel said with a delicate shiver.

"None o' us do," Nate said.

"She said that she would find a way to regroup. That it wouldn't be the end of her." Bertie looked at her father through the ragged fringe of her bangs. "Someday . . . the two of you might . . ."

One second passed, then two while Bertie's thoughts ran rampant.

As a bird, he loved her. Is he more bird than man right now?

The Scrimshander caught her up and pressed her tightly against his thin chest. When she coughed, he loosened his grasp just enough to let her breathe.

"I am glad," he said against the top of her head, "that you are back, and you are safe. Whatever else happens, know that."

Then he was gone, slogging through the sand, headed back to his cave. Bertie watched his retreat, remembering her promise to Ophelia that she would bring him back to the theater.

"Dad," she whispered hoarsely, but he didn't hear or didn't mark her.

He could have asked me to take him through the portal. Except Sedna's no more than foam on the water right now.

Bertie looked at the dim light shining out of the mouth of the Aerie.

Seventeen years not knowing. And now that I know, nothing has really changed, has it? The cottage, the laundry hanging on the line, the Family Dog belong to another child. All I have are two parents trying to piece together broken memories. And then there's me, just as broken in some ways.

The fairies prevented her from dwelling on such morose thoughts, crowding as close as they possibly could, pushing and shoving one another.

"Get out of the way, you."

"I want to sit on her shoulder!"

"Oh, Bertie, your clothes are a mess." Peaseblossom peered at her. "Whatever are you wearing?"

The wedding dress was no more than a waterlogged rag, tattered white feathers trailing from scraps of silk. "Someone's idea of a joke. There were more costume changes than expected."

"You need to change again," the fairy said.

Nate snorted. "She's practically asleep sitting up. What she needs is food an' medicine."

Mustardseed bounced, looking pleased. "It took some doing, but we managed to drive the caravan across the sand!"

"What he means is, I drove," Waschbär hastened to reassure her.

Cobweb nodded. "And we sang for our suppers—"

"Supplies!" Moth corrected. "In the marketplace. We knew when you came back that you'd probably need cake."

"That was very optimistic of you," Bertie said.

Mustardseed grinned. "Even if you hadn't made it back, we could have eaten the cake."

"What did ye buy, besides sweets?" Nate demanded. The fairies led him off with screams of "pomegranate custard!" and "lovely meat pies" and Waschbär's murmured "I think there was a first-aid kit in there, somewhere. Check under the haunch of venison."

The moment they were alone, Ariel turned to her.

"My thanks," Bertie said before he had a chance to utter a word.

That surprised him. "For what?"

"For going with me through the stone. You didn't have to do that."

"Yes," he said with a long, quiet look that was only for her. "I did."

Bertie found she wasn't too tired to blush. "Did you dream anything? Before we woke on the stage?" Thinking of the forest, she felt a pull so strong that her head swam with the desire to step past the moss-curtain. She put her chin on her knees, refusing to acknowledge the lure of leaves that rustled, still within her reach.

"I was flying." Here he swallowed. "Looking for something, though I couldn't remember what. I don't think I've ever felt that sort of fear before . . . at least, not until your play had me walking the knife's edge."

"How did you find me?"

"The winds became a white horse that took me straight to your forest. The moment I passed between the trees, I was a knight." A smile flickered across his face. "That was your doing, I think."

"Not on purpose—"

Nate interrupted without apology, draping a woolen blanket over Bertie's shoulders and shoving a mug into her hands. "Drink that."

Ariel stood with visible reluctance. "I'll get you something to eat."

Bertie sniffed at the steaming contents of the cup, which reeked of ginger. The cuts from her palms burned against the hot ceramic. "You didn't get this from the lizard woman, did you?"

"Ship's cook's recipe. Ginger's good for stomach upset." Nate sat down next to her. "Helps th' circulation too, an' ye could do wi' a bit more color in yer cheeks."

"Am I still blue?" Bertie took a hesitant sip and felt her blood flare to life. The drink burned her tongue and scorched a fiery path to her innards.

Only after she'd consumed the entire mug did Nate speak again, turning his face into her hair to whisper, "Thank ye."

"Don't be silly." She tried to shrug, but didn't have the energy for it.

"Someday, I hope ye will learn t' accept thanks when 'tis offer'd."

"Maybe about the same time I learn to gracefully accept a compliment?" Bertie rested her head against his shoulder.

Nate snorted. "Mayhap."

The two of them stared at the sea, the calm surface of the water flat and the same gray as the early morning sky. With him leaning close, Bertie realized with a pang that Nate smelled of sweat and salt and seaweed rather than the detergent Mrs. Edith used in the Théâtre laundry.

He touched a finger to the medallion. "Ye can take that off now."

Bertie blinked. "Why would I want to do that?"

"Her magic's gone from it. I can't hear her callin' t' me through it anymore."

"Good." Bertie twisted her fingers around the chain, but made no move to take it off. "I don't need her magic."

I have my own.

"I didn't mean it t' be just a bit o' pretty jewelry." Nate looked at it and murmured, "I see ye replaced the chain."

Bertie refused to look abashed. "What happened down there? Between you and Sedna?"

He stiffened. "Ye cut right t' th' heart o' things, no?"

"She indicated she was quite charmed by you."

"An' what lass wouldn't be, I'd like t' know?" The words were jovial, but he looked bleak about the eyes.

Though Bertie didn't want to pry, she did anyway. "She was your goddess, Nate. It's not as if I would blame you, if something happened."

"A fair trade fer whatever happened wi' Ariel?"

The sudden appearance of the sneak-thief plopping down in the sand next to Bertie saved her from having to explain.

"I thought you might want this back," he said without preamble, holding out the journal. "The Scrimshander said he found it at the base of the portal."

Bertie was beyond thankful to see it, to hold it again in her hands. "How could it ever be an unwanted thing?"

Waschbär wiggled his toes, paying no heed to Nate's scowl. "Your Theater Manager wished it well away."

"This belonged to the Theater Manager?" The unexpected connection left her mouth hanging agape. "But where did he get it?"

Nate looked at it askance. "Perhaps the Properties Department?"

"Easy way to check that," Bertie said.

"Mr. Hastings's paperwork," all three of them said at once.

"Even so, why would he want to get rid of something with so much power?" The wind caught hold of the journal's pages, riffling through them like a burglar in search of gold coins. Bertie spotted several sheets that were filled edge to edge; some even sported notes in the margin. Phrases caught her eye:

BERTIE

I KNOW I'M SUPPOSED TO BE THE NEW MIS-
TRESS OF REVELS! BUT THAT DOESN'T MEAN I
HAVE POCKETS FULL OF MUFFINS!

Only a few pages further and she spotted another scene
she had not penned but remembered all too well:

(THE WATER BUFFETS BERTIE FROM ALL SIDES
WITH CHURNING FOAM AND BUBBLES—)

Not her handwriting at all, but bold, black lettering that
carried all the way through the confrontation with the Sea
Goddess:

SEDNA

I WILL REMOVE ALL THAT IS YOUR CURSED
MOTHER FROM YOU, LIKE CUTTING THE SOFT
BRUISES FROM THE FLESH OF AN APPLE.

The journal had recorded their every line, their every
cue, arranging it around the bits of narrative Bertie had
written. Her handwriting had disappeared, replaced with
printed flourishes and curlicues. There was no mystery
as to where she'd seen this formal typeface before. She

closed her eyes and imagined the stage back at the Théâtre, the heavy red velvet curtains that flanked the proscenium arch, the golden glow emanating from Stage Right.

The journal was transforming into something like *The Complete Works of the Stage.*

"What's th' matter?" Nate leaned closer, but Bertie closed the journal firmly.

"Nothing that can't wait for another day," she said, praying she spoke the truth.

"Speaking of another day," Waschbär said, "Aleksandr also sends word that he'd like you attend rehearsals for the Brand-New Play."

"Careful now," Bertie warned, "you almost sound like a manager."

"Manager, eh?" The sneak-thief paused to consider her words, clapping his hands against his knees. "That's something to consider. In any case, Aleksandr fears the wedding scene needs some work."

Ariel returned, handing Bertie a metal plate piled high with bread, cheese, and rough slices of an exotic fruit. "I thought the ending was perfect."

Nate was immediately suspicious. "Really, an' why's that?"

"Because she married me. Bride-clad, with a *proper* ceremony before a priest."

"That thing wasn't a real priest—" Bertie protested, but Nate was already speaking over the top of her.

"She can't ha'e married ye when she already married me."

Clenching the plate, she tried to decide which boy to smack first. "Quit circling and snarling at each other like a set of dogs. You"—she pointed at Nate—"I didn't realize I was marrying, and you"—another poke of the finger for Ariel—"never kissed the bride. Both of you tricked me, and neither ceremony is legal or binding here, so I am not married to *anyone*."

"Not yet," said Ariel, as indefatigable as one of the fairies in pursuit of pie. "All you have to do is pick one of us."

Nate's hand clenched into a fist until he glanced at Bertie's face. Marking the expression she wore, he relaxed a fraction of an inch. "What ye feel is in equal parts, no? That's why Sedna didn't send ye back here wi' one o' us."

"That's the truth of it." She split a stern look between them. "So you can both relax long enough for us to eat something."

Waschbär wove a random path, distributing gently steaming pies that he'd warmed over the fire. Pip Pip and Cheerio emerged from his pockets to partake of buttery crust, blinking their little black eyes at the group as he noted, "A troupe needs both stage and coin to get along, especially when it wants feeding as often as this one does. You'd do well to consider Aleksandr's offer."

"Are you seeing this to the end, then?" Bertie asked, only half teasing.

The sneak-thief paused to consider the question, looking a bit surprised by the answer he gave next. "I do believe I am. And you?"

Bertie thought of the play, of being trapped in that hellish nightmare with Ariel, and the equally horrifying idea of watching it unfold every night onstage. "I'm contemplating early retirement."

"Stop talking nonsense and have a pastry," Moth said.

"I'll share my chocolate with you, Bertie!"

"Have a bit of marshmallow."

That the fairies were so eager to share their sugar with her warmed Bertie better than the ginger drink. They gathered around, shoveling bits of sweet stuff in her mouth, patting her cheeks with sticky fingers, playing hide-and-seek in her hair until it was a right mess.

Perhaps there's a real Turkish Bath in the Caravanserai.

"You've rescued your friend," Waschbär said with a nod to Nate. "Would you rather get back to the Théâtre?"

Bertie glanced up at the Aerie, thinking of her promise to Ophelia. "Not quite yet."

"So we stay with the Innamorati?" Moth asked with a bounce.

"For a bit," Bertie agreed.

For as long as it takes to persuade the Scrimshander to come back with us.

"I think it's a good plan." Peaseblossom clasped her hands. "Perhaps Chef Toroidal can make me another Henry."

"I'd like him to make me a Henrietta," Moth said.

"Yeah, what could be better than an edible girlfriend?"

"*Two* edible girlfriends?"

Bertie knew better, but said nothing, instead breaking apart a small fruit pie as she took inventory: fairies, furry friend, father. Both boys, neither bleeding for the moment. A truce called.

"Yer thinkin' hard about something." Nate's eyes crinkled with a laugh that caused her heart to squeeze in her chest, this time in a wholly welcome fashion.

"It's a lucky soul who can greet the morning surrounded by smiling faces," Bertie said, returning the grin. "Now which of you wants to slog back to the Caravanserai to get me a cup of coffee?"

CURTAIN

Acknowledgments

The Management at the Théâtre Illuminata would like to express its gratitude to the following Patrons:

My family, who offers the nonstop stream of love, support, hugs, coffee, and baked goods required to produce a finished manuscript. And all my love to Teddy Bear, the first family dog. Our hairy miscreants are my real-life fairies, and she was the Peaseblossom of the group. Princess, you are missed.

My publisher, Jean Feiwel, and my editor, Rebecca Davis, as well as the entire team at Feiwel and Friends; they are the stage ninjas, working behind the scenes to ensure the production is flawless.

Jason Chan, for his captivating artwork.

Friends first, beta-readers afterward: Sunil Sebastian,

for knowing the difference between the nib and the barrel; Tiffany Trent, for the conversation about cutlasses and cuirasses; Glenn Dallas, for his keen eye and all the great vocabulary words I ended up stamping on the Innamorati's luggage; Stephanie Burgis, for encouraging me through the earliest of drafts; Jenna Waterford, for asking if she should just wait for the newest revision; Michelle Zink, for acting in all ways like my writerly twin; target audience members Noel Furniss, Michelle Joseph, and Cheryl Joseph, for their enthusiasm and typo catches.

Daniel Erickson, for inspiring Valentijn, the Strong Man and Keeper of the Costumes.

All the wonderful librarians, booksellers, bloggers, and readers who demonstrated such incredible enthusiasm and love for *Eyes Like Stars*.

A special round of applause to Cirque de Soleil and Lucent Dossier Vaudeville Cirque, whose costumes and various acrobatic acts inspired the Innamorati. The Wheel of Death performance from Cirque de Soleil's *Kooza* was particularly important to this book.

The legend of how Sedna became a Sea Goddess is told in various forms by the native peoples of the Arctic Circle. I wish to particularly thank Mr. Zachary Jones of the SHI Special Collections Research Center for his information about this story and other tribal matters. For more information about the Tlingit, Haida, and

Tsimshian people of Southeast Alaska, please visit the Special Collections homepage at: http://www.sealaskaheri tage.org/collection/index.htm.

Also, special thanks to Maria Williams, author of *How Raven Stole the Sun,* for her graciousness and time taken to answer my questions.